Mon

Under a Siena Sun

T.A. Williams lives in Devon with his Italian wife. He was born in England of a Scottish mother and Welsh father. After a degree in modern languages at Nottingham University, he lived and worked in Switzerland, France and Italy, before returning to run one of the best-known language schools in the UK. He's taught Arab princes, Brazilian beauty queens and Italian billionaires. He speaks a number of languages and has travelled extensively. He has eaten snake, still-alive fish, and alligator. A Spanish dog, a Russian bug and a Korean parasite have done their best to eat him in return. His hobby is long-distance cycling, but his passion is writing.

Also by T.A. Williams

T.A.WILLIAMS

Under a
Siena Sun

CANELO

First published in the United Kingdom in 2020 by Canelo

This edition published in the United Kingdom in 2021 by

Canelo
31 Helen Road
Oxford OX2 0DF
United Kingdom

Print ISBN 978 1 80032 293 6
Ebook ISBN 978 1 78863 764 0

Look for more great books at www.canelo.co

Printed and bound in Great Britain by Clays Ltd, Elcograf S.p.A.

I finished writing this book one month before Covid-19 made an appearance in our lives. In the light of what has happened since then, I am immensely pleased that I chose to make my main character a doctor. This book is dedicated to all those selfless front-line health workers who have been devoting themselves to keeping us safe. Thank you.

Prologue

Lucy knew it was time to leave when a burst of machine-gun fire smashed the windows and tore through the tin roof of the clinic. They had been hearing sporadic gunfire for hours now, gradually approaching, but this was the closest by far. As pieces of molten metal and glass showered down into the room, she took refuge under the operating table and clenched her teeth to stifle the scream that had been building inside her. She was bathed in sweat, partly because of the high temperature here in the tropics and partly, she knew full well, out of sheer unadulterated terror. She glanced across at Nicole and Geneviève, both huddled together under the worktop, between the steriliser and the drug cabinet. They looked as frightened as she felt.

'You okay?' She was surprised to hear her voice sounding, not normal, but not nearly as raucous as she had feared. She saw Nicole nod and did her best to offer them both some reassurance. 'The helicopter should be here any minute now.'

'As long as it doesn't get shot down.' Geneviève had always been a glass half-empty sort of girl.

Lucy managed to produce a little smile. 'Don't worry, Geneviève, it'll come. I'm sure.'

'And if it doesn't?'

And if it doesn't? For a few seconds, Lucy's resolve faltered and she allowed herself to consider the fate that might await them if help didn't come in time. She had seen enough of the horrific results of violence perpetrated upon women in this war-torn part of Africa by both sides in the conflict to have no illusions as to what to expect. The red cross on her T-shirt would cut no ice with the men with the guns and machetes, many of them hopped up on drugs. It took a massive effort of self-control to relegate these thoughts to the back of her mind – for now.

The radio crackled into life and she crawled across the floor towards it, doing her best to avoid the broken glass and jagged pieces of metal littering the floorboards. She picked up the microphone and pressed Transmit.

'Hello, Kisangani, this is Mabenta Clinic, Mabenta Clinic. Come in, Kisangani. Can you hear me? Over.'

'Reading you loud and clear, Mabenta.' She recognised the voice coming out of the loudspeaker. She and Sergeant Chaudhary of the UN Peacekeeping Force had never met, but they had spoken so often she already thought of him as an old friend. 'Helicopter will be with you imminently. Be ready to leave as soon as you see it. Over.'

Lucy shot a glance across the room towards the two nurses to check that they had registered the message and pressed Transmit once again. 'Message received, Kisangani and thank you. Tell your men there's a machine gun not far away. We're under fire. Over.'

'Message received, Mabenta. Appropriate action will be taken.' His voice became a bit less formal. 'Not much longer, Lucy. Hang in there, you'll be okay. Out.'

As she dropped the receiver back on the floor, Lucy thought she could hear something. Still on her hands and knees, she made her way to the door and very cautiously pulled it open. As she did so, there was sudden deafening roar and an attack helicopter came past fast and low, its rotor blades almost skimming the rooftops. As she clasped her hands to her ears, its cannons opened up on targets in the trees barely a few hundred yards away and the whole building reverberated with the noise.

As it disappeared from sight, another helicopter appeared in its wake, this time the more utilitarian type they had come to recognise over the months they had been here. The side door was open and she could see a soldier wearing a light blue UN helmet standing there, gripping a machine gun mounted on a bracket. The MONUSCO logo of the United Nations was clear to see on the side of the helicopter and she heaved a heartfelt sigh of relief. She waved and received a wave in return. The pilot was clearly in a hurry as he jerked the nose up to reduce speed and then dropped like a stone towards the open courtyard.

Lucy turned back towards her two companions.

'Come on you two. We need to get out of here right now.'

Nicole and Geneviève needed no prompting. As the dust cloud thrown up by the rotors came swirling towards them, reducing visibility to a few feet, they rushed out and ran madly in the direction of the noise. Lucy swung her little bag onto her shoulder, took one final look at what had been her home and place of work for two years now, and followed. As she ran across the courtyard she felt terribly vulnerable but nobody fired at her. She almost bumped into the side of the helicopter, her eyes and her throat filled with dust. Strong arms caught hold of her and pulled her in. The Indian peacekeeper in the blue helmet bent over and put his mouth close to her ear.

'Hello, Doctor Young. Are you the last?'

Lucy saw Nicole and Geneviève already in there and nodded. 'Yes, I'm the last. There's nobody left there now.' The remaining local staff and patients had disappeared into the forest several hours previously. Lucy had hugged each and every one of them and wished them well before they left. Miriam, the clinic manager, who had become her closest friend, had opted to go with the group in the hope of helping them. When Lucy had offered to go too, she had been told firmly to wait for the helicopter with the two French nurses. Miriam and the others knew only too well that three foreign women would stick out a mile in the bush – and would make valuable hostages… if they were lucky. If not, their fate would have been too terrible to contemplate. Repressing a shiver, Lucy once more spared them all a compassionate thought and hoped they would be able to stay hidden, and survive.

The dust cloud swirled in through the door and as she erupted into a fit of coughing, she heard the soldier shout something and return to the machine gun. The engine note increased as the helicopter took off again, rising painfully slowly, or so it felt. Lucy crouched with her arms round her knees, head down, braced for incoming fire but, mercifully, none came. Hugging the treetops, the pilot speeded up and they gradually escaped the combat zone, the vegetation below them flashing past ever faster as the helicopter accelerated away.

'Here, doctor, put this on.'

A crewman handed her a headset and she did as instructed. The earphones cut out much of the noise of the engines and she gradually allowed herself to begin to relax. Her heart was beating frantically and she was glad of the support of the utilitarian seat beneath her. She

4

looked across and saw the other man pull the weapon back inside and slide the side door closed. This, plus the headphones, reduced the noise level to something approaching normality. Lucy roused herself.

'Thank you so much, guys.' She had to cough a few times before she managed to speak properly and she could feel the dust sticking to her eyelids. The microphone in front of her mouth was evidently working well as she saw both men turn towards her and smile.

'You're very welcome, doctor.' The taller of the two crouched down in front of her, steadying himself as the pilot swerved to avoid something. 'That was a close call you had back there.'

Lucy nodded. 'Far too close for comfort.' She surprised herself by managing a little smile. 'I used to be scared of helicopters, but at least this little escapade has resolved that. I love helicopters now. Thanks again, guys and, captain, if you can hear me at the controls, thank you and all your colleagues for risking your lives to get us out.'

The pilot's voice came back clearly in her headphones.

'You're very welcome, doctor. It's the least we could do. You MSF medics are amazing.'

The two crewmen helped Lucy and the two nurses strap themselves in and then sat down opposite them. Lucy turned towards her two companions and did her best to sound reassuring.

'I'm glad that's over. How're you doing, girls?'

Nicole answered for both of them, an unsteady smile of relief on her face. Beside her, even Geneviève was smiling now. 'Fine… now. I was scared stiff back there. We only just got away in time, didn't we?'

Lucy managed to smile back at them, but she was in no doubt that she would relive the past twenty-four hours in her dreams – or more probably nightmares – for a long time to come. 'But we got away, and that's what counts. I just hope Miriam and the others managed to get far enough away as well.'

The helicopter made another sudden change of direction and she caught hold of the side of the seat for support. Determined to do her best to keep her companions – and herself – feeling positive, she decided to move the conversation on.

'What are your plans now? A holiday?'

Geneviève shook her head. 'I'm getting out. I'm afraid I've had enough. I've been thinking about it for months now, but this was the last straw.'

'What? Giving up MSF?'

'Afraid so. I've served my time. You've been at it even longer than me, haven't you? Don't you want to get out?'

Lucy hadn't had much time to consider her future recently. For the past couple of fraught days it had been the present that had fully occupied her mind. She leant back and thought about it. Médecins Sans Frontières had been her life for the past four years. It was almost two years since she had been back to the UK and since then she had been here in Mabenta. She knew she needed a break. Even before this latest offensive, she had been feeling very run-down and she had no doubt that any doctor would have diagnosed her as suffering from acute mental and physical strain and probably the onset of exhaustion. She had self-diagnosed extreme stress, but had chosen to tell nobody and had resisted the temptation to raid the medicine cabinet for tranquillisers. One thing was for sure: she needed to take it easy for a bit. Whether the time had come to follow Geneviève's example and pack it in completely was something she would have to think about. Seriously.

'I'm not sure how long I want to go on, but I certainly think it might be a good idea to take a break. Maybe I'll take a holiday.'

'That sounds good. Where'll you go?'

That wasn't so easy. Her mum and dad had sold their little house and moved to the seaside town of Budleigh Salterton in Devon a couple of years ago and Lucy had only been there once for a week. Their new flat was very comfortable and it had lovely views of the English Channel, but it didn't feel like home and Lucy had been bored out of her skull within days. Of course she would go and see them, but then she knew she would need a real holiday somewhere where the average age wasn't in the late sixties. She only had a few friends back in London, none especially close, so she could pretty much choose to go wherever she wanted. One thing was for sure – it wasn't going to be Africa, at least not for a while.

'I'm not sure.' Then it came to her. 'Wait a minute. What am I talking about? Of course I know where I'm going. I've got a really close friend in Italy who's getting married next month. I told her I wasn't going to be able to go to the wedding, but maybe I can now if I'm out of a job for a while. I'll have to talk to the powers-that-be in Kinshasa.'

'Whereabouts in Italy?' Nicole was from southern France, not far from Avignon. 'I've never been to Italy, but our town's full of Roman remains and I know I'd love to visit Rome.'

'A bit further north. My friend Daniela lives in Tuscany. Ever heard of Siena?'

'Yes, of course, and I've seen photos. Isn't that where they have the crazy horse race around the main square?'

The engine note suddenly changed as the helicopter banked sharply to the left and they clung onto each other for physical and moral support. Maybe, Lucy thought to herself, she had been a bit hasty in telling the pilot how much she now loved this form of transport. Trying hard to sound resolute, she did her best to carry on the conversation as if nothing had happened.

'The Palio, yes. That takes place every summer. I've only ever seen it once, but it was exciting and historically fascinating.'

'You've always had a thing for history, haven't you?'

'If I hadn't done medicine, I'd have loved to do a degree in history. Yes, I find it riveting and Tuscany's got so much history connected to it. Anyway, Daniela, my friend, lives in a little village in the hills outside Siena, and that's where the wedding's going to be.'

The more she thought about it, the more the idea of a trip to Tuscany to see one of her oldest friends appealed. A lot. She felt her spirits begin to rise.

'I can go to the wedding and then maybe find somewhere over there to take a real holiday. That part of the world's very lovely. It's quiet, safe, and nobody's likely to be shooting at me for a change. Yes, I think that's what I'll do. What about you, Nic?'

'I'm going home. François's been on at me to come back for months now. I'm pretty sure he's going to propose, and if he doesn't I probably will.'

Lucy was delighted Nicole was sounding brighter and looking more relaxed as they put distance between themselves and the fighting.

'Lucky you.'

'And really no boyfriend waiting for you, Lucy?'

In fact, Nicole and Geneviève already knew the answer to that one. When you live in such close proximity for two years, effectively cut off from the outside world by hundreds of kilometres of dirt roads, scrub, forest and jungle, there are very few secrets. Lucy shook her head.

'Nope. Nobody, not now.'

The sudden demise of her relationship with Charles four years earlier had been one of the main stimuli in her decision to leave Europe. Since then her itinerant lifestyle had made any meaningful relationships almost impossible and, if she was honest, Charles's infidelity had left her emotionally scarred, with little desire to launch herself once again into a relationship with any man.

She felt a tap on her shoulder. It was the Flight Engineer and he brought very welcome refreshment in the shape of three bottles of ice-cold water.

'The captain thought you might like a celebratory drink. Sorry we don't have any champagne on board.' He gave them a big smile. 'I'm sure you all deserve a celebration and a good holiday. I envy you your trip to Tuscany, doctor. I'm sure it'll be a wonderful place for you to escape to.'

Escape to Tuscany – that sounded good. And the cold drink sounded even better. Lucy gave him a weary smile, sat back and tried to relax.

Chapter 1

The sun was remarkably hot for early May and even the locals were complaining, but to Lucy it felt wonderful. Compared to the humidity of Africa, she loved the dry heat that was doing a magnificent job of soothing her nerves, recharging her batteries, and helping her to get the rest and recuperation she knew she needed. R&R was what her boss in Kinshasa had called it, but he had always liked acronyms and abbreviations.

'Get yourself some R&R for now. There'll be plenty of time to talk about your future with us in a month or two. You've been hard at it for almost four years now and you've recently been through a very tough experience; you need to rest and recuperate. Leave the DRC and go get some R&R – that's what you need.'

She hadn't disagreed with him.

She stretched in the hammock and turned slightly so that the gentle breeze blew across her cheek. It felt good. She had arrived at Daniela's house a week earlier, after six days in Budleigh Salterton with her parents, deliberately playing down her hasty exit from the latest flare-up of hostilities in the Democratic Republic of the Congo. To her irritation, her airlift to safety in the nick of time had been picked up by the mainstream media back in London. There had even been reporters and a TV crew waiting for her as she emerged bleary-eyed into the Arrivals hall at Heathrow airport. She had muttered a few comments about her good luck, her concern for the fate of her patients and colleagues left behind, and her desire to take a break, and then had had to suffer sitting next to her parents that evening as she saw her face on the six o'clock news. Was she really that skinny and did her hair really look that unkempt?

Inevitably her mother had homed in on the fact that she had lost a lot of weight in Africa, but Lucy had been able to reassure her that she had every intention of remedying that during her visit to Italy.

And she had been true to her word since arriving here in Poggio San Marco.

Daniela's mother had insisted that Lucy stay with them in their rambling old farmhouse and had reacted in exactly the same way as Lucy's own mother had at the sight of her, throwing up her hands in horror at her emaciated appearance and insisting on force-feeding her mountains of home-made pasta, local ham, cheese from their own goats and enough steak to keep an American football team happy. In fact, Lucy didn't need to be *force*-fed. The food was excellent, especially when accompanied by home-made ice cream and Daniela's uncle's red wine, and she had let herself be spoilt rotten. In return, she had been helping with getting everything ready for the wedding that was coming up in just four days' time and doing her best to stop Daniela from freaking out.

Now, as the pounds – or at least ounces – started to pile back on, she could feel her energy levels rise once more. Things would have been perfect if it hadn't been for the recurrence of blood-soaked dreams involving machetes, machine guns and worse. She was still waking up almost every night, bathed in sweat, her mouth wide open in a silent scream. During her four years in Africa, two of them out in the wilds of Mabenta, she had seen too many of the appalling injuries and deliberate acts of mutilation inflicted upon men, women and even children – many of whom had died without her being able to save them – and these graphic images returned night after night. It then often took a long time for these horrific memories finally to subside and for her to able to drift off to sleep once more. Still, she told herself over and over again in the welcome light of the following dawn, this was to be expected after her close call at Mabenta, and everybody knew that post-traumatic stress needed time.

As she began to feel better physically, she started to give serious consideration to what she should do after the wedding was over. Her intention had been to take a holiday for a few weeks, but, nice as it might sound just to lie about in the warm Tuscan sunshine without a care in the world, she knew she would soon be bored. Maybe she should do something practical like improving her Italian with a course at one of the language schools in Siena, or volunteering for an archaeological dig or some such to keep her occupied. The more she thought about it, the idea of just heading for the beach or the depths of the country and doing nothing wasn't going to cut it.

And then there was the question of what to do after this period of R&R. After what had happened in Mabenta, she knew she didn't feel like taking on another mission to such a remote and dangerous location – at least not for a good long while. MSF operated in over seventy different countries all over the globe, from South America to Asia, and she felt sure it should be possible to find something a bit less stressful if she asked for it. The complication was that since returning from Africa she had started giving her future serious thought, and not only as far as her medical career was concerned.

She would be thirty-six in six months' time and it hadn't taken her mother's far-from-subtle interrogation last week for her to realise that she rather liked the idea of a 'normal' life; preferably involving a permanent address, a partner, children – one of each – and a dog or a cat or both. A few roses around the door wouldn't go amiss either. On one level this almost annoyed her as she had always thought of herself as a self-sufficient kind of woman who was quite happy without the usual trappings of conventional life. Now she wasn't so sure.

Her introspective reverie that afternoon was interrupted as Daniela returned from work.

'Ciao Lucy. Had a good day?'

Lucy opened her eyes and smiled. 'I've had a very good and very lazy day and, for just about the first time in two weeks, I've started thinking about work again. How was yours? Been busy?'

Daniela was a journalist with a Tuscan newspaper, based in Siena, and Lucy knew she enjoyed her job.

'Not too bad, thanks. Tomorrow's my last day in the office for a few weeks and I've spent today handing over to Tommy who's going to be standing in for me while I'm away on our honeymoon.' Daniela perched on the table alongside the hammock which was strung across the open-sided loggia. This veranda, shaded from the direct sun, had a spectacular view down over the olive groves and across the valley to the city of Siena on the slopes of the next hill. 'So, what have you decided about work? Don't tell me you're thinking of going back to Africa.'

'No, that's definitely off the agenda – at least for now. I'm still having bad dreams about the place. No, I've been thinking about something a bit closer to home.'

'MSF are active in southern Italy, aren't they? Your Italian's good enough. Why don't you see if you can get a transfer over here?'

Lucy's mother had been friends with Daniela's mother since university and over the years when their daughters had been growing up, the two families had often holidayed together here in Tuscany. As a result, Lucy spoke fairly reasonable Italian, although her years in Africa had tended to favour her French to the detriment of her Italian, but now that she was here again for the first real holiday in over ten years, it was quickly coming back. She nodded.

'I was wondering about that. There's been a big MSF operation in Sicily for quite a few years now, looking after the flood of migrants coming over from North Africa. Now that Italy's got a much more right-wing government, they're clamping down on immigration, but I imagine there'll still be a need for medics for some years to come.'

'Pietro and I'd happily come and visit you in Sicily if that's where you end up. It's a gorgeous part of the world and we're going there for our honeymoon. For now, the important thing is for you forget about Africa and just relax.' Daniela reached over and squeezed her hand. 'And don't worry, the bad dreams will stop, I'm sure. Just give it time.' She pulled out her phone and consulted it. 'Anyway, listen, I'm meeting Pietro in Siena in an hour. He sent me a message ten minutes ago. Here, let me read it to you.' She scrolled through to the message. 'Here it is. *Ciao Danni. See you at six. Bruno's going to be there. He remembers Lucy from years ago and wants to catch up with her again.* Why don't you come to Siena with me? What do you say? You haven't seen Bruno for a long time, have you? You'll be surprised by him now. He's moved on a lot since you last saw him.'

Lucy sat up – or rather, she tried to sit up in the hammock but failed. Instead, she had to lift her legs out and slide somewhat inelegantly to the ground beside her friend. She straightened her crumpled clothes, stretched and smiled.

'Bruno? I'd love to see him again. He was always great fun when we were playing together as kids. He was forever telling jokes and getting into trouble. Do you remember when he stuck an egg up the priest's exhaust pipe and spray-painted half a dozen nuns?'

'How could I forget? But, like I say, he's moved on a lot since then.'

'I suppose he must have done. A lot can happen in, what, fifteen or twenty years since I last saw him?'

Chapter 2

And a lot had happened in the intervening years.

Bruno had indeed moved on and had morphed into a good-looking grown-up. Lucy could hardly believe it when she and Daniela got to the café in Piazza del Campo to meet the two men. This was right in the heart of Siena's *centro storico* and she spotted them sitting outside at a table in the shade directly opposite the iconic Palazzo Pubblico on the far side of the piazza. This stunning medieval building, built partly of stone and partly of brick, dominated the square. Rows of arches made up the front and jagged crenellations on the top attested to Siena's often troubled history. Although Lucy had been here numerous times, she never tired of the views all around this fan-shaped, sloping square with its herringbone pattern of red bricks paving all but the edges. But this evening her attention was drawn by the tall, dark-haired man who jumped up to greet her. Daniela was right. Bruno certainly had moved on from his days as a spotty teenager – but then, of course, so had she.

'Lucy, ciao. Wow, you look amazing!'

He just stood there and gawped at her and, for a moment, she had a flashback to the teenage Bruno who hadn't been able to keep his eyes off her but, to her chagrin at the time, had lacked the courage to do anything more than stare. Somehow, she had a feeling he might no longer be so reticent. She went over to greet him with a broad smile on her face.

'Ciao, Bruno, how great to see you again after so long.'

She leant towards him and kissed him on his stubbly cheeks. Then she felt his hands catch hold of her shoulders and he stepped back, his eyes studying her. To her surprise he was a good bit taller now. Clearly he had had a late growth spurt. Finally he managed to stop gawping enough to address her again.

'I would have recognised you, Lucy, I'm sure. Pietro told me you'd changed, but it's still you underneath. Your hair's the same and your blue eyes are the same. Yes, you look terrific.' He released his hold on her, kissed the tips of his fingers and fanned them outwards in true Italian style, murmuring an awe-struck, '*Bellissima.*'

She gave him a grin and then went over to kiss Pietro. He and Daniela had started dating way back when they were teenagers and had been living together now for the best part of ten years. Lucy was delighted they had decided to tie the knot and she had no doubt they would spend the rest of their lives together. As ever, she felt a little twinge of jealousy at their luck in finding each other. She rather liked the idea of having a Pietro of her own. Still, she told herself, one thing was for sure: she was much more likely to find somebody suitable here in Siena than in a little jungle encampment in the middle of a war zone. Thought of the war zone brought its own disturbing memories and she had to make a conscious effort to brush them away.

'So, tell me all about you, Lucy.' Bruno waved her into a seat next to him, so that she had a view of the square and of the crowds of tourists milling around. It was still only May and it was already busy. She knew from experience just how much more crowded it would become here as the season progressed. Still, crowds or no crowds, the view across the square to the medieval buildings in front of them was as stunning as ever.

'Well, Daniela and Pietro may have told you I'm a doctor now.'

To her surprise, she saw him nod enthusiastically. 'Me too.'

'Really? You a doctor?' She was genuinely surprised. The last time she had met him he had been much more interested in sticking lizards into unsuspecting ladies' handbags or worms down girls' necks – hers included. 'When did you decide to go into medicine?'

'To be totally honest, it was when Daniela told me that's what you were going to do. I thought if that's what you'd chosen as a career, I'd better do the same.'

Lucy was touched. 'And where are you practising these days? Here in Siena?'

'Yes, well almost. It's a private hospital just outside of town.'

'It's terribly exclusive and astronomically expensive.' Pietro cut in with a few words of clarification. 'And he gets to treat all kinds of celebrities, but he refuses to tell us who they are.'

'I'm not *allowed* to tell you who they are, Pietro.' Bruno glanced back at Lucy. 'But I imagine they're a bit different from the average patient you've been treating in Africa. Pietro told me all about you working for MSF. *Complimenti*. That's impressive, especially in a war zone. It can't have been easy.'

As they chatted about their jobs, Lucy's eyes ranged over the square, alighting upon the famous Torre del Mangia, rising like a finger pointing into the sky from the side of the imposing Palazzo Pubblico. At the top, the red brick shaft gave way to a white stone section that flared out into an observation platform with a slim belfry sitting on it. The tower was over a hundred metres high and Lucy had only climbed the four hundred steps to the top once in her life and had no intention of repeating the experience. The view from up there had been spectacular, but the steep, narrow staircase hadn't been much fun. Chatting to Bruno here this evening, on the other hand, was bringing back a lot of memories and proving to be a lot of fun.

As the sun sank lower behind them and the shadows lengthened, she studied him more closely from behind the anonymity of her sunglasses. She noticed that he wasn't wearing a wedding ring, and there was no mention of a wife. Apart from his being taller than she remembered, he now had a rather alluring stubbly chin and impeccably styled wavy black hair that really suited him. He was wearing a pristine blue short-sleeved shirt and his tanned arms were strong and his shoulders broad. There was no doubt about it; Bruno was a handsome man who looked after himself but, somehow, the attraction she had felt for him as a teenager hadn't carried through into adulthood. He was a very nice guy but, for whatever reason, she was surprised to find she no longer saw him in a romantic light.

He was also evidently no fool. She felt sure that only the best doctors would be employed at the sort of upmarket private hospital where he was working. As their conversation proceeded, she learned more about his work and it was clear that some very important – and demanding – people passed through that establishment, although by the end she was no closer to finding out the identity of any of the famous patients. She respected his discretion and didn't press him, but one thing was for sure:

there was clearly a social and financial abyss between his patients and the ones she had treated in Mabenta.

Once again she thought with affection about some of the lovely people she had worked with and looked after over there and wondered what they would have made of the luxurious surroundings of a private hospital in Tuscany. And once again she also wondered how they were faring without her little clinic to look after them and with so many awful things happening around them. It soon became clear that this was a subject that was on Bruno's mind, too.

'And the place where you were working, Lucy, what's happened to it since you had to be airlifted out?'

She had been corresponding regularly by email with Geneviève and Nicole since coming back to Europe and had heard the news only this morning. Nicole, now happily engaged to be married to her beloved François as predicted, had directed her attention to a recent internal MSF bulletin. This announced that the decision had been taken, with regret, to abandon the Mabenta clinic indefinitely as serious conflict in what was often referred to as Africa's World War was still raging through the area. She did her best to explain.

'It's gone, at least for the time being. Although we don't hear much about it here in Europe, there's been a war going on in Africa for years now and it shows no signs of stopping. The government of the DRC – you probably know that's the Congo – is supported by Angola, Namibia and Zimbabwe, while the rebels are backed by Uganda and Rwanda. The Congo's rich in all manner of natural resources from diamonds to rare metals, so there are lots of different foreign interests jockeying for position there as well – like the Chinese for example – which muddies the waters further. That whole area of North Kivu – that's where I was working – is a war zone and it's just too dangerous to go back there.' She sighed. 'So there's nobody there to look after the local people any more. It's tragic.'

'And would you like to go back?'

Lucy paused for thought. 'For the sake of the locals, yes. I met some wonderful people there – patients and staff – but I just don't think I can stomach the thought of going back until it's safe again. I saw some horrific injuries over there and they're still fresh in my memory. I still get bad dreams, even now after coming over here to Tuscany. I'm sure I'll get over it all in time, but I had a really close call.'

Bruno reached over and laid his hand on top of hers for a few moments. 'Experiences like that are enough to give anyone bad dreams. You're far braver than I am. Far braver than most people. Everybody must be immensely proud of you.'

She gave him a little smile. 'I was only doing my job. I just hope things calm down soon, or an awful lot more people are going to die over there.'

'And what sort of cases were you dealing with?' His professional curiosity was evident in his tone.

'I trained as a surgeon back in London, and in Africa I found myself dealing with everything from gunshot and machete wounds to childbirth. Thank God I didn't come across any cases of Ebola – and there was an outbreak only a few hundred kilometres from us – but I've dealt with most everything else. I bet you don't have to treat many cases of snakebite here in Tuscany. I had one recently where the patient's friends helpfully brought the snake in with him so I would know which vaccine to use.

Unfortunately they only stunned it and the damn thing woke up and slithered away between my feet while I had the patient on the operating table.'

She saw Bruno shudder at the thought. 'Way out of my league. I spend most of my time dealing with breast enhancement, rhinoplasty, liposuction and sporting injuries. No gunshot wounds or snakes so far, I'm glad to say.'

Daniela moved the subject on to where to eat. After a brief discussion, during which Lucy tried her hardest to insist that she be allowed to treat them all to dinner, but in vain, the decision was taken to walk just a couple of hundred metres down to Piazza del Mercato. It was beginning to get dark as they strolled across the square and down a narrow road alongside the massive walls of the Palazzo Pubblico before emerging into a smaller piazza with another imposing medieval building directly ahead of them, also made of the same sun-bleached red bricks as so much of the rest of Siena.

Just a little way down from there they came to the restaurant. Although the sun was by now blotted out by the tall buildings all around them, Lucy could still feel the heat radiating upwards from the road as they walked along. From the look of the cloudless sky, it was a safe bet that tomorrow was likely to be another beautiful day and she smiled happily to herself. At her side, Bruno was also smiling and she wondered what was going through his head.

They chose a table on the terrace outside the restaurant, with five chairs around it. From there, they had a stunning view across the old market square with its covered central area supported on hefty brick pillars. Beyond it was a mix of buildings, all different shades of pinks and browns, built over the course of the last seven or eight centuries, no two alike. In the far distance were tree-covered hills crowned with ancient churches, farmhouses and towers, and framed by the ubiquitous cypress trees so common here in Tuscany. Lucy sat back and relaxed. She was still relaxing when the significance of the fifth chair at their table was revealed to her.

'*Ciao a tutti.*'

A very glamorous woman with a sumptuous mass of jet-black hair appeared and immediately draped herself over Bruno. Lucy's eyes instinctively checked out her ring finger but here, too, there was nothing. Was this his wife who didn't go in for jewellery or just a friend – a very affectionate friend? After giving Bruno a big kiss on the lips, the new arrival went round the table kissing the others on the cheeks until she reached Lucy. Daniela made the introductions.

'Virginia, this is Lucy. She's English and she's one of my oldest friends from way back. Lucy, this is Virginia. She's Bruno's girlfriend.'

'Ciao, Lucy.' Virginia and Lucy shook hands and then Virginia slipped into the empty chair on the other side of her boyfriend and caught hold of his bicep with both hands. Proprietorially.

Lucy reached for her glass and took a sip of wine. Somehow she wasn't surprised that a good-looking doctor in his thirties was already taken. She had only been with Bruno for an hour or two tonight but she had been getting on so well with him, even if she no longer saw him in a romantic light. Seeing as he was pretty clearly hooked up with Virginia, this was for the best. She took another sip of wine and reflected that there would be other fish in the sea for her, although a handsome doctor was pretty high

24

up the food chain and not to be found in large shoals. She set her glass down and looked across the table.

'So what do you do, Virginia?'

'I'm a hospital administrator.' She had a local accent, like the others.

'Virginia and I work in the same clinic,' Bruno was quick to explain. 'Her father's the big boss.'

'The owner.' Virginia caught Lucy's eye for a second and there was no missing the challenge. Lucy didn't react, reminding herself that having a jealous woman across the table from her was far less daunting than having a two-metre-long, potentially deadly, black mamba slither over her foot.

'Bruno's been telling me about it. It sounds like a lovely place to work. Certainly a lot more civilised than my last place of work.'

'And what do you do, Lucy?' Now that the pecking order had been established, Virginia was also smiling now.

'I'm a doctor… well, a surgeon actually.'

They had an excellent dinner. The restaurant special-ised in grilled meats and Lucy chose delicious lamb chops, accompanied by asparagus and roast potatoes seasoned with rosemary whose enticing aroma arrived before they did. The conversation, after the initial marking of her territory by Virginia, ran smoothly and Lucy and the others were soon reminiscing about the good times they had had together as kids growing up. For some reason Virginia seemed to disapprove of stories of practical jokes carried out by her boyfriend and did her best to keep returning the conversation to the present day. Pietro and Bruno, on the other hand, spent the evening recounting tall tales of adolescent mischief and Lucy had tears of laughter in her eyes.

It was a great meal and a memorable evening and Lucy was sorry when it came to an end. It had been really good to catch up with old friends and even Virginia had mellowed as the night progressed and as she recognised that Lucy did not have designs on her man. They walked back to the cars together and as they said goodnight, Virginia even kissed Lucy on the cheeks, as did Bruno. As he did so, he told her how much he looked forward to seeing her again on Saturday at the wedding.

Chapter 3

Daniela and Pietro's wedding went very well, although for Lucy it took an unexpected turn. The service was held in the local parish church in Poggio San Marco and the bride looked stunning in a simple but elegant white silk dress complete with veil. Everybody commented on how well she looked and how she positively glowed. Lucy was one of the very few to know that Daniela was now over three months pregnant and she had even dutifully held her friend's hair this morning as she threw up in the toilet. Still, the service went ahead without any hiccups – or nausea – and the reception in a nearby hotel was perfect.

It was another beautiful warm spring day and Lucy was wearing her recently purchased, smart summer dress. In her escape from Mabenta she had lost almost all her clothes – although in truth there hadn't been much requirement for more than shorts, T-shirts or surgical scrubs while she was there – and she had spent an enjoyable day in Siena earlier in the week replenishing her wardrobe. This dress and shoes hadn't been cheap in a town centre boutique, but she had money in the bank. Although the pay with MSF wasn't fantastic, the trade-off was that there had been very few opportunities to spend it, and so she knew her savings account was healthy enough to support her for a year or more if she wanted, before having to return to work.

As she stood at the back of the room and listened to the speeches, she reflected yet again on what she wanted to do. Being back in Italy felt very comfortable, so maybe she should look for a job over here, either with MSF or some other organisation. Although the nightmares were becoming less frequent, she knew she didn't want to go anywhere too scary until she was once more back to normal. At the same time, there was no doubt in her mind that she had enjoyed working with people who so desperately needed her help and she wondered if a return to 'ordinary' medicine was what she wanted out of life. But before that decision had to be taken, she first had to come up with something to do over the next few weeks to avoid getting too bored while she enjoyed her period of R&R.

Her reflections were interrupted by a voice at her ear. She turned her head and saw an unfamiliar face. It was a friendly-looking man with dark hair. He was probably around her age or just a little older, impeccably turned out and with the whitest teeth she had ever seen. They were very much on display as he treated her to a beaming smile.

'Hi, I'm Tommaso, but everybody calls me Tommy.' His accent was Tuscan, probably local. He was brimming with confidence and looked like the kind of man who knew his way around members of the other sex – or thought he did. 'I work with Daniela and I'm covering for her while she and Pietro have their honeymoon. You must be her English friend.'

Comprehension dawned. 'Hi, Tommy. I'm Lucy. I remember Danni mentioned you.' They shook hands. 'How did you recognise me?'

He grinned at her. 'Daniela told me you were drop-dead gorgeous, so it was easy.'

Lucy seriously doubted whether her friend had said anything of the sort, but it didn't stop her blushing. It also confirmed her initial impression of Tommy as a player. 'You journalists do have a tendency to exaggerate, don't you?'

He didn't get a chance to respond as a burst of applause indicated that the speeches were over and the bride turned to the crowd and waved her bouquet of roses in the air. Unmarried women, from teenagers to pensioners, were pushed to the front and Lucy found herself among them. She gave Tommy a helpless look and went with the flow.

Daniela caught Lucy's eye before turning her back on them and lobbing the bouquet into the air, suspiciously in her direction. Lucy was still trying to work out whether to make a lunge for it when a purple flash blotted out the light and Lucy saw none other than Virginia leap athletically into the air right in front of her and grab the flowers as they fell. A cheer went up all round as Virginia collected herself, checked that her daring décolleté was still structurally sound after her exertions, and looked across towards Bruno with an expression of triumph on her face. However, he was on the phone and barely noticed her achievement, just giving her a little wave of the hand.

Lucy gave them both a smile and headed across the room to where the Prosecco was being dispensed. She was standing there, sipping her wine, when she felt a hand on her shoulder. She turned to find it was Bruno, with Virginia clinging, limpet-like, to his arm.

'Congratulations, Virginia. That was quite some leap you made there. Have you ever played volleyball?'

Virginia contented herself with a shake of the head and a little smile as Bruno, to Lucy's surprise, started talking shop. And not just any old shop.

'Lucy, could we have a word with you?'

He sounded unexpectedly serious and she immediately nodded. 'Of course, Bruno. What is it?'

She saw him exchange glances with Virginia and then indicate the French windows that led to the charming formal gardens surrounding the hotel. 'Would you mind if we go outside?'

Together, the three of them walked out into the full heat of the sun and Lucy was glad she had gone for the lightest possible material for her new dress. Although it was still just May, it was really hot. As soon as he was satisfied that they were not being overheard, Bruno started.

'You said you were a surgeon with experience of gunshot wounds, didn't you?' He didn't wait for Lucy's answering nod. 'Well, you see… we would welcome your help.'

'With a gunshot wound?' Lucy was genuinely amazed. 'Isn't that something that should be handled by a major hospital? The police, even?'

Virginia, now no longer smiling, took over. 'Absolutely, under normal circumstances, but these aren't normal circumstances. You see, it has to be kept very confidential.'

For a moment an image of a nineteen-twenties gangster with a violin case in his hands crossed Lucy's mind and she took a step backwards. 'Not normal circumstances?'

Her uncertainty must have been plain to see and Bruno was quick to explain in more detail. 'It's nothing criminal. I've just taken a call from the clinic. It's one of our regular outpatients. He was at home, fiddling with his gun, and it went off, wounding him in the side – apparently not too seriously as he's sitting up and talking. His housekeeper called us and they're bringing him in as we speak. The thing is, we'd be grateful if somebody with more experience of gunshot wounds than we have could take a look at the extent of the damage and maybe be there to help me with the procedure.'

Lucy nodded hesitantly. 'Of course, but why all the secrecy?'

Again the two of them exchanged glances. 'He's very well-known. Not just here, but all over the world. Although it was an accident, the publicity would be colossal. He's very keen to avoid anything like that.'

Lucy made a quick decision. 'Of course I'll help. I suppose that means we should go now, doesn't it? I'll just pop over and tell Danni. I'm sure she'll understand.' As Bruno nodded solemnly, she gave him a smile. 'It's just as well I've only had a small sip of Prosecco.' Sometimes being a doctor could seriously interfere with your private life, but Lucy knew that was part of the fascination of her chosen profession.

Virginia drove them to the clinic in record time. She was a good driver but she was going a hell of a lot faster than Lucy would have liked. As they screeched to a halt outside the hospital, Lucy barely had time to register that it was housed inside a charming and no doubt ancient Tuscan villa, and under other circumstances would have been delightful. As it was, she didn't stop to admire it as they hurried up the steps and in through the main doors. Virginia disappeared through a door marked *Private*, while Bruno led her into the lift and down to the operating area in the basement, where a nurse was waiting for them.

After scrubbing up and donning gloves, they went through into a very smart modern operating theatre.

The patient was laid out on the table and as soon as she saw him, Lucy recognised him. It was none other than former tennis world champion, David Lorenzo, from the USA. Lucy had played a lot of tennis when she was younger and she was very familiar with his triumphant career over the past decade or more, although she had rather lost track of the whole tennis scene while in the depths of Africa. He was conscious and as he saw them, he even managed to hoist himself up onto his elbows, albeit with a grimace. Recognition appeared on his face as he saw Bruno.

'Bruno, hi. Listen, I've done something very stupid.' He sounded anxious, but under control.

'Hello, David, don't worry. We'll sort you out.' Lucy was mildly surprised to find that Bruno spoke unexpectedly fluent English. So far she had only ever heard him speak Italian. 'This is my colleague, Doctor Young. She has a lot of experience of gunshot wounds and she's going to take a look at you.'

Lucy walked over to the table and set about examining him. There was a blood-soaked towel strapped to the left side of his chest, just below the ribcage. She asked the nurse to expose the wound and, as the bandages were being removed, she introduced herself.

'Hi, my name's Lucy Young. I gather you somehow managed to shoot yourself. How did you do that?'

All she got back from him was a shake of the head. 'I dropped it. It's complicated. It was an accident.' His American accent had been softened by years of international travel, but was still there. His eyes suddenly focused on her. 'Are you sure you're old enough to be a doctor? You're not a medical student, are you?'

Now, when you are thirty-five, it can be rather nice when somebody thinks you are ten years younger, but when you're an experienced surgeon and your credentials are questioned, it's a different matter. Consciously keeping her tone sweet – he had just shot himself after all – she replied.

'Thanks for the compliment, Mr Lorenzo, but I'm older than you think and, don't worry, I'm well qualified.'

The nurse removed the blood-soaked towel and revealed the wound. Lucy's first reaction was one of relief. Unlike so many wounds she had seen over the years, there was just a little blood oozing from a neat hole surrounded by the trademark burns associated with a bullet wound at close range. She went over and bent lower to inspect it more fully. She reached round his side and found the exit wound reassuringly close-by. She got him to roll to one side so she could examine it more closely and she was heartened by what she saw. It looked like the work of a relatively small calibre, high-velocity bullet and it had come out leaving an exit wound that was almost as neat as the entry wound. It had gone straight through him and, with any luck, it had done so without hitting any vital organs. She glanced up to see him staring down at the wound in morbid fascination.

'Good news, Mr Lorenzo. It looks to me as though you haven't done yourself too much damage. I think you've been very lucky.'

'Me, lucky?'

You didn't need to be a qualified psychiatrist to hear the dejection in his voice. With all his success and all his millions, she wondered what he had to make him unhappy. Deciding to leave any consideration of his mental health to somebody else, she carried on in her most reassuring voice.

'All we need to do now is to give you a scan to be sure there's no serious internal damage and that it's all clean in there and then we'll sew you up again. You'll be back on your feet in a day or two and as good as new in a few weeks.'

There was no answer so she and Bruno headed back to the anteroom to change into surgical gowns and masks. As they did so, David Lorenzo was wheeled off for a CT scan before surgery could commence. The scan revealed nothing too sinister and it turned out to be a very quick routine operation, all over in less than half an hour. In deference to Bruno Lucy let him do most of the work while she kept a weather eye on his progress. She was pleased to see that he was very thorough and painstaking and his stitching was as good as she had ever seen. As the patient was wheeled away to a room to recover, she peeled off her mask and gloves and dropped them into the sack. As she was taking off her gown, she glanced across at Bruno, pleased to see the smile back on his face.

'That was brilliant, Lucy. Thank you so much. As it turned out, it was no big deal, but I'm really grateful you were here to hold my hand. I'm sorry I spoiled your afternoon.'

'You're very welcome. Congratulations on your surgical skill – very impressive. And you didn't spoil anything for me. If I'd stayed at the wedding, I'd probably just have been standing in a corner drinking too much Prosecco.' She caught his eye. 'Listen, as far as the whole gunshot thing's concerned, back home in the UK we'd have to inform the police. I don't know if the same applies

34

here and I don't want to know, all right? All I would say is I think you should keep an eye on Mr Lorenzo. He says it was an accident, but there was something about him, something in his eyes, that worries me. Can you tell me what you've been treating him for?'

Bruno nodded. 'Two things: widespread damage to the torn cruciate ligaments in his left knee, and serious depression.' He shrugged his shoulders. 'The two are linked. We've operated on the ligament twice in an attempt to resolve the problem which wasn't helped by a previous unsuccessful operation done in Paris almost three years ago, but with only limited success. It looks like his career's over. That's why he's depressed.'

Lucy nodded as she vaguely began to remember hearing something about this while she was in Africa. For a top-level sportsman to find himself invalided out of his chosen sport while still at the peak of his career must have been a bitter pill to swallow. Little wonder he was suffering from depression.

'Thanks, Bruno, and you have my word none of this will go any further. But just keep an eye on him, would you? And I think it'd be a very good idea if you told his housekeeper to lose the gun.'

Chapter 4

Back at the wedding the first thing Lucy did was to hurry across to apologise to Daniela for having had to run off. On the way back in Virginia's car – thankfully at a more sedate pace – they had concocted a story involving a very demanding British patient who had insisted upon speaking to a doctor in his own language. Daniela gave her a big smile and told her not to worry and the story appeared to be accepted by everybody. Pietro even did his unsuccessful best to wheedle the name of the fictitious patient out of her.

Amazingly, they only missed the antipasti. All in all, their excursion to the clinic had only taken little over an hour and Lucy was able to take up her place at table number six just in time for the *panzanella*. This typical Tuscan dish had always been one of her favourites and she helped herself with relish. Served straight from the fridge, this was an aromatic mix of dry Tuscan bread, tomatoes, cucumber, lettuce, red onions and basil, all mixed together with extra virgin olive oil and red wine vinegar.

She found herself sitting at table along with what she first thought to be four strangers, but she soon found she did after all know two of them. The couple who looked vaguely familiar turned out to have been part of their gang way back in her teenage years, when they had spent the summers splashing about in the little stream down in the valley. They were soon reminiscing and the girl, Annarosa, told Lucy something surprising.

'I'll tell you something about Bruno. I bet you didn't know he was head over heels in love with you back then, did you?'

'Bruno in love with me? I had no idea.' Lucy grinned at them. 'Pity he didn't say anything. I quite fancied him myself when I was fourteen or fifteen.' She glanced around the room until she spotted him over on table four, positioned next to Virginia who was pressed tight up against him. 'Still, it seems like he's found himself a new love now. They look good together.' And they did.

Annarosa lowered her voice, although they had already worked out that Daniela's Auntie Rita alongside them was as deaf as a post and her husband far more interested in emptying the bottle of Chianti Classico on the table in front of him. 'They've been together for about five years now but he still hasn't asked her to marry him and they don't even live together. I think Virginia's getting a bit fed up.'

'Well, at least she can't accuse him of rushing into anything.'

'That's for sure. So, Lucy, how long are you staying here in Tuscany?'

'I'm probably only here for a few more days and then I'll be off again.'

Annarosa looked disappointed. 'Oh, I was hoping you'd come back to stay. Why don't you stay? We'd all love it if you did. It would be just like old times.'

'I need to work, I'm afraid, and I doubt there's anything for me here. Daniela and I were talking the other day. I might apply for something in Sicily, though. That's still Italy, after all.'

Annarosa gave a dismissive wave of the hand. 'Sicily's hundreds and hundreds of kilometres away. You might as well be back in England.'

Lucy nodded sadly. Annarosa was right.

As soon as they had all finished their coffees, glasses of sweet Vin Santo and cantuccini biscuits, waiters arrived and started moving the tables to the sides of the room, revealing the dance floor. The band arrived and set up their instruments and soon the stage was set for the happy couple's first dance together. Lucy joined in the clapping as Daniela and Pietro performed the dance she had seen them rehearsing for hours over the past week. In view of the fact that Daniela was expecting, they had deliberately chosen a slow, romantic waltz and they performed it gracefully and impeccably. Lucy was as relieved as they appeared to be when it went off without a hitch. After that, most of the guests headed for the dance floor and Lucy found herself dancing with a gangly fifteen- or sixteen-year-old who bore a passing resemblance to Bruno himself all those years ago. He even had the same spots on his cheeks. How strange that with the passage of the years, her attraction to Bruno had waned. She was still pondering why this should have happened as the music came to a halt and her partner thanked her awkwardly and led her back to her seat.

Before she could get there, however, she felt a tap on her shoulder. She turned to find Daniela's smooth-talking colleague, Tommy, standing there, that same cocky smile on his lips.

'Hi, again, Lucy. Would you like to dance?'

She couldn't really say no, so she followed him out onto the dance floor and danced a couple of numbers with him. There wasn't much opportunity to chat, but she could tell he was very interested in her and she found herself evaluating him. He was fairly good-looking in a showy way, definitely a charmer – but that probably came with the job – and he was a good dancer. She quite enjoyed being with him but that was as far as it went. There was something about him that jarred just a bit. He never seemed to stop smiling and he was so damn attentive it just felt fake. Although there was a tradition in some circles for bridesmaids to end up in bed with unattached male guests, she knew this wasn't going to happen, so she danced with him, but knew that nothing was going to happen. She hoped he would gradually get the message.

After a quarter of an hour or so, as the music slowed, she decided to return to the table where she had left her glass just in case Tommy decided to get any more intimate. Before she could get there, she heard another voice.

'You're not giving up already, surely?' Her immediate reaction was one of relief. It was Bruno, a smile on his lips.

'Care to dance?' He looked over at Tommy. 'You don't mind, do you? We're old friends and we've got a lot of catching up to do.'

Tommy gave them a resigned smile and bowed out. Before going back onto the dance floor with Bruno, Lucy instinctively glanced around to see if Virginia was watching from the wings, but she failed to spot her. Bruno must have realised her concern as he was quick to offer reassurance.

'Virginia's popped back to the clinic to check on a couple of things… like our tennis player for example. So, come on, let's dance.'

They danced together to the slow tune, which lasted barely a couple of minutes before the band launched into a lively and noisy version of some indecipherable Italian pop song. The next dance was another far slower, softer affair and they ended up holding each other, and she felt his mouth close to her ear.

'This is nice. When I was a teenager I often dreamt about dancing with you like this, Lucy. Who says dreams never come true?'

'This *is* nice and it's been lovely to meet up with you again, Bruno. It's a pity I'm only here for a few more days. It would have been nice to have dinner with you and Virginia again.' His reaction was surprise and maybe disappointment.

'A few days? I thought you were here for a good long holiday.'

The more Lucy thought about it, the more she realised that now that Daniela was going off on her honeymoon to Sicily, it would be a bit weird to stay on with her mum. She did a bit of quick thinking.

'I've decided it's time I learned to scuba dive.'

In fact, this was something she had often considered doing – particularly when she had found herself pretty much bang in the middle of Africa, about a thousand miles from any ocean – although the idea had only just returned to her this instant. She quickly ran through her knowledge of Italian geography in her head before plumping for one of the Tuscan islands in the Mediterranean to the west of here. The one that immediately came to mind was the one where a massive cruise liner had gone aground some years earlier.

'I've been checking it out on the internet. There's a place on the Isola del Giglio that does diving courses. I think I'm going to head off there in a few days once I've finished helping Daniela's mum clear everything up.'

He was still looking disappointed so she gave his shoulders a little squeeze. 'I'll be back sometime though. Maybe for your wedding to Virginia?'

'Maybe.'

She spent the rest of the dance in silence and, as the music came to an end, he led her back towards her seat. Before they got there, she pointed across the room. 'Now, if you don't mind, I can see the bridegroom on his own and I promised him a dance.' She reached up and planted a little kiss on his cheek. Pulling herself away, she added. 'And do let me know if you and Virginia feel like dinner one night, depending on when I leave – but no arguments, this time I'm paying.'

Chapter 5

Giglio was lovely, and very different from Poggio San Marco and the area around Siena. Only an hour by ferry from the mainland of Tuscany, the whole feel of the place was radically different. Here, the sea was omnipresent and Lucy went to sleep each night to the sound of waves lapping on the beach below her window. Her recurring bad dreams were continuing to diminish in frequency and these restful surroundings only increased her sense of well-being. She took photos and sent them to her parents and to Geneviève and Nicole. As far as she could tell, the two nurses were also managing to put the scary experiences behind them and get on with their lives although Geneviève, like Lucy, admitted to still having bad dreams. Unfortunately, neither of them had any news about their former colleagues and patients, particularly Lucy's close friend, Miriam. Lucy sent off yet another email more in hope than anything else. Weeks had passed since she had last seen her, and the news from Mabenta was still grim.

Here on the tree-covered island, however, it was altogether very relaxing and Lucy had plenty of time to read up on the history of Giglio as well as taking diving lessons each morning. She made a point of driving up and down the very few narrow, winding roads of the little island in her hire car and spending her afternoons visiting Roman and Etruscan ruins around the rocky coastline.

Seagulls screamed above her head as she climbed the narrow paths while, below her, gorgeous rich red flowers clothed the rocky shore. The crystal clear water, viewed from the cliff tops, revealed every rock on the sea bed for a long way out. The little fishing village, now turned holiday resort, where she was based was small and charming, although at this time of year the population of the island appeared to be pretty much in the Budleigh Salterton age bracket. This didn't bother her as she wasn't there for the nightlife. It was a wonderfully quiet, peaceful place and she was pleased to see that no trace now remained of the wrecked cruise ship that had hit the rocks, and the headlines, in 2012.

The diving school was owned and run by a German couple and they did a very good job. As Lucy reached the end of her course, she was already beginning to feel quite comfortable underwater, without any of the ear problems some of her fellow trainees had been suffering. It had definitely been a good choice to come here. While on the island she had had enough to do to stop her feeling bored, but at the same time she had been able to continue her programme of R&R. As the days went by, she felt her batteries recharging, no doubt fuelled at least in part by the excellent seafood on offer in the island's restaurants.

Then, on the final evening of the course, as she was sitting at a table with the other members of the group, proudly clutching her precious PADI Open Water diving certificate, she received a phone call. It was Bruno.

'Ciao, Bruno. How're you and Virginia?'

'Lucy, ciao. It's good to hear your voice. We're fine, thanks. How's life on the island?'

They chatted for a minute or two before he came to the point of his call.

'I… we were wondering if you had made any decisions about your future. Are you going back to Médecins Sans Frontières?'

'To be honest, I haven't really come to any conclusions, but I imagine unless something else comes along I'll go back to MSF and ask to be sent to somewhere a bit safer.'

'I see. Right, well, you see, it's like this. A vacancy's come up here at the clinic and I mentioned your name to my boss in case you might feel like coming to work with us. He's very keen to meet you.'

Lucy waved apologetically at her fellow diners, got up and walked down the wooden steps that led to the beach. As she moved further away from the noise of the restaurant, she asked him for more information.

'We have an opening for a general surgeon. This is not to replace somebody who's leaving, but a brand-new position. The problem with Mr Lorenzo and the gunshot wound has brought home to us that we may have got too specialised over the past few years and we need to broaden our base. The director's decided we don't just want to focus on cosmetic surgery, orthopaedics and physical rehab. We need to be able to respond to all sorts of cases – although hopefully no further shooting incidents. He thinks – and so do I – that your qualifications, background and wide experience are exactly what we're looking for. If you think you might be interested – and I really hope you will be – he says he'll get somebody to email you all the details. Do you think this might be something that appeals to you?' He sounded genuinely keen.

Lucy perched on a rocky outcrop and thought about it. On the face of it, it sounded wonderful. If she took the job she would find herself in a state-of-the-art hospital, set in just about her favourite place in all the world, and it promised to be a rich and varied position and, most important of all, without black mambas and with nobody trying to kill her. What did worry her, however, was the idea of going into private medicine which, by definition, would be reserved for the privileged few, when she felt sure her heart lay in helping those less fortunate than herself. Would she be ignoring all her natural instincts? She decided to buy herself some time.

'Thank you so much, Bruno, that really does sound most attractive. I don't want to let anybody down so I need to speak to my boss at MSF first to see that they haven't already made plans for me, but, in principle, I'm very interested. If you'd like to ask the director to send me the details, I'll think it through and I'll send him over a copy of my CV. I'm still here tomorrow, but I'll be heading back to Siena on Friday so I could come and see the director then if he's still keen.' She dictated her email address and rang off.

Before returning to the dinner table she sat for a good long while looking out across the sea towards the twinkling lights of the Tuscan mainland in the far distance. Back in war-torn Africa, when she had thought about escaping to Tuscany, this sort of job would have been beyond her wildest dreams. In so many ways, it was too good to turn down, but there was the major stumbling block of her reservations about private medicine. Presumably she would find out how she would react only when she got there, but it worried her. When she finally roused herself and returned to her now cold grilled sardines, she was still turning it over in her head.

When she got back to her room, she found an email from Virginia, whose official title turned out to be Senior

Administrative Officer at the Siena Clinic. The contents of the email suddenly made Lucy's decision a whole lot easier. The salary they were offering was over twice as much as she had been earning with MSF and that made the job much more difficult to turn down, even though deep inside she was still worried at the sort of people she would find herself treating. Would she be selling her soul to the devil if she accepted? Still, she reflected as she drifted off to sleep, on a salary like that she would be able to afford to buy herself that little house she had dreamt of for so long. And the first thing she would plant would be a rose bush by the door.

She didn't sleep very well that night, despite being untroubled by gruesome nightmares. Instead, her subconscious had been turning this exciting new proposal over and over again in her mind. Next morning she emailed her boss at MSF in London, indicating that she had been offered another job in Italy, but specifying that she didn't want to let anybody down. To her delight, barely three minutes later, she received a call back from Dr Brown herself. Lucy had received a couple of emails from the UK Director General since her return from the Congo, but it had been a while since she had heard her soft Scottish accent.

'Lucy, so good to hear from you. How are you after your experiences in the DRC?'

Lucy told her that she was recovering well and didn't burden her with an account of her bad dreams. She told her a bit more about the job offer at the Siena Clinic and Dr Brown sounded very supportive.

'You're free to decide to do whatever you like, Lucy. We would love to keep you on here at MSF, and the very least we can promise you would be a position somewhere well away from any form of conflict. But I would equally understand if you decided this was the time to make a change. Please choose whatever road you think will suit you best.'

Lucy felt she had to tell her what was worrying her most. 'The thing is, I've always got a kick out of helping the poor and the dispossessed. I suppose I'm worried I might find such a big change distasteful. I need to be true to my principles.'

'I know what you mean, Lucy, but remember, they're still people who're sick, who need your help. The fact that they can pay for it doesn't reduce their need. From what you tell me, the position's for a general surgeon, so you wouldn't just be pandering to rich people's vanity but looking after patients with real medical problems to be solved. Besides, I happen to know Michelangelo Gualtieri, the Director of the Siena Clinic, and I have nothing but respect for him as a doctor and as a man of principle. You're a very talented surgeon, Lucy. Everybody says that, and you know there'll always be a job with us if you change your mind. If you do decide to take the Italian job, give Michelangelo my name as a referee, and whatever you do, don't think that you're selling out if you choose to go into private medicine. They're still patients in need.'

By the time she put the phone down, Lucy felt reassured that she wouldn't be burning her bridges with MSF and a bit more confident that she wouldn't be betraying her principles. She sent an email to Professor Gualtieri, telling him she was very interested indeed, giving him the email address of her boss in London for a reference, and offering to come in for interview. She was booked onto the car ferry next morning and it was only a two-hour drive from Porto Santo Stefano back to Siena, so she told them she could be there after lunch. The reply came back almost immediately and they arranged that she would drive up to the clinic at three o'clock the following afternoon.

–

This time her arrival at the clinic was a lot slower than on the previous occasion and she had time to take in the scale and the beauty of the hospital and its scenic location on the hillside looking down on the red roofs of Siena. Beyond the city were the Tuscan hills where Daniela's mother's house at Poggio San Marco was clearly visible near the top of the first of these. A steel and glass sign at the gate indicated the name of the hospital simply as the Villa delle Ginestre, with the discreet strapline beneath it in English: The Siena Clinic. The villa was built in the classic Tuscan style and was probably several hundred years old, although a large ultramodern extension had been built at the back. The walls of the villa were white, the louvred shutters a tasteful pale blue-grey, and the surrounding park with its specimen trees a delight. As a place to work, it definitely beat the hell out of the clinic in Mabenta.

Inside, she found Bruno waiting for her with a welcoming smile on his face. He accompanied her along a series of corridors to the office of Virginia's father, Professor Michelangelo Gualtieri Della Torre, the founder and owner of the Siena Clinic.

He was probably well into his seventies, but he still had a healthy head of hair, albeit steel grey, and his eyes were bright and shrewd. He greeted Lucy with a broad smile and soon put her at her ease as he asked her a number of insightful questions about her background and her recent

49

experience with MSF. It turned out he knew Dr Brown in London very well and he had been impressed by the glowing reference she had provided this morning. As Lucy relaxed in his company, she took a distinct liking to him. This came as a relief as, in spite of Dr Brown's words, she had been fearful that he might have turned out to be just a money-grabbing ogre. Such was quite evidently not the case.

They talked for the best part of an hour before she shook hands with him and told him she would be very happy to accept the position, starting in two weeks' time so she could complete her prescribed course of R&R first. After joining them in a cup of Twinings English Afternoon Tea and a little piece of super-sweet *panforte* to celebrate her appointment, she turned the conversation to her recent patient.

'And how's our tennis player? Has he got over his gunshot wound?'

Professor Gualtieri nodded. 'It's all healing very well. Between Bruno and yourself, you did a great job. Thank you again for your help with that, Doctor Young. We appreciated it massively. He was up and walking the very next day. He discharged himself and went back to his home and he's been off any form of painkillers for almost a week now.'

'That's excellent news. Do please give him my best wishes next time he comes in.'

Bruno checked something on his clipboard. 'If you like, you can tell him yourself and take a look at the wound. He comes in three times a week for physio sessions and he's upstairs now.'

Lucy shook hands with Professor Gualtieri and followed Bruno to the lift. As they reached it, he gave her an apologetic smile. 'Virginia's away today so I'm afraid I have to get back to something urgent, but if you take the lift up to the third floor, you'll find the physio department. I'll call to tell them you're coming to see David.'

The huge stainless-steel lift, built to accommodate a patient in a bed, took its time getting up to the third floor and when the doors hissed open, there was a woman in a stylish blue tunic already waiting to greet Lucy. She had evidently been well primed by Bruno.

'Good afternoon, Doctor Young. My name's Louisa Verdi. I work in the rehabilitation department. If you'd like to follow me…'

They shook hands and as they made their way down a wide corridor, Lucy took the opportunity to sound her out about the tennis champion.

'How's Mr Lorenzo doing?'

The physio gave that same shrug that Lucy had noted from Bruno. 'Physically pretty good. He's a very fit man, as you would expect, and his injury doesn't stop him walking, driving, doing most things normal people do on a daily basis. The problem is that he isn't a normal person. Unfortunately, Doctor Saeed and Doctor Lanslebourg say his knee problems mean he'll be out of competitive tennis for at least another year or two, quite probably forever, and that's taken its toll on him emotionally.'

Lucy's ears pricked up. The name she had mentioned was far from common, even in France. 'Dr Lanslebourg? I don't suppose that's Doctor *Charles* Lanslebourg, by any chance? Tall French guy, blond hair, good-looking.'

The physio shot her a quick sideways grin. '*Very* good-looking. Yes, that's him. So you know him?'

'I know him.' Lucy was genuinely staggered. The world of medicine was a small one, but even so… 'He and I were both in Médecins Sans Frontières together in Greece four years ago.'

'So you must know him well.'

Lucy definitely knew Charles Lanslebourg well. Although their free time in Lesbos had been limited, she and he had hooked up, and there had been a time when she had been pretty sure she was falling in love with him. Then there had been that unforgettable night when she caught him with one of the nurses and she had requested an immediate transfer to a different continent. She hadn't spoken to him since.

'Yes, I know him well, or at least I did.' Suddenly her dream job was looking far less inviting. 'Is he here this afternoon?'

'No, he doesn't usually work on Fridays. He'll be in on Monday though. Would you like me to tell him you send your regards?'

There had been a time when a black mamba in a box would have been all Lucy would have wanted to send him, but four years had passed and the hurt had diminished, so she just shook her head. 'That's okay, thanks. I'll tell him myself when I see him.'

'David's in here.'

Lucy noted the use of his first name. Clearly, the tennis champion was a familiar face around here. Louisa opened the door and ushered Lucy inside. David Lorenzo was sitting on a weights bench, wearing just a pair of black spandex training shorts. He was facing away from her, hands gripping a steel bar above his head, so she had a moment to study him before walking across to his side. As Louisa had said, he looked very fit. There wasn't an ounce of excess fat on him and as he pulled and released the bar above his head, lifting a staggeringly heavy load of weights each time, it was clear that his upper body was every bit as muscular as his powerful legs.

Quite unexpectedly Lucy felt a spark of what could only be explained as attraction at the sight of his naked back. It had been drummed into her from her very first year as a medical student that involvement with a patient was one of the cardinal sins for any doctor. This feeling of attraction was instantly followed by a wave of annoyance – at herself. Apart from being forbidden fruit because of her Hippocratic oath, he also undoubtedly came from a completely alien world of riches and celebrity, exactly the world of excess and wealth she had so feared when considering accepting this job. She told herself in no uncertain terms that she would do well to think of this man as just a patient. Period.

She walked over to him and positioned herself by his injured side, pleased to see the entry and exit wounds now well on the way to healing up and no longer needing to be dressed. He was sweating profusely and pushing himself hard, his eyes closed, his teeth gritted, and she counted twelve reps before he finally released the bar and stretched. As he did so, he opened his eyes and saw her. To her surprise, considering he must have been in shock when they had met before, he not only recognised her, but also remembered her name.

'Dr Young. Come to check up on me?'

As before, there was little or no warmth in his voice. Still, he wasn't the first grumpy patient she had come across, so she just smiled sweetly.

'I had an appointment with Professor Gualtieri Della Torre and I thought I'd come and see for myself how you were doing.'

'And now you've seen.'

His tone was dismissive and, in spite of her best intentions, she felt a surge of annoyance that she managed, with effort, to control.

'And now I've seen, and I'm pleased everything's healing up nicely. Does it cause you any discomfort?'

He shook his head, but made no response. Feeling that it would be best if she left him to it, she turned for the door, pausing only to wish him well. Once again she was met with sullen silence.

She murmured a few choice words under her breath as she closed the door behind her, reflecting that he was doing a very good job of helping her suppress that initial spark of attraction she had felt for him. Yes, he had a great body and a handsome face, but what lay within appeared to be anything but appealing. Besides, a grumpy tennis player was the least of her worries now. Her problems would begin when she met up with Charles Lanslebourg again.

Chapter 6

The following day she decided to start looking for some-where to live. Daniela's mum insisted that she continue to stay with them but Lucy didn't want to impose any more, so she drove into Siena and headed for an estate agency she had seen near Daniela's place of work to see what was available. Although she needed a rental property in the first instance, she now realised that her dream of having her own place, a fixed point after years as a nomad, could hopefully come to fruition.

The man who greeted her was very helpful as she explained her situation and the sort of thing she was hoping to find.

'I'm just starting a new job at the Siena Clinic – you know, the Villa delle Ginestre.' She paused to check that she saw recognition in his eyes. 'I'd like somewhere within, say, a fifteen- or twenty-minutes' drive from there if possible. It doesn't need to be very big and I don't want anywhere flashy – somewhere old would be fantastic. Ultimately I'd like to buy, but for now I need somewhere to rent until I find the right place.'

He nodded a couple of times as he thought it through before coming to a conclusion. 'I think I may have just what you want. It's an old farm cottage on the edge of a big estate in a village called Castelnuovo Superiore. It's a lovely spot and it's no more than fifteen minutes from the Villa delle Ginestre. It's been immaculately refurbished from head to toe and it's available to rent immediately. The thing is, though, I'm pretty sure the owner's also keen to sell. Just give me a moment to check and, if it appeals to you and the price is right, you could move in as a tenant until the sale goes through and then it'll be yours.'

After a few seconds on the computer, he gave a satisfied grunt.

'That's right: rental or sale. Here, take a look. See what you think.'

He turned the screen towards her and she found herself looking at half a dozen photos of a charming old brick cottage. She didn't hesitate.

'That looks perfect. When can I see it?'

'How would three o'clock this afternoon suit you?

As she left the agency and came out into the narrow street, she heard somebody call her name and turned to find a familiar, though not terribly welcome, face. It was Daniela's journalist colleague, Tommy. She hadn't seen him since the wedding and he appeared delighted to bump into her. She was less delighted, but didn't let it show. He did work with her best friend after all.

He immediately insisted upon taking her to the bar across the street for a coffee and she couldn't think of a convincing reason to say no. As she sipped her little cup of powerful espresso coffee *macchiato* with the addition of a drop of cold milk, she told him about the house she was going to view this afternoon. When he heard the name of the village, he nodded enthusiastically.

'I know Castelnuovo Superiore well. My aunt and uncle live there and I often go to see them. It's a super little place. Let me know if you decide to take the house and I can introduce you to the locals. They're all very friendly... at least most of them.'

They chatted over their coffees and this only confirmed her impression that, as at the wedding, he had got her firmly in his sights. He wasn't unpleasant by any means, but he just wasn't her type. At the end, when she stood up to leave, he asked her if she would like to come out for dinner with him some time and she prevaricated, saying she would be very busy getting everything sorted out over the next couple of weeks. She hoped he would get the message without her having to spell it out for him.

--

The old house was on the edge of a pretty little village and, to her relief, it wasn't completely isolated in the middle of nowhere. Castelnuovo Superiore even had a general store and a bar/restaurant. The village was situated partway up one of the hills to the west of Siena and all around were olive groves and vineyards, interspersed with clumps of trees and scrub. Bright yellow broom bushes – the *ginestre* that gave their name to her future place of work – were in flower, and the scent was all-pervading as the man from the agency drove her up the winding road with the car windows open. Tommy had been right about it being lovely. The views that stretched out before them were stunning.

The house was quite simply gorgeous and Lucy fell in love with it as soon as she set eyes on it. It wasn't grand or ostentatious. It had apparently been built at the end of the eighteenth century and it had clearly once been the home of a farm worker and his family. It looked pleasingly modest but comfortable, and that suited her perfectly. Her parents had never been very well off, and funding her long years of medical studies had been a struggle for all of them, and she had always instinctively avoided ostentation – be it with regard to accommodation or, indeed, men. Thinking back on it, that was one of the things that had always bothered her about Charles, and after their split-up she had vowed to go for plain, simple men in future.

Like so many of the properties in this area, this cottage was built of old bricks and had arched doorways, while dusty louvred shutters hung at the windows. The roof was tiled with sun-scorched curved red pantiles and the top floor opened onto a covered loggia supported by brick pillars which would provide shade and allow the breeze to blow through, just like Daniela's mum's house.

Inside, it was immaculate. Whoever had been respons-ible for the restoration had done a wonderful job and hadn't spared any expense. The floors had been retiled using antique – or at least antique-looking – terracotta, and the hefty timbers supporting the ceilings had been sandblasted to return them to their original appearance. The kitchen had granite worktops and a fabulous bank of built-in cupboards and appliances. A picture window in the far end wall looked out over the hills. It was superb and she thanked Federico, the man from the agency, warmly.

'What a place! Are you sure you've got the price right?'

He grinned at her and nodded. 'A bit cheaper than London maybe?'

She grinned back. 'A bit? A house like this in or around London would cost three, four times as much. And the rent would be astronomical. It's unbelievable.'

Upstairs there were two good-sized bedrooms, each with its own en-suite bathroom, and a landing from where a door led out to the loggia. The views from outside on the covered terrace were spectacular. From here she was looking straight out over row upon row of gnarled old olive trees that clothed the curves of the hillside and disappeared down towards the valley below. She did a quick count and found she could only see five other buildings dotted among the trees and vines. Siena, she knew, was in the next valley, along with the autostrada. Here the only noise she could hear was the tweeting of little birds and the rumble of a distant tractor some way away in the fields. Best of all, she reckoned it was barely five or six kilometres in a straight line from here to work, although the winding roads to get there would probably add up to almost double that distance. Even so, it was going to be a very easy, and very scenic, commute.

The house was empty so she knew she would have to buy everything and furnish it herself, but this really appealed to her. After years of living in rented property and sleeping and eating on other people's furniture, it would be wonderful to be able to make a fresh start. She breathed deeply. Her escape to Tuscany was really taking shape.

Outside to the rear there was a small garden that backed onto the estate to which it had originally belonged, and the backdrop of olive trees, cypresses and lines of vines reinforced the rural feel of the place. The garden was little more than a mass of straggly weeds and she could tell that she would have her work cut out for her in that department, but this didn't intimidate her either. With a garden to create and tend, and knowing she would be living in one of the most historically interesting parts of Italy, she would have more than enough to fill her free time. And there was even a bare patch of soil alongside the back door just crying out for a rambling rose bush. It was perfect.

'Why are they selling a gorgeous place like this? It's not on the San Andreas fault or anything, is it?'

The house agent shook his head. 'Most of Tuscany's designated a seismic region, particularly as you get closer to the Apennines, and there are little quakes around Siena from time to time, but there hasn't been a serious earthquake in this area for ages. Just think of the centre of Siena – the buildings around Piazza del Campo have been standing for six hundred years. The way I look at it, as long as the Torre del Mangia stays upright, there shouldn't be too much to worry about. No, I believe the vendor's selling this place because he's got all he needs with the villa.' He pointed up the hill. 'That's the Villa Castelnuovo up there. I've never seen it, but I'm told it's beautiful.'

Lucy followed the line of cypress trees marking the driveway as it curled up the hillside until she could just make out a broad red-tiled roof barely visible above the tops of a little copse of more cypresses and umbrella pines about half a mile away. Not as big as the Siena Clinic villa, it was still a sizeable place, with a little tower sticking out of the centre of the roof in classic Tuscan style. She had no doubt a house like that would be worth many millions; definitely the sort of ostentatious place where she would never feel comfortable. Still, she thought to herself with a satisfied grin, as long as they were happy to sell her this little cottage, she would be well pleased.

They drove back to agency where she wasted no time in signing the rental agreement and paying the deposit. They also discussed making an offer to buy the property and she decided to take the plunge. The place had just felt so right. They agreed a figure and she crossed her

60

fingers under the table as Federico emailed it through to the vendor's solicitor.

While waiting for a decision, Federico gave her all sorts of useful information about opening a bank account, arranging a mortgage and getting fixed up with all the complicated paperwork involved with settling in Italy. He also gave her some excellent advice about a number of antique shops and regular markets in and around Siena where he told her she should be able to find furniture at a fraction of the original price.

She was still scribbling the information down when the phone rang. He gave her an enthusiastic thumbs-up. They had accepted her offer.

-

The next week was a busy one for Lucy, but she wouldn't have wanted it any other way. She went on a spending spree that included a second-hand Fiat 500 that had allegedly belonged to one careful lady owner. After seeing the way Virginia had thrown her car about as they raced up to the clinic from Daniela's wedding, Lucy took this with a pinch of salt, but the Fiat garage offered a year's guarantee, so she suspended her disbelief.

She found a lovely old farmhouse table and eight straw-upholstered chairs in an antiques warehouse, along with a fairly battered but solid sofa. She splashed out on a brand-new double bed for herself although she had no candidate for filling the other half of the bed at this moment. Not, she told herself, that this bothered her in the slightest. For now, she just wanted to concentrate on her new house and her new job. There would be time to think of men once everything had settled down. Apart, of course, from

Charles. There was no doubt her forthcoming reunion with her former lover rather took the shine off an otherwise alluring future for her, both at home and at work.

An old wooden bedstead with a new mattress for her guest room cost a lot less than her new bed, but it looked and felt serviceable. She was quite sure her parents would be over to see her before too long and would approve of her not throwing her new-found salary around. Nevertheless, she went on to make a major investment in bed linen, crockery, cutlery, pots, pans, cups and glasses, along with a slick new coffee machine. Her savings took a hefty hit in the process, but she felt sure her amazing pay at the Siena Clinic would soon restore them to their previous level, if not more.

Everywhere she went, she arranged for the stuff to be delivered to Castelnuovo Superiore the following Monday when she would take possession of the keys.

She also wasted a considerable amount of time setting up a bank account, getting a *codice fiscale* which was essential so that she could purchase the house and start employment, and organising the utilities, including setting herself up with a new phone and internet contract. All in all it was a very hectic week but as Moving Monday loomed, she felt confident she had done all that was necessary. Even better, all this activity was having a positive effect on her recurring bad dreams and she hadn't been woken in blind terror for some time now.

That weekend saw the return of Daniela and Pietro from their honeymoon in Sicily, looking tanned and happy. They all went out for dinner together in Siena on the Sunday night, along with Virginia and Bruno. Lucy had the impression that Virginia was a bit more tense than the last time she had seen her and she wondered what was bothering her. She hoped there wasn't trouble brewing between her and Bruno.

Daniela and Pietro were delighted to hear about her new house. It turned out they also knew Castelnuovo Superiore well and they insisted on coming round the following night with food and wine to celebrate her moving day. Bruno also sounded interested in coming but Virginia, with a shake of the head, told her she regretted they wouldn't be able to come after all. Daniela and Pietro were also fascinated to hear about Lucy's new job at the Siena Clinic and the fact that this meant she would now be taking up full-time residence in Tuscany. For her part, Lucy realised she would be able to visit them regularly when the baby was born, and she promised to make sure he or she would be thoroughly spoiled by his English auntie, *Zia* Lucy.

Later on, after Bruno and Virginia had left and Pietro had gone off to pick up the car, Daniela demonstrated that she knew her friend very well indeed. She gripped Lucy's arm and leant close towards her in the darkness.

'So, are you going to be all right working in a private clinic? It'll be very different from what you've been doing for the past few years.'

'I've been wondering that myself. Virginia's father struck me as an honourable man, and my former boss in MSF said the same thing about him, so I'm confident it shouldn't be too bad. Yes, of course it'll be different but if Bruno can work there and enjoy it, I'm sure I'll be okay.'

'So you're not too worried about the sorts of spoilt patients you'll find yourself treating?'

'We'll see. I expect I'll cope.'

'Well, at least you should be working alongside some nice people. Bruno says they're a good bunch.'

'That sounds promising.' Though there was one very big black cloud on the horizon as far as her future colleagues were concerned. For a moment, Lucy thought about telling her friend about her discovery that she was about to find herself working with her former French lover, but it was too late at night. She had drunk too much red wine and she really had no idea what sort of impression Charles would make on her again after four years – and after so much hurt.

Chapter 7

The move to Castelnuovo Superiore went smoothly and, by the time Monday evening came, Lucy had washed the floors, cleaned the cupboards, and made a start on unpacking bits and pieces into the kitchen units. Vans from the different shops had delivered their goods as promised and with the help a couple of very obliging delivery men she had managed to arrange the furniture in the different rooms. Although she was still surrounded by boxes by the evening, it was already starting to feel like her dream home.

She stood by the window, admiring the view across the hillside and reflecting upon her good fortune at having found a safe refuge from the war zone while so many of her former patients and colleagues were not so lucky. The stories coming out of North Kivu were truly frightening and her heart went out once again to all the innocent civilians caught up in the slaughter. Unbidden, barbaric images of mutilation came piling back and she had to steel herself not to dissolve into tears. Although she managed to keep her emotions under control, it was a struggle and she found herself in a reflective mood.

Daniela and Pietro turned up at eight o'clock and the sight of them shook her out of her reverie and helped to cheer her up once more. They brought a roast chicken, salad, ice cream and half a dozen bottles of wine. She gave them a guided tour of the property and they looked and sounded most impressed. They all went up into the loggia where she opened a bottle of Prosecco for Pietro and cold mineral water for Daniela, and they sat looking out as the sunset turned the hills across the valley crimson. She counted her blessings once again as they toasted the new house.

One thing Daniela said that evening came as no real surprise.

'I think you've made another conquest.' Seeing Lucy's eyebrows raise, she elaborated. 'Tommy's been spending most of his time wittering on about how gorgeous you are.'

Lucy almost choked on her wine. 'I rather thought that might happen, but he's not really my type.' She caught Daniela's eye. 'A bit too slick for me. I don't see him as Mr Right, somehow.'

'Plenty more fish in the sea. You never know, you may end up with one of the other doctors from the Siena Clinic. You medics do tend to marry other medics after all.'

'Oh, dear God, no.' Realising that this had come out way more forcibly than she had intended, Lucy ended up breaking the news about her former lover now going to be her future colleague. She had already told Daniela ages ago all about what had happened in Greece, and Daniela had no doubt about what would happen now. Her friend's tone was sceptical.

'You won't go back to him. I know you, Lucy Young. He's in the past and I don't see you going back to him after he broke your heart. And I certainly hope you don't.' She glanced across at Pietro who was wisely staying out of the conversation. 'If Pietro did the same thing to me that would be that.'

That night Lucy went to bed with the window open and lay there for a good long while, listening to the sounds of the countryside. Although the village was probably home to a hundred people, maybe more, the only evidence of human activity was an occasional car in the distance and a lone scooter that came whining up the road outside. Hers was the last house in the village and there was just open country on three sides. On her left was another old cottage, but the shutters had been closed all day and there were no lights to be seen. Presumably it was either empty or the inhabitants were away or, quite possibly, it belonged to people who only used it as a holiday home.

As she lay there, listening to what she had first interpreted as silence, she realised that there were noises to be heard after all. Apart from a few creaks as the timbers inside the house settled after the heat of the day, she distinctly heard the scratching of claws on the roof tiles at one point, followed by the hoot of an owl so close by it made her start. There were occasional sounds of rustling from the fields as little – and not so little – animals went about their nocturnal business but, in spite of the solitude, she wasn't afraid. After living for years in an environment containing spiders that could paralyse you, snakes that could kill you, and armed men who could do unspeakable things to you, this really was heaven. Yes, she thought to herself as she drifted off to sleep, her escape to Tuscany was turning out to be everything she had dreamed of and more.

In spite of being on her own, she was delighted to find she was untroubled by bad dreams of evil men with machetes that night and slept soundly. Next morning she didn't need an alarm clock. In fact, she was woken at a quarter to six by not one, but a chorus of cockerels. This, in turn, set the village dogs off and, after lying there for a while, she decided there was no way she was going to be able to go back to sleep so she might as well get up. After another few hours unpacking and tidying, she decided to go for a little walk around the village. This proved to be instructive.

As she was turning to lock the front door, she heard a voice.

'*Buongiorno, Signora.*'

She turned to find herself being addressed by a little old lady who barely reached up to her shoulder. Her hair was white, her clothes a sombre black, but there was no mistaking the sparkle in her eyes or the smile on her face. Lucy found herself smiling back at her.

'*Buongiorno a lei.*' Lucy held out her hand in greeting. As the old lady shook it, she waved vaguely towards Lucy's house.

'Are you living here now?'

Lucy nodded. 'Yes, I moved in yesterday. My name's Lucy.'

'I'm pleased to meet you, Lucy. My name's Margherita Bianchi. I live in the white house on the corner by the church. But Lucy isn't an Italian name, is it?'

Lucy explained that she was English, but that she was about to start a new job here. The old lady nodded approvingly.

'That's very good to hear. So many of the houses round here are closed up for months on end and only get used in summer by rich Florentines trying to escape from the heat of the city.' She smiled up at Lucy. 'Or by foreigners who only come for a week or two. It's good to know the village will have a bit of young blood.'

They stood and chatted for a while before the old lady set off up the road, remarkably nimbly, and Lucy headed down into the village. Despite the fact that the first part of the name of the village, Castelnuovo, translated as 'new castle', she found no trace of any fortifications. Her historical curiosity was kindled and she resolved to do a bit of research to find out what had been here, if anything. All she found was a sweet little Romanesque church, but with the door locked. Just beyond it, on the corner of a modest-sized piazza, was the village shop. It was open and she decided to do a bit of shopping to help the local business. She walked in through a multi-coloured plastic fly curtain and found herself in Aladdin's cave.

The ceiling was low and the walls were lined with shelves all the way up to the top. On these were items as varied as tinned beans, firelighters, shovels, barbed wire and grappa. Definitely the place for anybody planning a siege. Thought of sieges and castles reminded her once more of her resolve to find out more about the origins of the village and she decided to ask the shopkeeper for any information. Pots and pans hung from hooks driven into the ancient beams that supported the ceiling and directly underneath, in the middle of the shop, there was a deep-freeze. This was packed with everything from octopus to ice cream, with joints of meat and skinned rabbits jockeying for position alongside frozen peas, prawns and what looked like home-made lasagne. At the rear of the shop was a long counter heaped with fresh fruit and vegetables and, behind it, a lanky man whose head almost grazed the ceiling. He was smiling.

'*Buongiorno, Signora. Posso aiutarla?*'

On the counter behind him was a leg of dry-cured ham set on a metal rack, with a long carving knife lying beside it. Lucy liked the look of that and she asked for a dozen thin slices and then watched as he carved them by hand with the precision born out of many years of experience. While he was working, she asked if he knew the whereabouts of a castle round here and he nodded.

'Up on the hill by the Villa Castelnuovo. There's not much left there now – just a few old walls and a heap of rubble. We used to play up there as kids, but it's all private now that the villa's been restored.'

Lucy resolved to do her best to go up and see the ruins one of these days. She continued with her spending spree and by the time she left, she had also bought half a big round loaf of unsalted Tuscan bread – he had happily chopped one in two for her – along with a bunch of lovely little fresh artichokes with spiky points, a slab of home-made pâté, a bag of local cherries, a washing line and, just in case, a pack of candles and a big box of matches.

Most surprising of all was a book, found on a shelf containing an eclectic selection of dusty books in Italian as varied as *War and Peace* and *50 Shades of Grey*. Unexpectedly, one book was in English and it was entitled *The History of Tuscany*. It was written by somebody with a Scottish name that she didn't recognise. She queried what an English book was doing here, and all the shopkeeper could do was shrug. Still, seeing as the book was in English and she had just been wondering about local history, she took it as a sign and purchased it.

As she got back to her house, she had another surprise. Trotting happily down the middle of the road towards her was a handsome-looking young black Labrador with a smart red collar. Fortunately, in spite of being a big dog, he looked friendly, unlike the packs of near-feral dogs she had learnt to avoid back in Africa. There was no sign of his owner and she wondered if the dog had escaped from somewhere. She was loaded with bags so she ignored him for now and turned to unlock her door. As she pushed it open, she felt a hairy body slip past her bare knees and she found herself with an uninvited, but unthreatening, guest in the house. She set her purchases on the kitchen table and crouched down beside the dog who wagged his tail affably and licked her hand. His nose then stretched towards the table top and she knew he had smelt the ham or the pâté or both.

'So where have you come from, dog?'

He sat down with a thud and scratched his ear with one of his back paws, his tail wagging and polishing the floor tiles for her as it did so. She checked his collar and spotted a silver medallion. On it was a phone number. She went across to the door and looked up and down the road once more, but there was still no sign of the dog's master so she called the number. It was answered by a female voice.

'*Pronto?*'

Lucy explained where she was now living and that she had found their dog. She heard the lady give an exasperated sigh.

'I'm so sorry you've been bothered. Boris is normally very good but he hasn't been out for a long walk for a couple of days, so he's probably just restless. I'll get my husband to come down and pick him up straightaway. Thank you so much for calling.'

Lucy dropped the phone back on the table and set about putting the food away in the fridge. The dog watched her every move with rapt attention and it reminded Lucy of their old Lab, back when she was growing up. He would have sold his soul for food and she knew it was typical of the breed. Finally taking pity on this one, she offered him a bread stick. He took it delicately, settled down on the floor with it wedged vertically between his front paws and crunched it up. In return she was on the receiving end of a broad canine smile and a sloppy lick.

Five minutes later she heard a vehicle pull up outside and she went across to open the door. The dog trotted out beside her and, when he saw who was driving, ran over and stood up on his hind legs, tail wagging, poking his shiny black nose through the open window of the little white van. The driver patted the dog's head, climbed out, and came across to where Lucy was standing. He was a friendly-looking middle-aged man with a weather-beaten outdoorsman complexion and in his hand a bulbous straw-covered bottle of wine. These real old traditional Chianti flasks were almost unobtainable these days and Lucy was delighted if it was intended for her, resolving to put it on display somewhere in the house.

'Doctor Young? I meant to come down to see you yesterday, but something came up. My name's Armando. My wife and I live up at the Villa Castelnuovo. Thank you so much for calling about Boris.' He handed her the bottle of wine. 'Ignore the label, this is our own wine from the villa.'

Getting over her initial surprise that the Labrador belonged to her landlord, Lucy held out her hand. 'I'm very pleased to meet you, Armando, please call me Lucy. And thank you so much for this gorgeous bottle of wine, but there was no need. I was thinking about coming up to the villa one of these days to say hello.'

She saw a shadow cross his face. 'It's probably best if you don't. The owner doesn't like visitors.'

So Armando was the hired hand, not the proprietor. 'Oh, dear, I'm sorry to hear that. It would only have been a courtesy call, but of course I'll keep my distance.'

He looked relieved. 'You can always get me or Fioretta on the number you called. We'll be only too pleased to help. Is everything all right here? You're the first tenant we've had.'

'Everything's marvellous and everything works. Can I offer you a glass of wine or a cup of coffee? It's a new machine and I'm still getting used to it, but it seems to make pretty good coffee.'

He readily accepted the offer of an espresso and she ushered him and the dog inside. While she made the coffee, he looked around appreciatively.

'It's good to see the old place lived in. It was almost falling down before the builders started and they were here for four, five months, getting it back into shape.'

'They've done a marvellous job. I love it.'

'And I understand it's your intention to buy it.'

'That's right. I can't wait. And do you know the first thing I'm going to do? I'm going to plant a rambling rose outside the back door. Call me old-fashioned, but I've always wanted a home with a rose around the door.'

She saw him smile. 'Well, in that case, let me offer you one of mine. As well as the vines, I take care of the gardens up at the villa and I've got a number of roses that I've grown from cuttings. There's a very unusual pink and white one with a wonderful scent that would be perfect for what you want. I've no idea of its name but it's a vigorous climber and it'll flower throughout the summer. Would you like that?'

73

'I would love that. Thank you so much, Armando.'

As they drank their coffee, he told her what he could about the history of the place. The villa had been built three hundred years ago alongside the ruins of the original Castelnuovo. He couldn't tell her much about the castle itself, seeing as it had been razed to the ground centuries earlier. From the size of the foundations, he said it was clear it must have been a building of some importance, but he knew no more than that, apart from the fact that it had given its name to the village and the villa. This only whetted Lucy's appetite to visit the ruins even more, but clearly this wasn't going to be allowed by its reclusive owner. She decided she would, at the very least, check it out on Google Earth, although it would have been better to see it in the flesh.

Armando finished his account with recent developments up at the villa. 'The present owner bought the Villa Castelnuovo five years ago and he and his wife only moved in when the builders finally finished about three years ago.' He lowered his voice although there was nobody in the vicinity to overhear. 'He's not been very well. That's why he keeps himself to himself.'

'What a pity. Still, hopefully, living in a beautiful place like this will help him get better.'

'Fioretta and I do hope so. He's a good man. It pains us to see him so unhappy.'

'Is he from around these parts?'

Armando shook his head. 'No, he's not.' He didn't say where he was from and Lucy didn't dig. It was clear he and his wife were keeping a low profile. At least Armando had said he was a good man. She certainly didn't want to end up living next to a sleazy Russian oligarch or a drug baron on the run.

'And Boris the dog; does he have free run of the place?'

'Yes, and normally he's very good. He either goes for longer walks with his master or he just wanders around the estate if he's out on his own. It's twenty-five hectares in total and that's pretty big, after all. It's just that his master has been away these last few days and I've been very busy so Boris hasn't had his usual long walks.'

'So he's not your dog?'

'No, he belongs to the master.'

Lucy wondered why her landlord's wife hadn't been able to give the dog his walks, but she decided it had nothing to do with her. 'Well, if I see him wandering out on the road again, I'll give you another call.'

'Thank you, but hopefully he shouldn't come all the way down here again. His master is due back home this afternoon so Boris can return to his normal routine.'

It sounded strange to Lucy to hear him referring to his master, rather than by the man's name, and it reminded her of a Dracula movie she had once seen where the old butler had always referred to the vampire lying in the coffin in the crypt as the 'master'. Hopefully she wasn't living next to a vampire. There had been big bats in the Congo, but none of them addicted to human blood as far as she knew, and none of them dressed in a sinister black cloak. In spite of herself, she shivered.

Chapter 8

As it turned out, Lucy came within just a few feet of meeting the dog's reclusive owner the very next morning, but at that point she was in no fit state to greet him properly.

It was another fine, sunny morning and she woke up feeling relaxed after the third night on the trot without any bad dreams. The weather forecast was warning of rain on the way later in the day so she decided to go for a long walk around the area to get her bearings before the ground got too sodden. She set out at ten, determined to do a circular tour around the perimeter of the Castelnuovo estate to see if she could at least get a glimpse of the remains of the ruined castle. The previous night she had checked it out on Google Earth and had located what looked like the rough outline of a rectangular shape in the trees alongside the sizeable red-roofed villa but, as both the shopkeeper and Armando had said, it was very overgrown and there was precious little of it left to see. Interestingly, there was a bright red luxury sports car visible parked outside the villa and that confirmed her conviction that the owners of a place like that must be of the rich and flashy variety. Still, if they kept themselves to themselves, so much the better.

She stuck a bottle of water and a banana in her bag, slung it over her shoulder and set out. The air was more humid today and she felt sure the TV weatherman had got it right. She walked up a steep, narrow path through the middle of a grove of gnarled old olive trees, their grey-green leaves covered in dust. As she did so, she reflected that everything around here looked extremely dry, in spite of it only being late May. No doubt the olives, vines and other crops could all do with the predicted rain and would enjoy a good soaking.

As she climbed, the view around her broadened until she was looking beyond the valley and across row after row of tree-clad hills in all directions. In the far distance she saw what might have been the towers of San Gimignano – one of the must-see places in Tuscany that she had visited several times as a girl. Even back in those days the little town had been crowded with tourists and she had no doubt that visitor numbers could only have increased with the passing of the years. Up here there was a little bit more breeze and she could well understand why the builders of first the castle and then the villa had chosen to come up this high. As she knew from experience, Tuscany could become swelteringly hot in the summer months and the breeze would have been very welcome indeed – particularly back in the days before air con.

She was roughly following a new-looking wire fence, taller than she was, that surrounded the Villa Castelnuovo estate. She wondered if this had been put up to keep out animals or humans, and decided it was probably both. Peering through the mesh from time to time, she was unable to catch even a distant glimpse of anything that might have been a ruined castle, and even the villa itself was well screened from sight by rows of vines, olive trees and woodland. Lucy shrugged off her disappointment. After all, the view in every other direction more than made up for it. As rain clouds began to bubble up, the landscape was dappled light and dark as the clouds moved across it. An ancient chapel on a distant hill was bathed in bright sunlight in stark contrast to the darker shades of the woods around it. This piecemeal illumination lent an almost magical air to the panorama before her and she found herself smiling.

After fifteen minutes of steady climb, she emerged onto a flatter bit of hillside where she knew the villa and the remains of the castle lay. The trees here were thicker and she followed a series of animal tracks through the woods, pleased that she didn't need to worry about stepping on a deadly snake or being attacked by a ferocious carnivore – animal or human. Certainly Tuscany had its advantages compared to the Congo.

However, a few minutes later, as she was sitting on a fallen tree having a rest and nibbling her banana, she suddenly found that she was indeed confronted by a large carnivore – albeit not ferocious by any stretch of the imagination. She barely had time to turn her head towards the sound of something heavy crashing through the dry undergrowth in her direction when a big black shape emerged from the shadows and hurtled towards her. To her immense relief it was a familiar face that greeted her.

'Ciao, Boris. Fancy seeing you here.'

Boris the Labrador clearly recognised her as he bounded up and did his best to climb onto her lap, emitting happy little grunts and whines as he did so, his tail wagging furiously. After a struggle she managed to persuade him to get off her and sit down, but it took the bribe of a piece of banana. Needless to say, this disappeared down his throat in a flash. He licked his lips a few times, checked to see there wasn't any more coming his way and then stretched out on his back at her feet, his tail sweeping the pine needles beneath him into a fan-shape.

She bent down and scratched the young dog's tummy, wondering how he had managed to get through the fence. This gave her an idea. After finishing her banana – and giving him the last piece – she took a big swig from her water bottle and stood up. Boris leapt to his feet and beamed at her.

'Right then, Boris, let's see if we can find your way back home. Off you go, home!' For the avoidance of doubt, she also added the translation: '*A casa!*'

She set off back in the direction from which the Labrador had come and he immediately took the lead, pausing only to mark his territory from time to time as he went along. It took only two or three minutes for her to spot how he had managed to get out. A tree had fallen across the fence, flattening one of the posts and bringing down the wire, producing a simple way of getting in and out of the estate. She stopped by the breach and stared into the shadows of the woods ahead of her, but without seeing anything but trees. A vestigial path disappeared into the undergrowth and Boris happily skipped over the flattened wire and disappeared into the trees. Presumably home – and the ruined castle – were down this way.

Lucy stood there for a few moments, debating whether to trespass or not. Much as she would have liked to see the castle, she decided not to risk it. It would be highly embarrassing to be caught wandering about on private property and this might even enrage the owner so much he might turf her out of her new house and refuse to sell it to her after all. There was no further noise from the dog, so presumably he had headed off home so, regretfully, she turned away and carried on around the perimeter.

As she walked, she gradually became aware that it would have been a good idea to go to the toilet before setting off. No sooner did she start thinking about it than the urge got stronger. She stopped by the fence and listened. All she could hear was the incessant buzzing of the bees and a very distant tractor. There was no indication of any other humans in her vicinity so she pushed her way into the middle of a thick clump of broom bushes covered in aromatic yellow flowers and pulled down her shorts.

She was in the middle of doing what she had to do when she suddenly became aware of the unmistakable sound of human footsteps approaching. She crouched there, hardly daring to breathe, feeling terribly exposed, and tried not to make a sound as somebody came past her, just on the other side of the wire fence.

Unfortunately, her presence had been registered. She heard the now familiar mix of grunts and whines that indicated that Boris knew it was his new best friend who gave him bread sticks and pieces of banana who was squatting in the bushes, blushing like a schoolgirl. She even heard scrabbling, presumably as the dog tried to get through the fence, but, to her infinite relief, the human footsteps continued to recede into the distance. Finally, there was a piercing whistle and she heard the dog bound off through the undergrowth to join his master. She gave a little sigh of relief and wiped the back of her hand across her forehead. That had been close.

When she got back home later on she called Armando to tell him about the gap in the fence and he thanked her and told her the owner of the property had reported it himself only a matter of minutes earlier. As Lucy put the phone down, she reflected that it would have been highly embarrassing if her first encounter with her landlord had been with her pants around her ankles.

Just after lunchtime the rain started and it absolutely bucketed down continuously for four or five hours. Water came pouring off the rock-hard soil of the hillside onto the road and past her front door, four or five inches deep in places. Although she kept checking regularly, she was delighted to find that the house was well out of the way of the stream of water, and the new roof did a terrific job of keeping the elements at bay. Finally, just after six, the rain stopped, to be replaced by a symphony of drips all round, and within a very short space of time the water on the road had disappeared as if it had never been there in the first place.

She made herself a ham sandwich and picked up the history book she had found at the village shop. It was a hefty tome and, judging by the myriad footnotes, was meticulously researched. There was a detailed index at the back and she started there in the hope that this village or the old castle might be mentioned. Alas, there was no reference to Castelnuovo Superiore or the ruins, so she turned back to page one and started to read. She had barely got midway through the first chapter when she heard a car pull up outside and she peeked out to see who it might be. The car was a very smart silver Porsche and the driver was none other than Bruno.

Slipping a pencil into the book to save her place, she went over to open the door, wondering why Virginia wasn't with him.

'Ciao, Lucy. I came to wish you well in your new home.' He handed her a bottle of cold champagne and leant forward to kiss her on the cheeks.

'Ciao, Bruno. Thank you so much.' She stepped aside and beckoned him in.

'Wow, this is amazing!' He looked around appreciatively and she felt a little thrill of satisfaction that he appeared to feel the same way about this lovely little house as she did.

She gave him a tour of the property, hurrying him past the bedrooms and out onto the loggia. It was pleasantly cool out here now after the rain, and the air was crystal clear. It was so clear, in fact, that for the first time she could make out the vague outline of the Apennines against the far distant horizon. She left him there and went down to the kitchen to bring up a couple of glasses and the bottle of champagne. He took it from her, opened it without fuss and filled the glasses.

'So how's it going, Lucy? Are you settled in?'

She took a seat opposite him and they chatted. He told her Virginia had gone off to Rome for a conference and wouldn't be back until the day after tomorrow so he was very much in charge of things at the clinic. He then came to what was probably the main reason for his visit.

'I wanted to come and see you to find out if you knew you're going to be working alongside Charles Lanslebourg. I only discovered today that you know each other.'

'Yes, I had heard. It's quite a coincidence. So he told you he knew me?'

'Yes, this morning after our regular weekly meeting when it was announced that you were joining us. And you knew him well?'

'Yes, four years ago in Greece, we worked together.' She took a deep breath. 'But there was more to it than that.'

83

'He told me the two of you used to be an item. Is that right?'

She nodded. 'For about six months.' She looked up from her feet. 'Until I found one of the nurses wrapped around him.'

'Really? That's not the way he tells it.'

'Is that so? What does he say?' Lucy listened intently.

'He says you went off and left him for no reason. It broke his heart, apparently.'

'If no reason means catching him stark naked on a beach at ten o'clock at night with a naked girl, then he's right. Otherwise, he's wrong, very wrong. I believe the Romans invented the expression "in flagrante" so, as an Italian, you can probably imagine the scene, I'm sure.'

Bruno nodded slowly. 'That comes as no surprise. To be honest, we've been keeping an eye on him for a while now. He's got a thing for nurses – and they seem to find him very attractive as well. Although it's not against the clinic's rules, Virginia's father quite rightly frowns upon that sort of thing and woe betide Charles if he lays a finger on one of the patients.'

'What's that old saying about the leopard never changing its spots?' Lucy gave a little sigh and, to her consternation, Bruno suddenly asked her a tricky question.

'Did he break your heart?'

She took a couple of deep breaths. 'Pretty much; at least for a while.' She pulled herself together and tried to sound as positive as she could. 'But as it turned out, he did me a favour. Without him, I wouldn't have gone to Africa, and that was an unforgettable time of my life. Thanks for coming here to tell me, Bruno, but I'll cope. Don't worry,

I'm not going to borrow the tennis player's gun and shoot him.'

'That's good to hear, but we wanted you to know that we know. If he gets on your nerves, come to me or Virginia. The last thing we want is to lose you. He's very good at his job, but I wanted you to know that he's under observation. Okay?'

'Thanks, Bruno, that's good to know. And, yes, he *is* damn good at his job, so I promise I'll do my best to bury the hatchet – and not in the back of his skull.'

They continued chatting as the light began to fade. She refused a second glass of champagne, deciding to save some for the next day. As dusk fell, he stood up and looked at his watch.

'Well, it's been great talking to you, but I need to go. As Virginia's gone off to the Rome conference, I need to do the rounds and check that all's well.'

She accompanied him to the door, kissed him on the cheeks and watched as he returned to his very smart car and drove off. This evening's visit had reassured her – if she had needed it – that she was going to find him a good person to work with at the clinic. The looming problem, of course, was that in only a few more days she would find herself confronted by her former lover and, in spite of what she had told Bruno, she knew it was going to be far from easy.

Chapter 9

Lucy's first week at the Siena Clinic was... interesting.

She got there bright and early at seven thirty on Monday morning and found Bruno waiting for her. He gave her a tour of the hospital, introducing her to other members of staff and some of the patients. Such was her apprehension at the prospect of seeing Charles again, she barely registered that two of the patients were very well-known Hollywood stars – one male and one female – who had come in for surreptitious 'nips and tucks' at the hands of the cosmetic surgeons. Nor did the presence of a senior member of the British government here for much-needed liposuction do more than tickle her curiosity. Her whole being was consumed by the thought of Charles and what effect his reappearance in her life might have upon her.

In the end, as her anxiety continued to grow, it was almost a relief when she found him sitting over a coffee in the very swish staff canteen. As she walked in, he raised his head and a smile spread across his face. He looked just the same, as if the events of Lesbos had only happened yesterday. He jumped to his feet and hurried across to her, arms open wide. Bruno was at Lucy's side and she felt him tense. As for herself, she didn't know what to feel. Here was the man who had meant so much to her, but who had then betrayed her so callously. She took a deep breath and held out her hand.

'*Bonjour, Charles.*' He was French after all.

He pulled up a foot or two from her and she saw his eyes drop to her outstretched hand.

'*Bonjour, ma chérie.*'

As much for Bruno's sake as for her own convenience she switched to English, which Charles spoke fluently. 'It's just Lucy now, Charles. No more *ma chérie*. Okay?' She was delighted to hear her voice sounding firm. 'How are you?'

She saw his face fall as he took her outstretched hand and shook it formally. 'I'm fine, thanks… Lucy.' He hesitated, lost for words, and she suddenly realised that he had probably been dreading this encounter as much as she had. This bolstered her resolve and she even managed a little smile as she responded.

'Fancy meeting up with you here! It's a very small world, isn't it?' Without giving him a chance to reply, she glanced over at Bruno alongside her. 'It's all right, Bruno. I'm not going to scratch his eyes out.'

She saw him relax and smile back at her.

'Good to hear. Physical violence between staff members is never a terribly good idea.' He glanced at his watch. 'Well, I've got to do my rounds. Why don't I leave you two to get reacquainted and I'll be back in half an hour to talk you through this week's schedule.'

As he went off, Lucy went over to the very complicated-looking coffee machine and studied it. As she did so, Charles came up alongside her.

'It takes a bit of getting used to, but it makes good coffee. Can I help?' As if anticipating her refusal, he hurried on. 'It's all right. I don't expect you to say thank you.'

She stepped aside and let him point out where to position the cup and which buttons to press in order to obtain a perfect *caffè macchiato freddo*. This had always been her preferred coffee and she couldn't miss the fact that he had remembered, even after four years. As the process finished and she picked up her little cup, she turned towards him.

'Thank you, Charles.'

She saw just a hint of a smile on his face. 'You're welcome. Would you like to come and sit with me? Maybe we could talk?'

She had never seen him so humble, so hesitant. Maybe this was a sign of positive personal development. Much as she had no wish to rake up all the heartache of four years ago, she knew it would be better to get things out in the open, so they could then get on with their lives and work together without friction. So she said yes.

As she sipped her coffee, he began speaking. She listened intently but gave no response as he did his best to convince her that the girl on the beach in Lesbos had been a one-time thing, an aberration. She had meant nothing to him. He had been stupid, selfish, a thoughtless moron. The only woman for him was and always would be Lucy who, by the way, was looking gorgeous. He was remarkably articulate, apparently sincere, and he sounded genuinely remorseful.

But she wasn't buying it.

She felt quite sure that this particular leopard's spots would never change – not least after what Bruno had told her about Charles and the nurses here at the clinic. Satisfying as it might have been to pour all her scorn onto him in one big cathartic outburst, possibly accompanied by a kick to the groin or a cup of coffee in the face, she was acutely conscious that he and she would once again be working closely side by side, so she swallowed her anger and did her best to keep things civil.

'Thank you for trying to explain, Charles, but we both know that anything we had is dead and long gone. There's no way I could possibly trust you again after what happened. I'm over it now and I want to forget about it. That's all in the past and we've both moved on since then.'

'So does that mean you've found somebody else?'

The simple truth was that she hadn't, but that was no business of his. 'It means it's all over. You and I *were* together and now we aren't, and that's the way it's going to stay.' As she spoke, she did in fact feel a sense of release, of closure, and she drew strength from this realisation. 'We're both going to be working here and that's all. We're colleagues and whatever I may think of your behaviour towards me in the past, I have a lot of respect for you as a doctor. Let's keep it like that. Okay? *Compris?*'

'*Compris.*' He shook his head sadly but then looked up again, a brighter expression on his face. 'Still, it'll be good to work with you again. You're a great surgeon and I respect you a lot too.' He sat back and visibly relaxed. 'So tell me all about Africa.'

That afternoon Lucy found herself repairing a hernia and removing a gall bladder. She didn't recognise the glamorous owner of the gall bladder, but from the length of the woman's finger nails, this was somebody who didn't go in for manual labour. Mind you, she reminded herself, she was now in the realm of the rich and famous – or infamous. The operation went well and she felt sure the patient would feel a lot better as a result and that, she told herself, was all that counted. The hernia patient was a more famous face, this time a Jamaican athlete. When he came round from his anaesthetic she sat with him for some time, telling him that all had gone well and reassuring him he would only be out of his sport for a matter of weeks. He was very pleasant and very grateful and she reflected that if all the patients here were like him she wouldn't complain.

Thoughts of famous sportsmen took her up to the physio department at the end of the afternoon where she found Louisa and, with her, David Lorenzo. Considering how grumpy he had been the last time she had seen him, she found herself questioning why she should have chosen to visit him again. His wounds would be well healed by now. She was still trying to come to a conclusion when her eyes alighted upon him and, to her annoyance, that same little spark of attraction stirred within her. She did her best to suppress it as she studied him.

The tennis player was stretched out, face-down, with weights strapped around his ankles, engaged in a series of leg and knee exercises. Lucy smiled at Louisa and then waited until he had finished his set before speaking to him.

'Good afternoon, Mr Lorenzo. How's it going?'

He rolled over onto his good side and looked up. 'Doctor Young. I'm doing good, thanks.' As ever, his tone was detached, but at least he was being a bit more polite than the last time she had seen him.

He was wearing a T-shirt and shorts which meant that she couldn't see his scars this time. She was just wondering whether to ask if she could take a look when he reached down and pulled the T-shirt up, exposing his muscular abdomen and lower back.

'I suppose you want to check things out?'

She bent lower and was very pleased to see both scars now almost fully healed. She gave him an encouraging smile. 'That's great. It looks as though you're back to normal.'

A cloud spread across his face. 'My side, maybe. Just not the rest.'

All Lucy could do was to offer support. 'Well, if the side's anything to go by, you heal quickly. You'll get there, I'm sure.'

He caught her eye for a second or two, during which she read the depth of his despair, but then he rolled back down onto his front and started the knee exercises once more. Lucy exchanged shrugs with Louisa, bade them both farewell and left, determined to take a look at his records, just to see how hopeless his case really was.

As she walked off down the corridor, she found herself wondering whether the degree of closure she felt she had gained with regard to Charles might be responsible for the growing attraction she felt for this man. Whatever it was, she told herself it was just as well he was an out-patient so she wouldn't see him too often. Apart from being far too rich and privileged, he was a patient and she a doctor and that was that. Nevertheless, as his attitude towards her showed signs of mellowing, she had to accept that she rather liked this troubled man.

Chapter 10

The next weeks passed quickly and she found herself dealing with a fascinating mix of cases and, refreshingly, not a single one of them involved snakebites, parasites, or bullet or machete wounds.

She did her best to readjust to the luxurious surroundings, the magnificent state-of-the-art equipment and the many wealthy patients, but it still felt surreal to her. The fact that her whole operating theatre back in Mabenta, where she had carried out often life-saving surgery, would have fitted inside just one of the guest bedrooms was hard to believe and she often found herself reflecting upon the injustice of a world where money was in the hands of the very few.

She was relieved to find that most of her patients were, as her former boss at MSF had said, just normal people who needed her help, and she found herself warming to most of them, irrespective of the fact that they chose to pay for private treatment. From time to time she came across less salubrious characters who ranged from a South American dictator to a disgraced financier, but they were the exception to the rule. Apart from the patients, she enjoyed bonding with other members of staff, from the world-renowned Egyptian head of orthopaedic surgery – who it transpired had also spent several years working in Africa – to Ahmed, the Syrian night porter that she often met at the end of his shift as she arrived to start work in the early morning. So, all in all she began to settle in and did her best to reassure her conscience that she was doing the right thing.

Her personal life also settled down. She quickly formed a happy working relationship with Bruno, though Virginia herself was maybe a bit on the cool side. Lucy soon worked out that she was a bit snappy and a bit distant towards everybody for some reason. As for Charles, she saw him regularly and even had coffee with him on a few occasions. She still wasn't even close to forgiving him, but he behaved impeccably as far as she was concerned and she felt sure they would be able to carry on as work colleagues without it feeling too weird. Certainly, her desire to strangle him had diminished by now and she slowly began to settle into a routine, increasingly confident that he wasn't going to make her position here awkward.

As the days went by, she got to know many of the patients well. Some were only in for a day or two, while others were there long-term and some were regular outpatients like David Lorenzo. As far as the tennis player was concerned, she settled down one afternoon to review his notes and check out the results of his numerous scans. Sadly, she found that she had to concur with the orthopaedic surgeon's verdict that recovery – at least to the sort of stress levels of a professional athlete – was highly unlikely. Not having any good news to give him and wary that her feelings towards him might risk straying towards the unprofessional, she decided it might be better to steer clear of him, but she hoped his regular physio sessions would gradually manage to bring a smile back to his face. She noted that he was also receiving counselling from Franz and felt sure that would help.

Dr Franz Berlin, the resident psychiatrist, wasn't your stereotypical psychiatrist. He looked as different from Sigmund Freud as a person could get. He was probably little older than Lucy herself; tall, athletic and good-looking, with piercing blue eyes and blond hair. In spite of his name, it turned out he was Italian. He told her he came from the far north-east of the country, high up in the Alps, where people still spoke German as a first language alongside Italian. He smiled a lot and was very approachable, and Lucy often sat down and chatted with him when she saw him. Also, unlike many psychiatrists she had known, he was remarkably sane.

One of the first things he did was to point out to her that maybe she was drinking too much coffee and he introduced her to ginseng. Remarkably, this was available among the list of options in the all-singing and all-dancing coffee machine in the staff canteen and she soon developed a taste for it. It looked just like a little espresso but tasted strangely, but not unpleasantly, sweeter. She took Franz's advice and reduced her intake of caffeine and slept better as a result of this, but also as a result of her talks with him.

She found herself starting to tell him about her experiences in Mabenta and the fraught final days in particular, and he encouraged her to open up to him. His laid-back supportive manner encouraged her to confess just how terrified she had been as the advancing forces had been drawing ever closer. She also spoke to him about the horrors she had seen first-hand, talking about things she hadn't revealed to anybody, not even her parents, and after each session with him – even as brief as a few minutes – she emerged feeling liberated and restored. She was intelligent enough to realise that these chats were acting as a very valid form of therapy and were exactly what she needed in order to gain some kind of closure. There was no doubt about it: he was very good at his job, even when he was theoretically off duty. She felt a deep debt of gratitude towards him and, with it, considerable affection.

As she started sleeping better the memories of the Congo gradually faded away and she settled down in her new home. Speaking with Geneviève and Nicole, she was pleased to hear that they didn't appear to be suffering too many long-term stress issues either. In fact, Nicole was already planning her wedding for a Saturday in September and she told Lucy to save the date.

Most evenings after work Lucy called in to see Daniela or just went for a walk by herself in the fields behind her house. The rain had been swallowed up by the parched earth in a matter of days and it was now once again tinder dry. There was no sign of Boris the Labrador, and she rather missed him. They had always had a dog at home and she knew it would have been nice to have a dog of her own. The fact was, however, that she worked full-time five days a week – with a week of night duty once a month – and it wouldn't have been fair on the dog to leave him alone so much. Even without a dog, she enjoyed her walks in the hills and slept soundly afterwards.

All in all, her new life was working out fine, barring her concerns that a career looking after the rich and privileged was maybe not what she wanted in the long term. Still, she told herself, after her experiences in the Congo, she felt she had earned a bit of repose with so much less stress.

–

One July night she was invited to a party. It was Franz's thirty-ninth birthday and he was having people round to his apartment in Siena. Lucy accepted readily, delighted to be able to see more of the psychiatrist who had been helping her so much. The more she got to know him, the more she liked him, so as it was a very warm evening, she chose a smart summer dress she had bought in the market in Siena and even put her hair up. When she checked herself out in the mirror prior to going out, she reckoned she looked pretty good.

It was just as well she had no amorous intentions as her efforts would have been wasted on Franz.

She was met at the door of his top-floor flat by an equally handsome man who introduced himself as Franz's partner, Antonio, and the scales fell from her eyes. She gave him a big smile and pushed her way into the crowded flat to look for the birthday boy. She found him by the drinks table talking to, of all people, Charles. Her heart sank at the sight of her ex. She gave Franz a bottle of wine and he gave her a warm hug and pressed a glass of cold Prosecco into her hand. She thanked him and kissed warmly him on the cheeks.

'Happy birthday, Franz. I love your apartment.' She caught his eye. 'And thanks for being such a good friend.'

He grinned back at her. 'Any time, Lucy. I'm delighted to see you looking so relaxed. Sleeping well?'

'Sleeping just fine, thanks to you.'

In fact, with Charles so close-by, she wasn't feeling as relaxed as she might have been, but she managed to smile anyway and transferred her attention to her surroundings – deliberately turning her back on Charles. It really was a charming flat, perched on the rooftops of Siena, with a wonderful big terrace outside where she could see more people mingling. No doubt the view from out there would be lovely. Inside, it had been decorated with exquisite taste and when Franz explained that Antonio was an interior designer, it all fell into place.

She took a big mouthful of wine and reluctantly turned back towards Charles, noticing for the first time a diminutive, but very attractive, dark-haired girl hanging onto his arm. As her eyes landed on the girl's face, Lucy was unsurprised to see she was one of the junior nurses at the clinic and was probably at least ten years younger than Charles. Lucy nodded sagely to herself; the leopard was following its usual modus operandi. She steeled herself and gave them both a sweet, but totally insincere smile.

'Good evening.' She kept her tone studiously neutral.

He made no attempt to kiss her, which was just as well seeing as her glass was still almost full and this little scene had filled her head with a host of unpleasant memories. Something in her expression must have made him realise he was on thin ice as he took an uncertain step back and pointed vaguely across the room.

'Good evening, Lucy. Do excuse me. I have to...' And he disappeared into the crowd with his latest conquest in tow, much to Lucy's relief.

She took another sip of wine and wandered round the room, stopping to chat to a number of familiar faces from the hospital. After a bit she made her way over to the French window leading out onto the terrace. The view out there was as delightful as she had expected. The temperature was still high, but there was a hint of a breeze up here and she breathed deeply. The flat was situated just outside the *centro storico* and she found herself looking out over the roofs of the old heart of the town towards the unmistakable arrow shape of the Torre del Mangia, rising up vertically into the night sky. As she was standing there, taking it all in, she heard her name.

'Ciao, Lucy, fancy seeing you here. You're looking wonderful.'

She turned and discovered, to her surprise, that it was Tommy. She summoned half a smile and deliberately held out her hand instead of kissing him on the cheeks. She hadn't heard any more from him since they had bumped into each other and had coffee together well over a month ago, and she had been coming round to believing that he had got the message that she wasn't interested in him as anything but a friend. She was wrong.

'Ciao, Tommy. It's good to see you again. How do you know Franz?'

'I've only met him for the first time tonight, to be honest, but I've known Antonio for years. He and I were at school together and his company did the interior design for my sister's apartment and he's very good. Are you going to use them for your house?'

She shook her head. 'No, I'm fine with it as it is.' She held out her glass and clinked it against his. 'I love the place.'

'I thought of you last week.'

'Oh?' She braced herself for something romantic.

'It was the Palio di Provenzano and it occurred to me that you might enjoy watching the next one with me. The paper I work for is organising a party in an apartment right on Piazza del Campo on Palio day in August. If you'd like to come to that one, I could fix it.'

The two Palio races were the highlights of Siena's year. Horses representing the different *contrade*, the wards or districts of the city of Siena, were raced bareback around the main square by jockeys dressed in traditional bright team colours. These races were some of the oldest and most famous historic events in Tuscany and they always took place twice a year on the second of July and the sixteenth of August. Although she had been in the crowd at one Palio many years ago, at the time she had hardly been able to see anything and her lasting memories were of deafening noise, a crush of people and the overwhelming reek of sweaty horses – and humans – in the air. Seeing it from above did sound rather good, but she knew it would not be a good idea to humour Tommy.

'That was a nice thought, but I went to see the Palio some years ago, thanks. All a bit too claustrophobic for me.'

'Well, if you change your mind, the next one, the Palio dell'Assunta, is only just over a month away. Let me know if you're interested.'

They stood and chatted for a while until he asked her to have dinner with him yet again and, after a lot of pushing from him and a good bit of hedging from her, she finally ran out of excuses and decided she had to say yes. He did work with her best friend after all, and she didn't want there to be any bad blood between them. She told herself afterwards she was just being sociable and trusted he would realise this wasn't a real date – besides, he had said he could tell her all about Castelnuovo Superiore, seeing as his aunt and uncle lived there.

–

Sunday was another very hot, sunny day and she decided to go for a walk in the morning and then take refuge in the shade after lunch. She followed a slightly different path up through the olive groves until she found herself once again at the fallen tree where she had stopped for a banana the previous month.

History repeated itself. She had only been there for a few minutes, sipping water from her bottle and admiring the view, when she heard familiar paws running towards her and turned to see Boris the Labrador.

'Hello, dog. Haven't they mended the fence yet?'

This time he managed to scramble up onto her lap before she succeeded in shooing him off. There was no doubt he liked his new chum, even though this time she wasn't bearing a banana. As she was bending down to scratch his tummy, she heard footsteps and glanced up to see a tall figure walking towards her, limping slightly. Even in the shade, she recognised him immediately and it came as a major surprise.

Boris's reclusive master and her landlord was none other than David Lorenzo, the tennis champion. She stood up and realised this was the first time she had seen him on his feet and he towered over her – and she wasn't short.

'Good morning, Mr Lorenzo. Boris and I have just been renewing our acquaintance.'

He stopped and looked genuinely surprised. 'Doctor Young? And you know my dog's name?'

Keen to keep the conversation light, Lucy decided to tease him. 'He told me. I bet you didn't know I speak Labrador.'

She was delighted to see a hint of a smile on his lips and there was no getting away from the fact that beneath his normal air of gloom, he was a very good-looking man. He had a fine head of dark hair, a strong clean-shaven chin and, as she had already noted at the clinic, his body was very well-honed. He reached up and slid his sunglasses onto his forehead and she saw that his eyes were an attractive deep blue colour, although the dark rings beneath them were still there.

'A woman of many talents – not only speaking English and Italian, but Labrador as well. Good morning to you, Doctor Young. Fancy seeing you here.' Although his tone was formal and reserved, he sounded noticeably less grumpy than during their previous encounters. She decided she had better explain about Boris.

'I found him walking down the road outside my house when I first moved in and I phoned Armando who came to pick him up. So, I'm sorry to disappoint you, but I don't speak dog after all.'

Comprehension – and considerable surprise – dawned on his face. 'So you're renting the old cottage. And you're going to buy it as well, or so my lawyer tells me.'

'It was love at first sight, I'm afraid. Everything about it's just perfect. Please don't tell me you're going to change your mind.'

'No, I'm keen to sell, so if it suits your needs, then go for it. As far as I'm aware the papers are all going through.'

There was a momentary pause and she did her best to keep the conversation going before he decided to go off and leave her. Just why she wanted to keep talking to him was something she would ponder over the days to come. She glanced down at the dog sprawled across her feet.

'Tell me, why did you call him Boris? Has he got Russian roots?'

As she asked the question she remembered that Armando had mentioned that the dog's owner had moved into the house some years earlier with his wife. Maybe she was Russian. However, considering he was a tennis player, the answer should have been obvious.

'Armando got him for me from a local farmer who breeds Labradors and all the pups in that litter had names beginning with B. Armando said he chose him specially because the name would remind me of an old friend – Boris Becker. Heard of him?'

'Of course, but I didn't know he was part-Labrador.'

'Not that I've heard of, but it wasn't just that. I liked the idea of a name that would be the same in Italian and in English.'

There was another pause and before it could become awkward, she decided to turn the conversation to his wound.

'How's your side feeling now?'

'That's doing just fine – it's barely noticeable now – but unfortunately I'm having more trouble with my knee. I must have overdone things a few days back and I've been paying the price.'

'I saw you limping. That's tough. Cruciate ligaments can take a long time, I'm afraid.'

'Tell me about it! It's been almost three years now and still there's no light at the end of the tunnel.' The frustration in his voice was all too clear.

'I took a look at your records a few weeks back and I can see the problem. All I can tell you is that you're in very good hands. Doctor Saeed is an exceptional orthopaedic surgeon. If anybody can help you, he can.'

If he was surprised at her interest in him, he hid it well and gave no response. Keen to move the subject to less contentious matters, she decided to try history.

'I understand you have a medieval castle alongside your house.'

'I have the *ruins* of a medieval castle alongside my house, but there's precious little left. Half the houses in the village have been built with stones scavenged from the castle over the centuries. In fact, if you check out the back wall of your cottage, you'll find that a lot of it's stone, not all brick like most of the houses in this part of Tuscany.'

This was developing into by far the longest conversation he had ever had with her and she was happy for him. Communication with others is everything when dealing with depression. 'I hadn't noticed. I'll take a look this afternoon.'

'So, are you a historian who moonlights as a surgeon?' There might even have been a lighter note in his voice.

'The opposite. I'm a surgeon all right, but I'm also fascinated by history.' For a moment she wondered whether she could ask his permission to check out the ruins for herself, but decided this might be too much, too soon. Besides, apart from being a patient, he was presumably still married, not to mention from a different financial stratosphere. She would do well to keep her distance. She could see he wasn't completely comfortable with her either, so she kept the conversation light and general. 'That's probably why I fell in love with the cottage. And, apart from being a lovely place, it's perfectly positioned for me to get to work at the clinic.' Another thought occurred to her. 'By the way, have you had a chance to mend the fence? I phoned Armando ages ago when I spotted it.'

'Thank you for that and yes, it was all fixed last month. The only way out for Boris now is through the side gate I've just come through and so far he hasn't worked out how to unlock it.' He glanced at his watch. 'And now he and I have to go.' He turned away, but stopped and looked back. 'And thank you for what you did for me, Doctor Young. I don't think I ever said thank you. You'll have to excuse me.'

'You're very welcome, besides it was Bruno who did most of the work. And do, please, call me Lucy, seeing as we're neighbours.'

'That's good.'

He gave a low whistle and set off on his walk again, his dog running ahead of him.

As she watched him disappear into the trees, she found herself thinking back to their brief conversation and, in particular to the two words he had used right at the end.

Had he been commenting on the fact that she had told him to use her first name, or that she was buying his house, or was it about the possibility that they would see more of each other as a result of being neighbours? Though they had originally met under strained circumstances, she now felt sure she would like to see more of him – and not just because of his friendly dog – though she would have to be careful not to let things get too intimate. It would be awful if his wife were to react as Virginia had reacted when they had first met. The last thing Lucy wanted was a jealous woman living next door to her. So, she told herself sternly, she would do well to add David Lorenzo to the list of men with whom she knew she should never get involved. This simplified life, but she couldn't help a feeling of disappointment.

Chapter 11

Back at home, she made herself a sandwich and spent the afternoon out in the relative cool provided by the shade of the loggia. After a little snooze, she picked up her history book once more. She had been reading it bit by bit and she was now well into the turbulent history of this region and the regular squabbles, or worse, between Siena and its neighbours – most notably Florence – but also wars that involved larger powers such as Spain and even the Holy Roman Emperor, based far to the north in Bohemia. The Middle Ages and the Renaissance had been a time of great cultural achievements in the little republic, but also the time when so many fortresses and watchtowers had been built. There was no doubt the castle here had been designed with defence in mind. It was just a shame so little was known about it.

Her reading was interrupted by a knock at the front door. She closed her book and went over to the balustrade to look down onto the road. It was the elderly lady she had met on her first day here. Lucy gave her a little wave.

'*Buonasera, Signora Bianchi.*'

'Ah, there you are, Lucy. I've brought you a little housewarming present.'

Lucy hurried down and opened the door to find Signora Bianchi carrying an unlabelled wine bottle.

'Here, Lucy, I've been meaning to give it to you for weeks and weeks now, but I keep forgetting.' She smiled ruefully. 'I'm afraid I forget a lot of things these days.'

Lucy took the bottle from her and thanked her profusely. 'Can I offer you a cup of coffee, or tea, maybe?'

'That's very kind of you. If you're sure it's no trouble, I'd love to try a cup of real English tea if you have one. I went to London many years ago and I still remember the tea I had there.'

'Of course, and do sit down, Signora Bianchi.' Lucy gestured to a chair.

'Please call me Margherita. Everybody in the village calls me Margherita.' She sat down at the kitchen table while Lucy filled the kettle. 'You've got this place looking so welcoming. It's good to see it lived in once again. It's been empty since the war, you know.'

'That's what Armando told me. You know… Armando from the villa.'

'Of course I know Armando. I know everybody around here.'

'Have you lived here long?'

'Eighty-seven years, my dear. I was born here and I have no doubt I'll die here.'

As Lucy put the kettle on, a thought occurred to her. 'Can you tell me anything about the castle up by the villa? I'm interested in history, you see, and I'm trying to find out about it.'

Margherita shook her head slowly. 'Not very much. You know it's ruined, I suppose? All I know is that when I was a little girl, my grandfather used to call it the Englishman's castle, but I never did find out why he called it that.'

Lucy registered the information. That really was interesting and it just stimulated her historical appetite to find out more. While the kettle came to the boil, she dug in a cupboard for a packet of biscuits and put them on the table alongside the wine bottle Margherita had brought. It was only then that she realised that this didn't contain wine after all. The stopper was a small, wedge-shaped cork that barely sealed the top. She picked the bottle up, held it against the light of the window and tilted it, realising that it was full of oil, no doubt precious extra virgin olive oil. Setting it down again she returned her attention to Margherita.

'Is this local oil you've brought me? That's awfully generous of you. You really shouldn't have.'

'Not at all, Lucy, you're very welcome. It certainly *is* local and it's produced by my grandson. He took over the family farm when his father, my son, was killed in a terrible accident five years ago.' The elderly lady's voice almost broke. 'A runaway tractor crushed him to death.'

'How awful.' Lucy bent down and squeezed Margherita's shoulders. 'I'm so sorry for your loss. Was he your only son?'

'I'm afraid so.' She crossed herself and wiped away a little tear. 'He was my only child.'

'And your husband?' As Lucy asked the question she had a feeling she knew what the answer was going to be. She was right.

'He's passed away as well, but at least he reached a good age before he died.' But then, just as Lucy feared her guest might be about to dissolve into tears, the old lady straightened her shoulders, took a deep breath and looked up. 'But life goes on. My grandson, Roberto, is a fine boy – and the spitting image of his father. He's a great consolation to me.'

Lucy went back to the kettle which had come to the boil. 'And he farms around here?'

'Yes, you must have seen the farm. Just off to the left as you come up the hill into the village. Fattoria Le Querce; you can't miss it. You should drop in on Roberto one of these days and say hello.'

Lucy instantly recognised the farm from the description. She had often admired it. It looked like another very old, maybe even medieval, building and it was in a great position, no doubt with panoramic views of the valley below.

'I certainly will. Does he sell wine as well? I keep meaning to stock up.'

'Oh yes, and our vines are the best in the area.' A look of pride replaced the sorrow on the old lady's face. 'Even better than the vines up at the villa. Although I heard from Armando that the American has made him plant new ones.'

Lucy pricked up her ears. This would appear to show that David Lorenzo's presence here wasn't as secret as he might have hoped. She did a little bit of digging. 'Have you met him, the American?'

'Nobody has.' Margherita lowered her voice although they were the only people within a radius of a hundred yards or more. 'Do you know what I think? I think he's a New York gangster on the run.'

Lucy smiled at the thought as she made the tea. 'I actually did meet him and his dog briefly this morning and I'm sure I can confirm that he isn't a gangster and, from his accent, he isn't from New York either. By the way, I take my tea the traditional English way with a drop of cold milk. Is that how you like yours?'

'That would be lovely, thank you – with two spoonfuls of sugar, if you don't mind.'

As they sat and chatted, Lucy learned more about the village and, seeing as she was pretty clearly in the presence of the fount of all wisdom as far as Castelnuovo Superiore was concerned, she quizzed Margherita about the house next door.

'It's all locked up. Do you happen to know who it belongs to?'

'Florentines…' There was a dismissive note in Margherita's voice. 'When old Signor Scandicci was alive, he was often here, but now it's passed to his son, we rarely see him. He never married and he works at the university, I believe.'

That sounded good to Lucy. She had been dreading discovering that her neighbours might turn out to be bagpipe aficionados or a bunch of rowdy teenagers. Hopefully there was a limit to the amount of disturbance a single academic could cause.

'And how about the restaurant? I keep meaning to go there. Is it good?'

Margherita beamed at her. 'It's very good. People come up from Siena and even all the way from Florence to eat here, you know. You should try it.'

Just at that moment, Lucy's phone rang. She apologised to Margherita and picked it up.

'Ciao, Lucy. It's me, Tommy.'

'Ciao, Tommy. Good to hear from you.' Although it wasn't, really. She had been expecting a call to tell her where and when he was taking her for dinner. Since saying yes, she had been having serious second thoughts about having accepted, in case he might think it was going to be anything but a casual friendly evening together, but it was too late now to pull out. 'Dinner on Wednesday night, I think we agreed?'

'That's right. I was wondering… have you been to the Cavallo Bianco just down the road from you yet?'

'The Cavallo Bianco? You mean here in Castelnuovo? I've got a friend here at the moment and she's just been talking about it.'

'So, would that be all right?'

'It would be super, thanks. I've been meaning to go there. My friend tells me it's very good.'

'You can judge for yourself. I like it a lot and I often eat there. My aunt and uncle own it.'

'Well, well.' Lucy remembered he had told her way back that he had relatives in the village. 'That sounds great. Would you like to come here for a drink first and then we can walk down together?'

'Terrific. Say, eight o'clock?'

When she rang off, she looked across the table at Margherita.

'Now, that's a coincidence.' She went on to tell her what Tommy had revealed and saw comprehension on the older woman's face.

'So you're going out for dinner with little Tommasino, fancy that.' Adding the suffix *–ino* to a word in Italian acted as a diminutive and as Tommy was the best part of six feet tall, it seemed a bit of a misnomer, but presumably Margherita had known him since he was a baby and still thought of him as a toddler. 'It was so sad what happened with him and his wife…' Her voice tailed off sorrowfully and Lucy found herself undecided whether to ask or not. In the end she felt she had to know.

'Did she die?'

'No, she left him when he had an affair. And with a German woman of all people!'

'Ah…' Lucy couldn't think of a follow-up to this but she filed the knowledge away for future reference. It sounded as though her first impression of Tommy had been right and he came from the same mould as Charles. She harrumphed to herself and wondered what sort of evening she was going to have on Wednesday.

Chapter 12

Tommy arrived bang on eight o'clock on Wednesday and Lucy gave him a glass of Prosecco as promised. Even up on the terrace it was a hot, clammy night as the end of July approached, so they stayed downstairs where the thick stone walls David Lorenzo had mentioned did an excellent job of keeping the temperature at an acceptable level. She told Tommy about her conversation with Margherita and he smiled at being referred to as Tommasino.

'I was born in Siena, but we used to come here to see my uncle and aunt most weekends. I know Margherita very well – ever since I was tiny. They had the local farm and we kids used to play in the olive groves and we'd often see her. I can't tell you how many glasses of home-made lemonade I've had from her. You heard about her son's accident?'

Lucy nodded. 'Yes, and all sorts of other stuff. She's a walking encyclopaedia. I reckon I now know everything about everybody around here – and if I don't, I know who to ask.' She wondered if he would register that this might well include him and his German lady friend, but he gave no reaction.

The restaurant was almost full, even though it was mid-week, and this confirmed what Margherita had said about its good reputation. Tommy was greeted with kisses by his aunt who then gave Lucy an interested look as she shook her hand. Presumably this wasn't the first time Tommy had brought a woman here for appraisal.

As they sat down, Lucy felt his knee rub against hers and she registered that it was remarkably hairy – surprising, seeing as he was wearing long trousers. A swift glance under the table revealed the culprit. A familiar-looking black dog had squeezed between them and was sitting at their feet, one paw scrabbling at Tommy's knees. Instinctively, Lucy looked around to see if David Lorenzo was in the room, but couldn't locate him.

'Bella, come out!' Tommy's aunt gave Lucy an apologetic smile. 'I'm sorry, she and Tommaso are old friends, so she's always around him.'

As the dog reluctantly heeded the command to come out from under the table, Lucy registered that this Labrador was not Boris after all. The sensation of disappointment this induced in her reminded her of the little shivers of attraction she had been feeling in the tennis player's company and she did her best to shrug off a feeling of regret – and guilt, seeing as he was a married man and she had strong views about that sort of thing. She gave Bella a pat on the head and turned her attention to the meal.

The menu was delivered verbally and she let Tommy and his aunt persuade her to try a starter of lightly fried artichoke hearts and courgette flowers. The combination of bright green and even brighter yellow on their plates looked alluring and the taste was excellent. After that they shared a hefty Florentine steak, cooked on a charcoal grill and sliced vertically into strips. Accompanied by a mixed salad consisting mainly of fresh tomatoes that smelt heavenly, it was an excellent meal. As they ate, Lucy did her best to keep the conversation away from anything too personal. The more she chatted to Tommy, the more convinced she became that nothing more than friendship was ever going to develop here.

Bella the Labrador came back partway through the meal – no doubt attracted by the smell of the grilled meat – and Lucy turned the subject to dogs.

'I'm pretty sure I met Bella's brother the other day. They're the spitting image of each other.'

'Who's the owner?' Tommy topped up her glass with the very drinkable local red wine, but she was deliberately going slow.

'My landlord, the guy who owns the Villa Castelnuovo.'

He looked up with interest. 'You've met the mystery man? Nobody around here's ever seen him. Nobody even knows his name.'

Lucy grinned. 'Margherita thinks he's a New York gangster on the run.'

'She's not the only one. So, what's he like? Do you know his name?'

Lucy reached for her glass and took a little sip to give herself time. She remembered that Tommy was a journalist, after all, so she decided to be economical with the truth.

'Everything's been done through Armando and the lawyer. As for meeting the mystery man, the closest I've got to him has been making friends with his dog.' Seeing as Boris, unlike his master, had actually climbed onto her lap she felt she wasn't being too duplicitous. She then went on to describe the time just after she had first moved in when Boris had followed her into her house and she had called Armando to come and collect him. She conveniently left out her chance meeting with David Lorenzo and the dog a few days ago. She didn't like telling lies, but she felt she owed it to him to keep his secret. If he wanted to be invisible, she had no right to give him away – especially to a journalist.

It was a pleasant evening and the food was extremely good. Although Tommy insisted upon paying, from what she had seen of the prices on the specials board it wasn't too expensive and she vowed to bring her parents here when they came over to visit in the autumn.

As they walked back up the road to her house, she debated how to break it to him that she wasn't going to invite him in for a coffee. She had decided just to harden her heart and send him packing as politely as possible when they reached her door and he did something she hadn't been expecting. He reached out and shook her hand almost formally, before stepping back.

'That was a lovely evening, Lucy. Thank you so much for your company.'

She was genuinely surprised that he was leaving without even an attempt to kiss her, and on such a formal note. Somehow she had been pretty sure she would have to fight him off. Still, she was relieved and she thanked him in her turn before watching as he climbed into his car and set off down the hill. She gave a little whistle of satisfaction that he had finally got the message.

The next day she met up with Daniela for an early evening *aperitivo* in the centre of Siena. They had arranged to meet at a little café in a side street just a stone's throw from the Duomo. Every time Lucy walked past this wonderful marble-clad medieval building with its amazingly ornate façade covered in carvings and statues, and topped with a triangle of golden mosaic, she couldn't resist stopping. This was something she had always done since she was a little girl. She would stare in awe at the intricacies of the decoration, always noticing something different she hadn't spotted before. This evening she tried counting the animal sculptures, ranging from lion-headed gargoyles with wide open mouths that would spew rainwater onto the streets below, to bulls and horses supporting plinths bearing yet more statues. She hit thirty and was still counting when she glanced at her watch, realising she was late meeting up with Daniela, and hurried off. When she saw her she was quick to apologise.

'Ciao, Danni, so sorry I'm a bit late. You know me and the Duomo.' She hadn't seen Daniela for a couple of weeks and this time she definitely noticed a change. 'Wow, you're looking seriously pregnant now.' Her bump was quite pronounced. 'How's it all been going?'

Daniela had bagged a table outside in the shade of an awning and there was even a little breeze blowing up the narrow street that was no doubt very welcome to a pregnant lady. As Lucy sat down beside her, Daniela brought her up to speed on her condition. All was going well with the pregnancy, now in its sixth month. She was drinking ice-cold mineral water and continually mopping her brow, complaining of the heat. Lucy opted for the same and had to agree with her about the temperature.

'This is almost equatorial heat today. If this was the Congo, we'd be in for a thunder storm and a torrential downpour.' Thought of Africa reminded her once more of all the friends she had left behind over there and the uncertainty of their fate at the hands of the different warring factions. For them, rain was the least of their problems. She dismissed their faces from her mind with difficulty. 'The fields around me at Castelnuovo badly need water and I certainly think we could do with a rainstorm to cool things down.'

'You can say that again.' Daniela fanned herself with the drinks menu and gave Lucy a little smile. 'Anyway, how did your date with Tommy go? I asked him today but he was being unusually coy.'

'It was a nice evening, and I'm pleased to say he appears to have realised that it wasn't a date. He didn't call it that, did he?'

'Like I just told you, he hardly said anything. So, date or no date, how was it?'

Lucy told her about the restaurant, the great meal, the Labrador, and the hurried handshake at the end without her having to put up a struggle for her honour. Daniela's smile broadened.

'I wouldn't be so sure. I think that means he thinks it was a date.'

'What makes you say that?'

'I didn't want to put you off as he claims he's turned over a new leaf recently, so I didn't say anything in advance, but Tommy's got a bit of a reputation. You know… with the ladies.'

'My spies did tell me about his wife leaving him after he had an affair with a German woman.'

'I'm impressed. You've managed to get into Castel-nuovo society double-quick and the bush telegraph is working well. In fact, the German woman – who, by the way, was a very nice lady – was just the last straw that broke the camel's back as far as Teresa, his wife, was concerned. He just couldn't keep his hands off other women and that's why she left him. Whether it's true he's a changed man now, I can't say.'

Lucy nodded to herself. She had been expecting something like this. 'So, if he's some kind of serial womaniser – or at least used to be – why didn't he try it on with me?'

'Because he likes you. It means he likes you an awful lot and he didn't want to risk frightening you off.'

'You're trying to tell me he didn't try to kiss me, because he likes me too much?'

'Pretty much. You wait. I'm prepared to bet you'll get a call from him, but it won't be immediately. I reckon he's going to play it really cool.' Daniela fanned herself some more. 'Which is more than I feel.'

Lucy sighed inwardly. Whatever he had said to Daniela, her instincts were telling her that Tommy wasn't to be trusted, so it looked like she had another few rounds in the ring with him still to fight. One thing was for sure; she could do without the attentions of another serial womaniser.

However, Daniela then turned the conversation to a subject that immediately commanded her full attention. Daniela had a problem – Pietro.

Lucy listened in disbelief as Daniela started to voice doubts about their relationship which had already lasted fifteen years or more.

'I don't think he finds me attractive any more, now that I'm pregnant.' Daniela took off her sunglasses and Lucy noticed how red her eyes were. Had she been crying? She was quick to pour oil on the troubled waters.

'Danni, this is Pietro you're talking about. Of course he finds you attractive. You two are the most stable, loving couple I know.' Seeing the empty look on her friend's face, she tried again. 'Why on earth should you think that?'

'It's just a feeling I've got. He sleeps on the far side of the bed and hardly even touches me, and he goes out every

Thursday night. He told me he was taking a furniture repair course – he's always been keen on carpentry – but the other night I was trying to contact him and he didn't pick up, so I called the institute and they told me the course finished for the summer three or four weeks back.'

'So where does he go on Thursday nights?'

'That's the thing – I don't know.'

'Haven't you asked him?'

Daniela shook her head and Lucy saw the tears spring to her eyes. 'I haven't asked him because I suppose I'm scared of what the answer might be.' She wiped the back of her hand across her face. 'In less than three months' time I'm having a baby. What if he goes off and leaves me? I'll be all alone.'

'He won't leave you. Don't be so silly. There has to be a simple explanation. Just talk to him. And as far as not touching you is concerned, he's probably just worried for the baby.'

But, try as she might, Lucy couldn't get through to her. Daniela steadfastly refused to bring up the subject with her husband for fear of getting the answer she dreaded. Lucy remained firmly convinced that there had to be a perfectly innocent explanation and in the end all she could do was to resolve to speak to Pietro herself, to see what was going on. Daniela was obviously – and quite normally – a bag of hormonal nerves at this point in her pregnancy and Lucy felt sure it would all turn out to be a big misunderstanding.

At least, she certainly hoped so.

Chapter 13

On Friday afternoon two things happened in swift succession. First, there was a text message from Tommy, asking if she felt like coming out with him the following evening. She was still mulling over how to tell him as nicely as possible that she didn't want to when she almost bumped into the tall figure of the tennis player in one of the corridors of the clinic. She barely had time to register that he was walking better.

'Hello, Mr Lorenzo. I'm glad to see you're no longer limping.'

A little smile spread across his face and her heart gave an involuntary leap. 'Hi, Doc. I'm feeling better.'

'That's great to hear. So the physio's been paying off. I'm happy for you.' And she was. 'How's your lovely dog?'

He was still smiling. 'Boris is great, thanks. Hey, listen, I've been looking for you and I'm glad I caught you. This is my last day here at the clinic and I wanted to say goodbye.'

'That's really good news – not that you're saying goodbye, but that you're well enough to give up the treatment.'

'I really feel a lot better.' He hesitated, but she was pleased to see a hint of a smile remain on his face. 'Not perfect, but better.'

'That's good. And, of course, we'll still be neighbours, so I expect I'll see you around.' She couldn't prevent a note of disappointment from creeping into her voice and she was quick to try to cover her tracks. 'Anyway, hopefully the sale of the house should be going through any day now. I thought I might have a little house-warming party when that happens. Maybe you and your wife might like to come round for a glass of something to celebrate when that happens.'

His face hardened in an instant and he shook his head, leaving Lucy wishing she hadn't mentioned the idea. Of course he wouldn't want to come to a party where he could be recognised. She could have kicked herself.

'That's kind, thanks.' She noted that he didn't say yes, but he also didn't immediately say no. But then, to her surprise, he came up with an invitation of his own. 'Anyway, you know you were asking about the ruined castle alongside the villa. I was wondering if you'd like to come up and take a look for yourself some time.'

'That would be amazing. I'm reading a book at the moment about the history of the region and I'd love to tie Castelnuovo into the events of the past, maybe even find out who the original builder of your castle was.'

'I'm trying to do the same thing and I've got a number of books of my own. I could lend you some if you like.'

'You're interested in history, too?'

'Always have been. I majored in history at college on a sports scholarship, though admittedly I spent most of my time on the tennis court rather than in the library. Still, I spend... used to spend a lot of my life in hotel rooms and on aircraft, so I've kept up my reading. The main reason I chose to come and live here in Tuscany – apart from my Italian roots – was the history of this part of the world.'

Lucy was genuinely surprised. Somehow she had always assumed that elite sportspeople just lived and breathed their chosen sport, to the exclusion of all else. 'How fascinating. Anyway, thank you for the invitation, I'd love to see the castle. Just tell me when's a convenient time for you. I wouldn't want to disturb you.'

His smile returned, but it was bittersweet. 'Nothing to disturb. I don't have a social life these days. Any time's good. How about this weekend? Tomorrow afternoon, maybe, if you're free? If that suits, why not come up at the end of the afternoon when it starts to cool down a bit.'

'Terrific. I could walk up at, say, half past five or six o'clock?'

'That's fine. So, I'll see you then.' He held out his hand. 'Anyway, professionally, this is it for now – hopefully – so thanks again for sorting me out.'

'You're very welcome.'

As he turned and headed for the exit, she was left with mixed feelings. On the one hand she was sorry she would no longer bump into him here from time to time, but on the other, the prospect of visiting the ruined castle was enticing. She had no idea how long the visit to the Castelnuovo might last. She might well be in and out in a matter of minutes. Alternatively, he and his wife might even invite her in for a drink and she knew she would love to see the inside of the villa. This reminded her of the other invitation she had received from Tommy. She pulled out her phone and started typing.

Hi Tommy. Thanks again for the other night.
Afraid I'm tied up on Saturday. Lucy.

He replied almost immediately:

How about the day after? T

She gritted her teeth and decided she had no choice but to take refuge in a little white lie.

To be quite honest, I'm seeing my boyfriend
this weekend so it isn't going to be possible.
Thanks for asking. L.

All she got back were three words.

Okay. No problem.

Hopefully, this time he had finally got the message.

–

At half past five the next day she set off and walked up the road to the gates of the villa. She had passed these hefty wooden gates numerous times before without stopping, but today she went over and pressed the bell set in one of the stone gateposts. A few seconds later a metallic voice answered from a brass grill. She immediately recognised it.

'Hi, Mr Lorenzo, it's me, Lucy, Lucy Young.'
'Hi, Lucy. Come on up.'
As he spoke, a yellow light on top of the gatepost began to flash and the gates started to open automatically. She heard them close behind her as she walked up the gravelled drive towards the distant villa. The drive curled its way up the hillside, flanked by a regular succession of the iconic Tuscan cypress trees. Some were as high as three-storey buildings and they had clearly been planted many years ago. As she walked in and out of the shade

provided by the trees, a strong scent of resin filled her nostrils and she became aware of the incessant twittering of little birds high in the dark green branches. At one point, a pair of red squirrels appeared above her, leaping from tree to tree, engaged in an enthusiastic game, and she stopped to admire the antics of these sweet little animals. It was a delightful walk, not least as the view opened up more and more behind her and she was forever turning her head to check it out.

As she neared the top, she heard the crunch of gravel ahead of her and saw the Labrador come racing round the bend towards her, having somehow worked out that he had a visitor. He bounded up to her, stood up on his hind legs and scrabbled at her with his paws, covering her and her shorts in dust – fortunately bone dry. She had agonised about what to wear but had decided to stick with her usual shorts, and as the dog jumped up at her she was glad she had resisted the temptation to put on the new pink and white dress she had recently bought. White cotton and dirty paws don't mix.

She was still bent down petting Boris – and brushing the dust off – when she heard another set of feet on the gravel and looked up to see the dog's master coming towards her.

'Hi, Mr Lorenzo. Boris appears to be pleased to see me.'

'And I'm pleased to see you, too, Lucy. And please stop calling me Mr Lorenzo. It's David.'

He came up to her and held out his hand. As she took it and shook it she once again felt that little spark of attraction she had sensed before. Growling at herself in annoyance for having such thoughts about a married man, and a rich one to boot, she searched for something suitable to say.

'It's a lovely day, isn't it?'

Her internal growl intensified. Talking about the weather? What was she, a tongue-tied teenager? She was a bloody surgeon for crying out loud.

David appeared to stifle a grin so maybe he had noticed she was sounding a bit awkward. 'It certainly is. The castle's up this way, if you feel like following me.'

He turned off the drive onto a narrow but clearly defined path and they both followed the dog who ran on ahead of them. The path wasn't wide enough for them to walk side by side so she had no opportunity to talk to him for several minutes as they climbed through the trees. On reflection, this was probably just as well as it gave her time to come up with a few other conversation topics apart from 'it's a lovely day'. Really, what had she been thinking? It also gave her the opportunity to observe his broad shoulders and the strong muscles in his legs as they flexed in time with his steps. From a professional point of view she was glad to see him moving almost normally. As a woman, the rear view of him was disturbingly appealing.

'Here we are.'

She was shaken out of her introspection by the sound of his voice and the fact that he stopped so abruptly she almost bumped into his back. Recovering her balance, she looked in the direction of his pointing finger. There, ahead of them in the thinning undergrowth, was the distinct outline of the remains of low stone walls, a few rising almost to waist height, but most barely reaching her knees. Beyond them was the cream-coloured side of the villa and, in the distance, what was unmistakably a tennis court, but she felt it tactful to avoid making any mention of this in view of his ligament problems. Anyway, for now he appeared to be in full archaeological mode.

'It takes a bit of effort to make it all out, but it's pretty clear the castle consisted of a rectangular outer wall running from here to that big clump of rosemary over there and then across almost to the side of the villa.' She followed his finger as it indicated the outline of the base of a sizeable fortress. 'And inside that was a circular tower or keep. See?'

Sure enough, this, too, was just about visible amid the bushes. She glanced across at him.

'Would you mind if I take a closer look?'

'Help yourself, but just be careful. Some of those little bushes have vicious thorns.'

She went across to one of the taller bits of ruined wall and studied it closely. As he had said, the bushes were very thorny and she felt them scrape her bare legs. She hardly noticed, captivated by the ruins. The stones, some of them as big as packing cases, had been very precisely cut and jointed and it was easy to imagine how impenetrable a defence the finished construction would have formed. She made her way slowly around the outside rectangle, noting the location of a wide gateway and what might have been the vestiges of a moat, or at least a ditch. The circular structure inside the outer walls was clearer to make out and she was able to create a good image in her mind of what must have been a formidable fortress.

She turned and looked back down the hill through the trees. There was no question it occupied a fabulous defensive position and she wondered, yet again, who or what might have been responsible for its downfall and destruction. Had it maybe been taken by treachery, rather than full frontal assault? She felt even keener to try to discover the truth. As she stood there thinking, Boris trotted up and nudged her with his cold wet nose. She glanced down at him and ruffled his ears.

'You're a lucky dog to be living here, Boris. But you know that already, don't you?'

She received a lick in return while his master came up and answered for him. 'He's a *very* lucky dog, but I'm very lucky to have him. There's no question about it: he's my best friend. I don't know what I'd do without him.' Although serious, his tone wasn't dejected and Lucy felt sure Franz, the psychiatrist, would be pleased to hear this if she decided to relay the news to him when she next saw him.

'You know what they say about man's best friend… Oh, I met his sister the other night in the local restaurant. She's the spitting image of him.'

'The Cavallo Bianco? What's the restaurant like? I've never been there.'

'It's really good. I had an excellent meal.' She went on to tell him what she had eaten.

'Did you go there by yourself?' He stopped and hastily corrected himself. 'I'm sorry, that's no business of mine.' He glanced at his watch. 'I don't know if you have plans this evening, but maybe I could offer you a cold drink?'

'That sounds perfect, thank you, and no, I wasn't on my own. I went there with a friend. It's his aunt and uncle who own the place and they've got the Lab.' For a moment she felt very tempted to specify that Tommy was just a friend and no more, but then rejected the idea as sounding far too needy. Instead, she returned the conversation to a less contentious subject – or so she thought. 'Does this mean I might get to meet your wife?'

She couldn't see his face as he had already turned towards the villa, but his voice sounded strained as he replied. 'She no longer lives here.'

Lucy wasn't sure what to say in answer to these few curt words, so she just offered a simple, 'Oh, I'm sorry' and left it at that. Her mind, however, was churning as she followed him round to the impressive stone stairway at the front of the villa.

Seen close up, the villa was charming. It was obvious that it had been redecorated recently as the light cream walls were still bright and they positively glistened in the evening sun. The louvred shutters had been painted a delicate light lavender colour and the whole place – which was quite a bit bigger than she had anticipated – looked like something out of a Millionaires' Homes television programme. But of course, she reminded herself, the owner of the house was without doubt a millionaire many times over.

He led her up the sweep of steps to the fine sculpted front door and into a large marble-floored entrance hall. The temperature in here was noticeably lower than outside, either as a result of the villa being insulated by massively thick walls or, more probably, air conditioning. Whatever the reason, it felt very refreshing after the cloying heat outside. In spite of her predictions to Daniela earlier in the week, no rain had come and it was getting more and more humid as the end of July approached and the potentially even hotter month of August dawned.

'If you don't mind climbing a few flights of stairs, I thought we could go up to the dovecot.'

Lucy remembered seeing the little tower that protruded upwards from the centre of the roof of the villa.

'Do you still keep doves?'

He shook his head and started to walk up the fine wooden staircase to the first floor.

'No, we converted it into a little lounge, seeing as the views are so great. Armando and Fioretta keep chickens round the back, but that's all the livestock we have here at the villa – apart from my four-legged friend here.'

'Do Armando and Fioretta live here with you?'

'Close by. We converted the old stables as a home for them. It's just behind the villa. They're lovely people and they've been invaluable to me. Armando looks after the gardens and, more importantly, the olives and the vines.'

'How wonderful to produce your own oil and wine. I might plant a vine against my back wall, but somehow I don't think it would produce enough grapes for me to venture into wine-making.'

'The red Armando produces is pretty good wine, but there were no white grapes here when we first moved in. The new vines are chardonnay and they went in three years ago so we're hoping to start production – at least on a small scale – next year. Tuscany's predominantly a red wine area and my wife preferred white, so that's why we planted a couple of acres of white grapes. Armando tells me the plants are coming on well so fingers crossed for next year.'

But now his wife was no longer here to drink the wine. Had she left him? Had he left her? Were they divorced? Had something happened to her? From what he had said, she was presumably still alive, but where was she if she no longer lived there? So many questions Lucy knew she would love to ask, but of course she shouldn't – at least not until she knew him a good deal better.

From the first floor landing he led her up another staircase to the second floor and then up another, narrower one, to the dovecot. Boris clearly knew his way around and hurried on ahead. He was waiting for them, tail wagging, as they reached the top.

The view from the little tower room was spectacular and Lucy stood wide-eyed and admired the panorama that opened out all around. From up here she could see over the next range of hills to the red roofs of Siena itself and, beyond that, the distant Apennines, shimmering in the heat haze. Everywhere she looked there were rows of vines, olive groves and ancient red-brick buildings and occasional light-coloured villas dotting the hillsides, with white gravel tracks – the famous *strade bianche* of Tuscany – weaving between them. Golden fields of ripening wheat, almost ready to be harvested, formed a checkerboard effect alongside rich brown patches of recently ploughed earth. She was entranced and she barely heard him as he offered her a choice of drinks.

'What would you like to drink? Something non-alcoholic, or a cold beer or, if you like champagne, I've got a cellar full of the stuff. One of my sponsors used to send me truckloads of it.'

She noted his use of the past tense but didn't comment, determined to keep the conversation light. 'I'm not sure I could handle a *truckload* of champagne, but I'd love a glass if you're sure.'

He opened a little door set low down in the wall beneath one of the lovely arched windows and revealed a fridge built into the wall. He hadn't been joking. The shelves were packed with gold-topped bottles stored on their sides. He pulled one out and made short work of opening it and filling two exquisite long-stemmed flutes. The wine was so cold that tears formed on the outside of the glass and ran down the stem. She took one from him and raised it in his direction.

'Cheers, David. Your very good health. Thank you so much for inviting me up here and letting me see your historic ruined castle.'

She found herself wondering if he made a habit of entertaining women up here now that his wife was no longer around. No sooner did the thought occur to her than she dismissed it. He was a secretive recluse, after all. He could hardly invite women home if he wanted to remain undiscovered. And, she reminded herself, he hadn't said where his wife was. From his tone she had inferred that the marriage was over, but this assumption might be completely wrong. Maybe his wife had merely moved elsewhere to look after her aged parents, or she might have a job that kept them apart – like being an MSF medic for example.

What was unquestionable, however, was that as views went, this one was very, very romantic. What if he had invited her up here today because he was interested in her? And if so, supposing that his wife was out of the equation, how did this make her feel? She was prevented from any further conjecture by the clink of his glass against hers and the sound of his voice.

'Cheers, and thanks again. I must confess I did have an ulterior motive in inviting you up here.' This very definitely attracted her full attention but it turned out his ulterior motive was anything but romantic. 'I thought you might like to see this.'

He opened a drawer in a fine old sideboard set against the back wall and pulled out what looked like a handful of rags. Parting them, he exposed a sinister-looking pistol, the black metal covered in a light sheen of oil. As she stared down at it, he explained.

'This is the culprit. It's a World War Two German Luger. It's all right, you can pick it up if you like. It's harmless now. Armando had the firing pin removed.'

She declined his offer to handle the weapon with a little wave of her fingers. 'Thanks, but I'll leave well alone. I hate guns. I've seen too much of what they can do to people. So how come you have it, and how did you manage to shoot yourself?' Hopefully this indicated that he hadn't tried to commit suicide, in spite of her original fears. After all, he would hardly show her his chosen weapon, surely?

'As somebody with an interest in history, you might enjoy the story. During the war, the villa was command-eered by the Nazis for six months or so from autumn 1943 until spring 1944 as a rest home for officers injured in the fierce fighting further south. Presumably one of the officers dropped his pistol over the banister up here and it landed down the back of a statue and he couldn't reach it. Here, look.'

He guided her over to the little landing at the top of the staircase, from where they could look down to the floor below. Standing on plinths protruding from the walls were three charming marble statues of scantily clad nymphs. He pointed down at the first of them.

'That's the one. We discovered the pistol jammed down between her buttocks.'

Lucy giggled at the thought. 'When did you find it?'

He looked shamefaced. 'Back in May. The day you had to come to the clinic and sew me up.'

'So what exactly happened?'

'Fioretta spotted the gun, and she went off to ask Armando to fetch a long ladder. While I was waiting here, I had what I thought was a brilliant idea. I dug out an old fishing rod and line and managed to hook the pistol and jerk it free. I reeled it in and it was as I dropped it into my lap that the damn thing went off. Who'd have thought it would still work after seventy years or so?'

Lucy nodded. As a story, it made sense and she was genuinely pleased for him that her suspicion of an attempt at suicide had not, after all, been correct. 'The bullet went right through you. Any idea where it ended up?'

He pointed back into the dovecot room. 'That's it there. I thought I'd leave it as a reminder to myself not to be so stupid another time.'

Sure enough, she could see a little hole in the plaster just above waist height, right beside one of the windows. Presumably the bullet must have embedded itself in the wooden frame.

'Well, as it turned out, it could have been a whole lot worse for you. You're all healed up now, I'm sure.' As far as the bullet wound was concerned. From a brief chat with the orthopaedic surgeon the previous afternoon she now knew that the cruciate ligaments, while a lot better than before, were never going to be able to stand up to the rigours of competitive tennis again. She was impressed at David's positive-sounding attitude, now that it had been spelled out to him that this signified the definitive end to his illustrious career. Franz Berlin must have worked his therapeutic magic on him and David had come a long way from his morose state when she had first met him back in May.

She returned to contemplating the view. 'I could stand here for hours. It's simply gorgeous.'

136

'I really do stand here for hours. I think I saw you working in your garden yesterday evening, didn't I?'

'Wow, your eyesight must be good.'

Sure enough, her little house and its back garden were just about visible, and she could even make out the darker rectangle where she had been removing weeds and preparing her first flower bed. Beside it was the sunbed she used for short bursts of sunbathing. Somehow, the idea that he had been watching her gave her a little thrill, although if it had been somebody else it might have been a bit creepy, but not him. Somehow she felt confident he didn't belong to the 'creepy' category. This little thrill took her back to the question of how she would feel if it turned out he was interested in her – and free to be interested in her. After all, he was no longer a patient at the clinic so, assuming his wife was out of the equation, there was no legal or moral impediment now. Mind you, she told herself, he had yet to give any indication of real interest in her as anything but a friendly neighbour. Besides, she reminded herself, he was a millionaire and he inhabited a very different world from hers.

'You've cut yourself.'

Startled out of her reflections, she followed the direction of his eyes and saw a trickle of drying blood on the side of her calf.

'It's nothing. It was probably those thorny bushes outside. You did warn me, but I was too engrossed with the ruin.'

'Stand still for a moment.'

Before she could stop him, he took a paper napkin from a pile on the sideboard and lowered himself onto his good knee. He tipped a splash of champagne onto the napkin and, holding her leg steady with one hand, used the napkin in his other hand to wipe the blood gently away. The cut was tiny and had already closed and no further blood emerged. She tried to tell herself that it was the bubbles in the wine that made her skin tingle, but deep-down, she knew it was his touch. She took a mouthful of Dutch courage and did her best to sound perfectly normal.

'Thank you. I think this rates as a medical first. It'll be interesting to see if champagne has healing properties.' As he rose to his feet, she gave him a little smile. 'If it gets into the Lancet, I promise I'll give you the credit.'

They chatted about history for a while as the sun began to drop towards the horizon and the memory of his touch against her bare leg gradually faded – at least for now. The dog stretched out on the floor at their feet with a heartfelt sigh and was soon snoring. After a while they abandoned the view and sat down on armchairs facing each other but with a chaste two metre gap between them. She mentioned what Margherita had told her about the name of the castle and she saw him sit up in surprise and heard him repeat her words.

'She said it was called the Englishman's Castle? I wonder...' He pulled out his phone and scrolled through until he found what he was looking for. 'Have you ever heard of John Hawkwood?'

'No. That sounds like an English name.'

'It is indeed, although he's better known over here by his Italian name, Giovanni Acuto. As you must know, *acuto* in Italian means wily or smart – and he was – but he probably got his Italian name simply because the locals couldn't get their tongues around Hawkwood. Acuto was as good as they could get.'

'So he spent time here in Tuscany?'

He looked back down at his phone. 'Yes, after fighting for Edward III in the Hundred Years' War in France, he joined up with a bunch of mercenaries called the White Company and followed them into Italy. He soon became their leader and he developed into one of the most famous and successful soldiers of fortune in Europe during the fourteenth century. He and his men fought for a lot of different masters, but he ended up as the hero of Florence and was even buried there, in the Duomo.'

'And you think this might have been his castle?' Lucy felt a surge of excitement.

'Who knows? It's a fact that he was gifted a number of properties during his time in Italy. Maybe this was one of them or maybe he designed it. Nobody seems to know in what year this castle was originally built.'

They talked and talked, and it was beginning to get dark when he looked at his watch and rose to his feet – using the arms of the chair to assist him, she noticed.

'I'm very sorry, but I have a conference call scheduled for eight thirty our time. That's the problem with having so many business contacts in the States. It would have been nice to continue our talk over dinner, but the last one of these I took lasted an hour and a half. Maybe some other time?'

'Any time you want to talk, just give me a call. Armando's got my number. And maybe you'll come round to my place next time. Don't worry, it's very discreet. Your secret will be safe with me. Nobody will know that the New York gangster who's been hiding here in the villa has been out and about.'

'Is that what people are saying?' He sounded genuinely astounded.

'That's what a couple of people in the village were saying.' She came close to asking the reason why he had chosen to turn his back on celebrity and hide himself away out here in the middle of the country, but she relegated that question to the heap of others to be asked when they knew each other better.

At the bottom of the stairs he looked out of the door at the gathering dusk. 'Are you going to be okay walking home on your own? I've got this damn conference call but I could ask Armando to give you a lift.'

She assured him she was fine, resisted the temptation to kiss him, thanked him again, and set off back down the drive.

Chapter 14

The following morning, as it was a Sunday, she sat down after a late breakfast and searched the internet. This was for two reasons. One was to read up about John Hawkwood, the medieval mercenary leader, and the other was to check out David Lorenzo.

She started with the tennis player and it didn't take long for her to discover the two main reasons why he had been suffering from depression. A feeling of pity spread through her as she read numerous newspaper articles going back over the last three years. First was of course the fact that he had been forced to give up tennis as a result of the knee problems suffered at Roland Garros in Paris, with which she was already familiar. As she had seen first-hand, the effect of this upon him had been crushing.

Second, and probably even more important, was the fact that his marriage had broken down not long afterwards. His wife had left him, but there were conflicting reports as to what had been the cause of the break-up, although they mostly seemed to agree that it had been his fault. Her feeling of pity for him turned to disappointment. Hypotheses ranged from physical assault to a naked sex romp with a bunch of cheerleaders in Orlando, and she shook her head in disbelief. As a result of the media hounding he had subsequently received, he had disappeared into thin air and his whereabouts were still unknown, although there was a theory he had left the US for Europe.

She sat back and stared blankly at the screen. This was all brand new to her – but of course, she had been in the middle of Africa at the time those events had taken place. Could it be that his wife had left him because he had been unfaithful to her? Did this mean he was no better than Charles, Tommy and maybe even Pietro? What was it about men that they couldn't understand, and stick to, the concept of monogamy? David had really struck her as a decent, straightforward guy, in spite of his initial grumpiness, but, alas, it appeared that this might not be the case.

Of course, she told herself, there were always two sides to every story and maybe his wife had been the cause of the breakdown of the marriage, but in her eyes, if it turned out he was the guilty party, there was no excuse. Just like Charles, if he could do it once, he could do it again, and she knew she would never be able to trust him if these reports were true – maybe as a neighbour and friend with an interest in history, but nothing more. Mind you, she reminded herself, there was no way she would have felt comfortable hooking up with a multi-millionaire anyway.

In an attempt to take her mind off the tennis player, she read about John Hawkwood. He had indeed been a very canny and a very successful general who had led from the front. A description of him remarked upon his broad shoulders and powerful physique. She had no doubt that would have been necessary at a time when the weapon of choice was a longbow or a two-handed sword a metre long which could decapitate a horse or a knight in steel armour. Either of these weapons required considerable upper body strength.

Over the course of his career Hawkwood had fought for and against the Pope, and for and against most of the warring city-states of northern Italy, before ending up as a faithful servant of Florence. As David had told her, he had been buried in the Duomo in Florence, although his remains had subsequently been returned to England at the express request of King Richard III. A fresco in his honour still stood inside the Duomo and she resolved to take a trip up there to see it one of these days. There was no mention of Castelnuovo, so she returned to her history book through which she was slowly working her way. The facts the author presented were interesting, but he had a lugubrious style and a love of never-ending sentences, so it was proving to be a long, hard grind.

Before she could read much more of it, there was a knock at the door. She went over to open it and to her surprise, she found Pietro standing there. Without Daniela.

'Ciao, Lucy. Are you free for a few minutes?'

She kissed him on the cheeks and waved him in, thinking that this was the perfect opportunity to talk to him about Daniela's suspicions, but he shook his head. 'There's something I'd like to show you. Would you mind coming with me? It's not far.'

Puzzled, but intrigued, Lucy grabbed her bag, locked the door and followed him out to his car. He drove back through the village, then, just as they left the last house behind, he turned off onto a *strada bianca* leading to what Lucy now knew to be Margherita's grandson's farm. As they bumped along the potholed track towards the farmhouse, she realised that her guess that it might be medieval was almost certainly correct. It was a charming old brick-built longhouse with stables and stalls for animals at one end and the farmer's accommodation at the other. Sitting on the front doorstep was yet another black Labrador.

Pietro drew up opposite the farmhouse and as Lucy climbed out, she was greeted by the dog. His greeting was less effusive than the one she was used to receiving from Boris, but his tail was wagging and he looked friendly. His nose hairs were just beginning to turn white and she calculated he was a good bit older. This made her wonder if he might be the father of Boris and the other Labrador she had seen in the restaurant. When he spotted Pietro, his tail started wagging more enthusiastically and he trotted round to jump up against him to be petted. Clearly, this Lab and Pietro were old friends.

'Ciao, Nerone. Have you been a good dog?' As Pietro patted the dog's head, the fly curtain at the door parted and a man came out.

He was tall, with a mop of dark hair hanging around his tanned, stubbly face and almost down to his broad shoulders. He was wearing scruffy shorts and a battered T-shirt that revealed his muscular forearms. Both these and his strong brown legs were covered in a mat of dark hair and Lucy had to admit he was a very good-looking man. As he saw Pietro, his face broke into a smile.

'Ciao, Pietro.'

'Ciao, Roberto.' With the dog bouncing at his side, Pietro went over to shake hands and make the introductions. 'This is Lucy. She's my English friend and she lives here now. She and Danni have known each other since they were kids.'

Lucy gave Roberto a little wave. He had to be Margherita's grandson. He came over and extended a welcoming hand.

'Ciao, Lucy. Good to meet you. You're living in the cottage at the far end of the village, aren't you? My grandma's told me all about you.'

'It's good to meet you too, Roberto.' She gave him a big smile. 'I love your home. And what a view!'

He nodded. 'I've lived here for forty years, but I never tire of it.'

Pietro cut in. 'I've brought Lucy here to show her what I've been making. I'll just take her round to the barn if that's okay.'

'Of course.' Roberto glanced at Lucy. 'And if you feel like calling in for a glass of wine afterwards, I'll be here.'

'Thank you. I've been meaning to come and buy some of your wine and olive oil. Your gran gave me some of the oil, which is amazing, but I'd love to try the wine.'

He gave her a little wave of the hand and returned to the house. The dog hesitated, torn between following his master or his friend, before deciding to head back and take up station on the doorstep once more. Pietro led Lucy around the back of the farmhouse to a more modern building. He opened a side door and waved her in.

'That's it. Over there, under the dustsheet.'

The room was clearly a workshop. The floor was covered in sawdust and wood shavings and there were numerous bits of new and antique furniture lying around. As Lucy followed Pietro over to the object under the sheet, suddenly everything became clear to her.

He pulled the cover away to reveal the sweetest little crib she had ever seen. It was made of highly polished new wood and Pietro had sculpted almost every flat surface with bunny rabbits, birds, dogs and cats. It was simply delightful and she knew that Daniela would fall in love with it.

'It's a secret because I want it to be a surprise. I've been making it over the past couple of months. It started out as a project at evening class, but Roberto, who's an old friend, said it would be okay if I brought it here to finish it off when the institute closed for the summer. What do you think?'

'I love it, Pietro.' Such was her feeling of relief to learn what he had been doing that Lucy went over and threw her arms around him and kissed him on the cheek. 'And Danni's going to love it, too.'

'Lucy, listen, I need your help. Danni's acting very strange. The way she's been looking at me over the past few weeks, the things she says, and the things she doesn't say, I'm beginning to wonder if she's fallen out of love with me. I know she's pregnant and that can affect her mood, but I've never known her to behave like this.' He looked up in real anguish. 'I don't know what to do, Lucy, honestly.'

Lucy took his hand and led him over to a bench where they sat down side-by-side. She kept hold of his hand in both of hers as she related everything Daniela had told her and she was delighted to see relief and real joy spread across his face as the significance of her words sank in.

'So she thinks I don't love her? That's crazy.'

'That's what I told her, but she wouldn't listen. Anyway, now that you know, I really think there's only one thing for you to do.'

'Tell her everything.'

'Absolutely. And, if you want my advice, I'd take her the crib and give it to her now, even if it's not completely finished.' She squeezed his hand a last time before releasing it. 'She'll love it and everything will be straightened out. I'm so, so glad for you both.'

She gave him a hand to carry the crib out to his little car. Together they folded the rear seats down and squeezed it into the back. He then led her over to Roberto's house where she found she was in for a treat. There, lying in a big wicker basket in the corner of the big old farmhouse kitchen was yet another Labrador and this one had half a dozen of the sweetest little puppies pressed up against her. Nerone, evidently the proud father to this litter of pups, trotted over to say hello again while his mate just lay there and let her tail wag lazily. Roberto looked up from the table.

'I don't suppose I can interest you in a Labrador puppy, can I?'

Lucy beamed at him. 'I would love a puppy, but I just can't. It wouldn't be fair on the dog. I'd have to leave it alone all day.'

'You live by yourself?'

'Yes, and I work across the valley at the Siena Clinic. I'm a doctor.'

After Lucy had spent a lot of time making a fuss of the little dogs and then, reluctantly, handed them back to their mother, Roberto led her and Pietro out and along the front of the building until they came to a glazed arch. In here was his farm shop and he insisted she should taste not only last year's red wine, but also his new development – a sparkling deep rose-coloured wine that tasted amazing. Lucy had no hesitation in buying a dozen bottles of each, along with a five litre can of extra-virgin olive oil.

As the crib was now occupying what little space there was in Pietro's Fiat, she told Roberto she would come straight back in her own car to collect her purchases. He told her not to worry, loaded them into the back of his battered old Land Rover and gave her a lift home with the wine. Before leaving the farm, she kissed Pietro on the cheek and made him promise to text her as soon as he and Daniela had had their talk, and asked him to have a think whether they might like to come out for dinner with her to celebrate.

When she and Roberto arrived at her house, he insisted on carrying the bottles into the kitchen for her. After setting the boxes down on the floor he turned towards the door. 'I'm afraid I need to get back. My wife's taken the kids into Siena to buy clothes and there's nobody back at the farm. I've no idea when they'll be home and I don't like leaving everything open. My daughter's thirteen, going on eighteen, and she takes forever to choose what she wants to wear.'

Lucy suppressed a wry smile. Just like David, this one was already married. As his car drove off and she closed the front door, she shook her head slowly. Why were all the good ones already taken? And why were so many of the others two-timing cheats? Still, she told herself, at least she now knew that Pietro was on the side of the angels.

Chapter 15

An hour or so later, while she was on her knees in the garden, tidying her new flowerbed, her phone beeped twice with one message from Pietro and one from Daniela within a matter of seconds of each other. The content was reassuringly similar: they had had their talk, everything was all right and they both sent their thanks for acting as go-between. Lucy immediately replied and managed to persuade them to go out for dinner with her to celebrate the fact that all was once again well between them.

Daniela suggested that they meet up in the local restaurant here in Castelnuovo Superiore, but Lucy hesit-ated before agreeing. The Cavallo Bianco belonged to Tommy's aunt and uncle after all, and she didn't really want to bump into him so soon after refusing his invitation on the grounds of her non-existent boyfriend. Still, she told herself as she finally texted back to say yes, if she were to bump into him, he was a big boy and he would get over it, and the food there was too good for her to avoid the place on his account.

It was still very warm at seven thirty that evening as she walked down the road to the restaurant, but tonight the clouds were starting to gather above the horizon. Lucy hoped this would signify the arrival of long-awaited rain – for her own little patch of garden as well as for the sake of the farmers around here. Even the hardiest weeds by the side of the road were dry and yellow, parched and burned by the sun, and there was no doubt the whole of Tuscany would give a huge sigh of relief when the rain finally came.

When she got to the Cavallo Bianco, she was pleased to see no sign of Tommy, although Bella the Labrador seemed happy enough to see her again. Daniela and Pietro arrived a few minutes later and they all had a lovely meal together. Tonight, Lucy went for the chef's take on the Spanish classic, gazpacho, and this cold tomato and cucumber soup was just what she wanted on such a sticky night. She followed this with home-made *pappardelle al cinghiale*. The rich gamey sauce accompanying the wide strips of pasta was made from the meat of the farmer's big enemy in this part of Italy: the wild boar.

Almost on a daily basis the local news was full of reports of vineyards devastated, crops uprooted, and even a few cases of people attacked by the huge wild pigs with their scary tusks which were multiplying at an alarming rate. Lucy had been pretty sure she had had one in her back garden the previous night but, by the time she looked out of the window, whatever it was that had been grunting and digging up her newly planted flowers had gone, leaving a trail of destruction behind that had taken her the best part of an hour to fix earlier this afternoon. As she savoured her pasta, she decided that wild boar appealed to her much more on a plate than in her garden.

Daniela and Pietro once again looked as loving and settled as ever and Lucy rejoiced for them, not without the usual little twinge of envy at their evident happiness. As the meal progressed, the conversation turned to Lucy and her new home. Once Daniela had heard that she had spent the previous evening with her mysterious neighbour – whose identity Lucy steadfastly refused to divulge –

Daniela spent considerable time digging, not so much to find out who he was, but to find out how Lucy felt about him.

'So am I right in thinking we're talking more than just good neighbours?'

Lucy did her best to play down any developing feelings she might have towards David, but Daniela wasn't a journalist for nothing and she managed to get Lucy to admit that she found him handsome, bright and good company. Reluctantly, Lucy repeated what he had said about his wife no longer living there and added the caveat that for all she knew, he might have been the guilty party responsible for the break-up. Daniela nodded sagely and gave her advice.

'You've got to find out. Why don't you ask him?'

'I don't know him well enough yet. Besides, if I start asking him that sort of stuff, it'll sound as if I'm after him.'

'And aren't you?'

'No... well, maybe. To be honest, I do find him very attractive, but nothing could ever develop between us as he's from a completely different world from me. The shoes he was wearing alone probably cost more than my whole outfit. I'd never feel comfortable alongside a millionaire.' Lucy saw that her friend was about to retort and did her best to change the subject. 'Besides, I'm quite happy without a man at the moment. To be honest, I'm more concerned about my job.'

'Why? Problems at work? I thought you said you'd cleared the air with Charles.'

'It's not Charles.' Lucy's voice tailed off and she glanced around but there was nobody within earshot. 'And it's not the work itself. I love the place. It's got the most amazing state-of-the-art equipment and excellent facilities. I get on well with my colleagues, the director and with almost all of the patients, but I suppose it's just this hang-up of mine. All men are supposed to be born equal but they aren't. I'm finding the disparity between these over-privileged few and the millions of less fortunate people in the world increasingly hard to come to terms with.'

'But didn't you say your boss at MSF told you not to worry about that sort of thing?' Daniela stretched out her hand and caught hold of Lucy's, giving it a little squeeze. 'I imagine you're often doing life-saving work, I'm sure. It's not as if you're involved with the cosmetic surgery side of the clinic, after all.'

'I know, but I still can't get my head round the inequality of it all.' She looked across the table and sighed. 'And, if I'm honest, there's something else. It's all too easy. I go into work, I do my job, I stop for coffee, I work some more and then I come home again. I wouldn't go so far as to say it's stress-free – of course it's not – but it's so totally different compared to the daily struggle I've been used to facing.'

'But isn't it good to get away from too much stress?'

'Well, yes, of course, but I felt so wedded to my job in Mabenta and I just don't feel it here.'

'And you miss the stress?'

'It's not that, really. Like I say, I like most of the patients – and I really wasn't expecting to – but it's something inside me. I honestly don't know if I'm cut out for private medicine.'

'So are you thinking of leaving? Going back to MSF?'

Lucy shook her head slowly. 'I really don't know.' Apart from anything else, leaving the clinic might well mean losing her little house and, for that matter, her handsome neighbour – millionaire or not, married or not, adulterer or not. 'Like I say, it's my problem. I've got to figure it out.'

'Please don't go off and leave us, Lucy. I know you're a great surgeon – Bruno never stops singing your praises – but if you really don't feel right working at the clinic, why don't you go down to the main hospital in Siena and see if they're recruiting? I bet they'd jump at having you.'

Any further conjecture was interrupted as the door opened and Lucy's face fell as Tommy walked in. Bella the dog ran across to greet him, tail wagging, but Lucy certainly didn't feel the same way. After kissing his aunt and petting the dog, he spotted them and made his way across to their table.

'Ciao, Daniela, ciao, Pietro.' He shook them by the hands and turned towards Lucy, as ever the big toothy smile on his face. 'And, Lucy, you look lovely. Has your boyfriend left?'

Lucy shot an admonitory look across the table towards Daniela and replied sweetly. 'Ciao, Tommy. Good to see you. Yes, he's just left.' She glanced at her watch. 'You're leaving it a bit late for dinner tonight, aren't you?'

'They'll make me some pasta, I'm sure.'

He stood there, showing no sign of leaving, quite possibly waiting to be invited to join them. Lucy didn't know what to do, but help was at hand. Daniela knew that Lucy had turned down his dinner invitation and she must have realised the situation as she pushed back her chair and stood up, grabbing the table for help as she did so.

'Well, Tommy, enjoy your meal. We've just finished.' She glanced down at Pietro who was looking surprised. 'I think I'll skip dessert tonight. It's terribly hot and I think I need a breath of fresh air.'

Lucy waved them away as she went to get the bill. By the time she had paid it, Pietro had collected his car and was waiting outside. Lucy saw Daniela into the passenger seat and kissed her goodbye, whispering into her ear as she did so. 'Thanks a lot, Danni. I owe you. I'll call you later.'

As Pietro set off downhill, she turned to walk home and found she had company in the shape of Bella the Labrador and, holding the end of her lead, Tommy. He grinned at Lucy and she distinctly felt him undressing her with his eyes – not for the first time.

'While my uncle's making me something to eat, I said I'd take Bella for a quick walk. I'll see you back to your house.'

Accepting the unavoidable, Lucy fell in beside him and they set off. He kept up a constant stream of conversation and she soon realised there was a common theme to it – her mysterious neighbour. He was evidently very interested to discover just who now owned the villa and she had to endure a serious grilling as Tommy the journalist did his best to wheedle any information out of her as to the mystery man's identity. By the end of the inquisition she was fairly sure she hadn't given away anything compromising, but he had been like a terrier, snapping at her heels and it had started to annoy her. This made it easier for her to tell him another little white lie when they got back to her house.

'I've been feeling a bit off all evening and I just need to go to bed. Goodnight, Tommy.'

And that was that. It wasn't as clichéd as saying she had a headache, but he didn't need to be Hercule Poirot to work out that his company was not required. To her relief, he told her he hoped she would feel better soon, and went off. She rather hoped this would be the last she would hear from Tommy.

Chapter 16

In spite of the clouds, it rained very little during the night and on Monday morning the sky was once again clear, the roads dry, and the temperature if anything even higher. It was a busy day, with a tricky bowel operation that took several hours. This was on an opera singer who was renowned internationally as much for his appetite for gourmet food as for his voice. She couldn't help comparing him to her average patient in the Congo, reflecting that a love of exotic food was a luxury few, if any, could afford over there.

When she got home from work that evening, feeling quite weary as well as uncomfortably sticky and hot, she was cheered to find a gift on her doorstep. It was a healthy rose bush, covered with beautiful pink and white blooms, in a hefty terracotta pot and there was a note with it.

> *Hi Lucy. This is a present from Armando (and*
> *me). We both hope you like it. David.*

She opened the door and carried the heavy pot through the kitchen and out to the spot beside the back door where she intended to plant it. The scent of the roses was intoxicating and she breathed deeply. Coming back inside, she poured herself a large glass of cold mineral water from the fridge and debated what to do to say thank you. She didn't have David's number, but she did have Armando's. An idea came to her and she reached for her phone. Armando answered almost immediately.

'*Pronto.*'

'Hello, Armando, it's Lucy from the cottage. I've just found the gorgeous rose you left me. It's absolutely perfect. Thank you so much. I was wondering if you and your wife might like to come down here one evening for a glass of wine so I could say thank you properly. Hopefully you might be able to persuade David to come too. I'd like to thank him as well for his hospitality the other day. Please tell him there won't be anybody else here. I'm free any evening this week. Tomorrow, maybe, or Wednesday? Whatever suits you.'

Armando reacted very positively and told her he would phone her back once he had spoken to his wife and to David. Barely a few minutes later, he called back to say that the three of them would be delighted to accept her kind invitation the day after tomorrow, Wednesday evening. They agreed upon six o'clock and Lucy had a last-minute thought. 'Do, please, bring Boris. I met his mum and dad yesterday, and it'll be good to see him again.'

On Wednesday afternoon on her way home from the clinic she dashed into the shop in Castelnuovo Superiore to stock up on food. She and Donatello, the shop-keeper, were good friends now and she bought more of his wonderful hand-carved ham, several different local cheeses, a lovely aromatic cantaloupe melon and a variety of crisps and crackers as well as some fennel-flavoured *finocchiona* and little wild boar salami. Back home she hastily toasted slices of bread, cut them into squares and covered them with cheese, pâté or sausage, before cutting the melon into cubes and threading these onto cocktail sticks together with rolled-up pieces of ham. She had put bottles of Roberto's sparkling rosé in the fridge the previous night and hoped her guests would approve.

She just had time to run upstairs and take a quick shower before they were due to arrive. She resisted the temptation to put on the smart frock she had worn at Daniela's wedding and went for her new white and pink dress instead. This was a bit short, but her legs were nice and brown by now after all her walks in the hills, so she felt confident she looked okay. Besides, she told herself, there was no point dolling herself up for David's benefit. Yes, as she had told Daniela, she really did find him very attractive, but she knew there could be no future for her with a millionaire, let alone one who might also be philanderer.

Shortly after seven she heard a car outside and went out to greet them. It was a sleek black Mercedes with heavily tinted windows. Evidently this was the way David managed to get around and maintain his anonymity. It was the first time she had met Fioretta and she took an immediate liking to this motherly lady. Before she could greet anybody else, she was assaulted – in the friendliest possible way – by the happy Labrador and she had to crouch down and make a fuss of him. When she stood back up again, she beckoned them all inside and made a beeline for the sink to wash the dog off her hands.

'Thank you so much for coming and thank you for the rose.' She opened the back door and showed them where she was planning on planting it. Armando, ever-helpful, had an idea.

'I've got some wire and some masonry nails back at the villa. If you like, I'll come round one of these days and pin up a framework for you to train the rose against when it starts going up the wall.'

Lucy thanked him warmly and turned to David who had been standing back, letting Armando do the talking. She noticed a bottle in his hand.

'Hi, David, you shouldn't have.'

He handed her the bottle of champagne and she was delighted to see him smile. 'Like I say, I've got cases of the stuff. You're very welcome.'

As it was another warm, sunny evening without much wind, she took them up to the loggia. Ignoring Lucy's protests, Fioretta picked up the biggest tray of food and carried it up the stairs, Armando took the rest and David brought the wine, leaving Lucy with just the glasses to carry. They settled down on her recently purchased chairs and David opened one of the bottles of Roberto's sparkling rosé. Boris positioned himself at Lucy's feet, his nose firmly pointed at the food on the table and did his best to look as if nobody ever fed him. Knowing Labradors of old, Lucy hardened her heart – at least for now.

As for David, hardening her heart wasn't so easy. He was looking very appealing. He was wearing a light pink polo shirt that was just tight enough across his chest to reveal his muscular frame. His strong forearms – she had always had a thing about men's forearms – were tanned and covered with light brown hair. There was something different about him and it took her a few moments to realise he had had a haircut. She had only ever seen him with fairly stylish, medium length hair before, but now it had been sheared to barely an inch. It looked good. In fact, he looked very good and she growled to herself.

It was a very pleasant evening. They all approved of Roberto's wine and Armando told her he was also hoping to try his hand at making some sparkling wine along with regular white wine when next autumn came around. David also had some good news for her.

'I heard back from my lawyer today. The notary says all the papers are in order so the sale of this place should go through later this week or early next week.'

Lucy beamed at him. 'That's great. I really love this house and the thought that I'm going to end up owning a historic piece of Tuscany is amazing.' Given her doubts about the probity of some of the patients and the nature of the job at the clinic, whether or not she would still be working at the clinic in a few months' time was a different matter entirely, but for now she did her best not to dwell on that.

In the course of the evening she was delighted to see David visibly relax and she couldn't miss the affection he had for Armando and Fioretta. It emerged that Fioretta was responsible for his new haircut and Lucy complimented both of them. David's Italian was unexpectedly fluent until he revealed that his grandparents had emigrated to the USA from Italy and he had been brought up speaking both languages in the house. The dog – once he had scrounged a couple of pieces of salami – behaved impeccably, and all in all it was a most enjoyable evening.

The not so nice part came right at the end.

As they were standing at the door, chatting and saying goodnight, a car pulled up behind David's Mercedes. To Lucy's horror, she saw that it was Tommy. She rushed over to try to head him off before he recognised David, but she felt pretty sure she saw what might have been a glimmer of recognition on his face, although she hoped that might have been for Armando and Fioretta.

'Hi, Tommy, I wasn't expecting to see you.'

'Hi, Lucy.' He leant towards her and kissed her on the cheeks before she could retreat. 'It's really good to see you too. I've just been having dinner with my aunt and uncle and I thought I'd pop up to see if you were feeling better.' His eyes once more flicked across to figures by her doorway. 'That's not your boyfriend, is it?' He didn't give her time to deny the accusation. 'Sorry to interrupt you if you've got company, but at least that shows you're feeling all right again.'

'Back to normal, thank you. Listen, I'm sorry to sound inhospitable' – she wasn't sorry in the slightest – 'but I'd better get back to my guests.' To her relief, he nodded.

'Of course. Anyway, I'm glad you're feeling fine again. Goodnight, Lucy.' And to her extreme annoyance, he tried to kiss her again, although this time she managed to avoid his advances.

As his car drove off again, she went back to the others. 'I'm really sorry about that. He's someone I know. He works with a friend of mine. His turning up here tonight was completely unexpected.' But of course she was in the presence of long-term Castelnuovo residents. Fioretta had already recognised Tommy.

'We know Tommaso, don't we, Armando?'

'Yes, we've known him since he was a toddler. He's a local boy, but you probably already know that.'

Lucy nodded. 'We had dinner together at his aunt and uncle's restaurant a week ago and he told me all about the village. He knows it well.' As she spoke, she caught a glimpse of the expression on David's face. If asked to define it, she would have struggled. It was part friendly, part interested, but also part jealous. Could that be? For a moment their eyes met and she realised she was actually blushing. Turning away hastily, she thanked Armando once again and then shook everybody's hand before seeing them back into David's car. As they drove off, she kicked the dust at her feet and snorted.

'Bugger!'

What was for sure was that David was probably now convinced that she and Tommy were an item and, even worse, there was a very real possibility that Tommy, the journalist, had recognised her reclusive neighbour.

As she stood there she felt a drop of rain on her face, then another and another. As the drops turned into a sudden torrential downpour, accompanied by a clap of thunder that rattled the window panes, she hurried back inside. This dampener on what had been a lovely evening might be welcomed by the plants in her garden, but it rather summed up the way she felt. If she had been responsible – albeit inadvertently – for revealing David's identity to the media, she knew she would feel awful.

Chapter 17

She got a text from Daniela next morning that completely spoiled her day.

> Ciao Lucy. Bad news. Tommy has found out that your neighbour is tennis star David Lorenzo and we're running a full page spread in tomorrow's morning edition and online. There's every chance the news will go viral. I spoke to the editor and tried my hardest to put a stop on it, but he's adamant. So sorry. Danni.

Lucy was sitting in the staff canteen with a cup of ginseng, taking a quick break in the middle of a long morning working alongside Dr Saeed, who was performing major leg reconstructive surgery. This complicated procedure – made necessary after the owner of the legs had crashed his million dollar supercar into the wall of a mosque – had been performed amid high security, as the patient was a prince from one of the Gulf States. It had been slightly unnerving to have to operate with two large men clad in long white robes standing impassively at the back of the room watching her every move. Still, she had told herself, compared to a black mamba they were small fry.

As soon as she read the text message, she knew she had to act fast – not least as she was due back in theatre in less than ten minutes. She immediately tried to get hold of Tommy, to see if she could persuade him to lay off. She dialled his number several times, but it came as no surprise to her when she heard it just ring and ring. Somehow she felt sure he wasn't going to answer. She sent him a text, asking him to think twice before revealing the information, but she had little hope of a positive response.

The next thing she knew she had to do was to contact David and warn him that his whereabouts were about to be revealed. As she considered this, she realised that this might result in his packing his bags and leaving in a hurry for an undisclosed location and she might never see him again. Whatever her continuing uncertainty about his marital integrity and her concerns about his obvious wealth, she would be very sorry to lose him from her life. Although she could hardly say she knew him well, the little time they had spent together had already earned him a special place in her heart.

She didn't have a phone number for him, so she called Armando but, frustratingly, his number also just rang and rang. She thought about sending a text, asking him to ask David to call her, but as she was about to disappear back into the operating theatre any minute, there was probably no point.

As she was still making up her mind about what else she could do, the door opened and Charles came in. Helping himself to an espresso, he came over to her table by the window, through which she noticed that the rain had finally stopped after bucketing down for twelve hours without halt.

'Hi, Lucy. Mind if I sit down?'

She nodded and waved him to a seat opposite her. 'Help yourself. I'm due back in theatre in five minutes anyway.'

Although relations between them never strayed beyond workplace matters nowadays, she and he had been managing to co-exist as colleagues without too much friction. As he sat down she saw that he was looking unusually troubled today. Had it been anybody else, she would have asked what the trouble was and offered to help, but seeing as it was her ex, she just carried on sipping her ginseng and waited for him to speak.

She didn't have long to wait. After draining his little cup of coffee in one, he set it back down again and looked across the table towards her.

'Lucy, I've got a problem.' He sounded unusually worried.

'If it's professional, I'm happy to help. If you've got some little nurse pregnant, you're on your own.'

'Nobody's pregnant.'

'Right, well, what is it, then?'

'It's this woman, you see.'

'Which woman?'

'A woman I've been seeing. Well, to be honest, we only slept together once, but the problem is I think I've fallen in love with her.'

In spite of her impassive exterior, this did in fact arouse more than a spark of interest in Lucy. Doing her best to sound disinterested, or at least neutral, she prompted him. 'So why's that a problem?'

'Because she doesn't feel the same way about me.'

'And why are you telling me this?'

'I thought you could help me, advise me...'

'Why on earth would I want to help you after the way you behaved?' She could hear her voice rising in tone and volume and she struggled to contain herself. The irony that her former lover, the man who had broken her heart, now found himself suffering in the same way as she had done, was not lost on her. Karma, she told herself, was definitely a thing. Very conscious she only had a few minutes before she had to return to the operating theatre, she swilled the last of her ginseng around the cup and swallowed before continuing in a calmer tone. 'Seriously, what do you expect me to do? Get on with it. I have to go.'

'Maybe give me some advice. It's complicated, you see.'

'Complicated?' She gave a hiss of frustration and then looked up as a glimmer of comprehension dawned. 'Don't tell me – she's married, am I right?' It didn't need the slight nod of his head for her to realise her guess had been correct. 'So you've fallen in love with a married woman and she doesn't love you back – at least, not enough to leave her husband for you? Is that the situation?'

'Not exactly married, but that's about the size of it, but it's more complicated than that…' His voice tailed off helplessly.

'More complicated, how?'

'I can't say.'

He hung his head and looked miserable but she was rapidly losing patience – and running out of time. 'Well, if you won't go into more detail, the only help I can offer is to advise you to sit down and talk it through with this woman, whoever she is.' She glanced at her watch once more and stood up. 'I'm due back in theatre right now. Just talk to her, okay?'

It was lunchtime before she was able to do anything more about Daniela's news and she had been fretting about it all morning. As soon as she came out of theatre, she went out into the gardens, now once again bathed in sunshine, but she barely registered the delightful display of roses in the big bed around the fountain. The important thing was that nobody else had chosen to come out into the burning midday sun, so nobody was here to overhear her conversation. The temperature was rising steadily as the overnight rain disappeared like magic into the parched ground, but, ignoring any thoughts of mad dogs and Englishmen, she called Armando and was greatly relieved to hear him answer the phone this time. She asked him if he could get David to ring her about a very urgent matter and the call came through less than a minute later.

'Lucy, hi. It's David. Is something up?'

'Hi, David. Yes, I'm afraid we've got a problem, a big problem, and it's my fault.' She went on to tell him about Tommy and his job as a journalist. 'It's my fault he came round last night and spotted you. I was out on Sunday and he saw me, but I didn't want to talk to him so I told him I wasn't feeling well. I should have guessed he might come to check up on me, but it never occurred to me, I'm afraid. I'm so, so sorry.'

There was silence at the other end of the line for a few moments. 'If he's your boyfriend, couldn't you maybe appeal to him to stay quiet?'

'He's not my boyfriend.' Lucy realised that this had come out a bit too loud and a bit too dogmatic, so she lowered her voice once more and explained. 'He's a friend of a friend and I only agreed to have dinner with him as his aunt and uncle own the restaurant and he said he could tell me all about the village. One thing's for sure – after this, he's definitely no longer even a casual friend. I've tried phoning him, but he's not picking up. I've left him a series of messages, but I fear in my bones that he isn't going to change his mind. As far as he's concerned, this is a major scoop and it'll be good for his career.'

'Right... I see...' She heard a long escape of breath. 'Listen, Lucy, don't beat yourself up. It wasn't your fault. It was bound to happen sooner or later. My lawyer knows who I am and where I live, as do the guys at the bank, lots of people at the clinic, and any number of others. It's been a long time coming but sooner or later it had to be revealed. I've been living on borrowed time.' She heard him take a deep breath. 'It was inevitable. I've been very lucky up till now, but it's time for me to face the music.'

'So you aren't going to run off somewhere else?'

'Absolutely not.' She couldn't repress a sensation of relief that he would be staying around. 'There are too many things, too many people, keeping me here.' She found herself desperately curious to know if she might be one of these people, but he hadn't finished. 'No, bring it on. Listen, I was going to call you to say thank you for last night. I had a really good evening and it reminded me what I've been missing in my self-imposed isolation. I was wondering, do you have any free time this week or at the weekend?'

'I'm actually off work tomorrow, before starting nights on Saturday.'

'Well, look, how about this as an idea? Would you feel like coming to Florence with me some time? I thought we could check out the memorial to John Hawkwood. It's something I've been dying to do for ages, but I've been so scared of being recognised. Now the cat's going to be out of the bag, so what the hell? What do you say?'

Lucy stood there for a few moments, lost in thought. It was going to be pretty well impossible for him to keep his identity a secret in the midst of the crowds of tourists who would be packed into the centre of Florence. School holidays had started all over Europe and further afield, and she had no doubt there would be thousands upon thousands of people there. The second thing going through her head was whether she wanted to spend a day in the company of somebody who was reputed to have cheated on his wife.

It didn't take her long to make a decision. When all was said and done, this was an innocent enough invitation and she couldn't deny a large part of her wanted to spend more time with this man. It wasn't as if he was inviting her to go off on a dirty weekend with him, or even go out for dinner. If she could say yes to dinner with a proven womaniser like Tommy, then there was no reason to reject David's offer, and there was always that thing about being innocent until proved guilty. And, apart from anything else, she really wanted to check out Hawkwood's memorial fresco as well.

'That sounds great. I'd love to go to Florence. I'm free tomorrow if that suits you.'

'Tomorrow's good for me. Okay if I pick you up fairly early? That way we might miss the worst of the crowds if we aim to hit the Duomo as it opens at ten. What time works for you?'

'As early as you like. I'm used to being at work by seven thirty so I'm not afraid of an early start.'

'We don't need to leave quite that early. Shall we say eight thirty?'

Chapter 18

She was ready for him well before eight thirty next morning, feeling surprisingly nervous as she heard his car pull up outside. To her horror, this turned out to be the very smart, but incredibly conspicuous, bright red Ferrari she had seen on Google Earth and her heart sank. She rolled her eyes and wondered what it was about rich men and fast cars. Not that she cared to know the answer.

She knew she was going to feel really uncomfortable being seen in such an obvious status symbol, whose worth was probably more than all the houses and all the belongings of the people around Mabenta put together. David was free to spend his money any way he wanted, but this gleaming car was making it impossible to avoid comparisons with some of the more unsavoury patients at the clinic. Somehow it felt improper, if not just plain wrong. Nevertheless, she gritted her teeth and mustered a smile and was immediately presented with another, more practical, problem.

As she wasn't working, she had chosen not to tie her hair back today and had let it hang around her shoulders, feeling pretty confident it looked good, not least as the sun had done a great job of bleaching it lighter, turning it from its usual mousy colour to blonde. The roof of the car was down so she had no doubt she would look like a haystack by the time they got to Siena, let alone Florence, after being buffeted by the wind at high speed. She gave David an apologetic wave and ducked back into the house to take remedial action.

She hunted around for a hair tie but couldn't find a single one. In desperation she located her only silk scarf and tied it around her head, although she felt sure it would make her look like her grandmother. A quick glance in the mirror confirmed her fears, but it was too late to change now. She locked the house and as she came round to the car door, another problem presented itself. She was wearing her new summer frock. The car was very close to the ground and, somehow, she had the feeling David was going to see a lot of her as she climbed in. In fact, it wasn't so much going to be a case of climbing in as *falling* in. She opened the door and put one foot tentatively inside. To her relief, he came to her rescue.

'Unless you have a crane, the best way to get into this thing is backwards. My wife had a system so trust me — ass first.'

She took his advice and turned her back on him, grabbed the door pillars and lowered herself into the seat, finally swivelling round, knees together, and tugging the hem of her dress down, relieved it hadn't ridden up any more than it had. She glanced across at him and there was an embarrassing moment when she wondered if she should kiss him on the cheeks or shake hands or do nothing, before he resolved things by pressing a button and starting the engine. There was a high-pitched roar and he set off, fortunately at a reasonable pace. The prancing horse on the steering wheel made it clear this was a car designed for raw speed and she hoped he wouldn't turn out to be a mad driver.

As he manoeuvred the surprisingly wide vehicle through the narrow streets of the village, she glimpsed Donatello, the shopkeeper, sweeping the pavement outside his shop, and she almost died of shame. The bright red Ferrari immediately drew his attention and he must have recognised her as he waved and, hesitantly, she waved back. She turned towards David.

'I'm afraid your anonymity isn't going to last long – especially in a red Ferrari.'

He shot her a quick smile. 'I'm sure you're right, but I reckon it's the only way. Would you believe this car hasn't been out of the garage for over two years? In fact I wondered if it would start this morning. But I thought, what the hell? Just like tearing off a Band-Aid, I reckon it's best to just go for it.'

'So you're happy to emerge from hiding, or should I say *burst* out of hiding in this beast?'

He nodded. 'It's time. I've been closeted away for too long. I need to get out. In a funny way, I'm almost grateful to your friend for giving me the kick I needed.'

'My *ex*-friend. And so you're choosing the nuclear option? A bright red Ferrari with the roof down will definitely draw a few eyes.'

'And don't forget the beautiful blonde in the passenger seat. That should definitely help in making sure I get noticed.'

Doing her best not to blush, she corrected him and saw him smile. 'The little old lady in the headscarf, you mean. I'm not sure how alluring I look.'

'Trust me, you look alluring.' This sounded like flirting to her, and it worried her. She would never in her life have wanted to be thought of as just a blonde accessory to a rich man and she felt almost sullied. Still, she told herself firmly, she had agreed to accompany him and she was stuck with it now. Whatever it might look like to other people, this was a day out with a friend, learning a bit of history. Nothing more.

The drive to Florence turned out to be really rather nice. He avoided the main road for the first part and took her along winding country lanes through the hills, passing through charming rural Tuscan scenery. Trees, fields, olive groves and vines surrounded them and they met very few other vehicles and saw very few other people. As a result, her sense of embarrassment gradually began to subside. David drove remarkably slowly and she relished the feel of the relatively cool morning air. When the stunning medieval walled town of Monteriggioni hove into view he suggested stopping for a coffee, but instead they decided to press on to Florence on the *superstrada*. To her surprise, even at speed on the highway, she barely felt the wind, and she was able to take off her headscarf after a while, letting her hair blow about gently in the breeze, confident she wouldn't end up looking like Worzel Gummidge.

The traffic as they drove into Florence was heavy but passable and it was here that she started to feel very uncomfortable once again. As she had predicted, the open-topped Ferrari attracted a lot of attention and she felt sure she caught recognition of David on a number of faces in cars alongside them as they crept in towards the city centre. The driver of one car in particular made a point of hooting his horn and pointing and waving enthusiastically in their direction and she cringed. There was no doubt that the combination of the flashy red car and his famous face made anonymity a forlorn hope – for him and for her.

Over the years, Lucy had been to Florence many times, but she was still looking forward to seeing the historic centre again. As the massive Fortezza da Basso appeared and David turned in alongside the railway line towards the main station, her anticipation grew, not least as she knew she would soon be out of this shameless status symbol.

He edged the very low-slung car gingerly down a steep ramp into an underground parking garage right at the edge of the pedestrian area and they emerged into the daylight at just before ten. He was wearing dark glasses and a baseball cap, but she felt pretty sure he would soon be recognised. However, they were able to walk past the front of the station and across the broad Piazza Santa Maria Novella without hindrance, passing the imposing church that gave its name to the square. They stopped to read the sign alongside the beautiful marble-clad façade and saw that, interestingly, it had been built around the same time as John Hawkwood had been active here. Lucy rather liked the idea that their man had maybe ridden past this very spot on his horse and had actually watched the workmen labouring to build this beautiful structure.

As they reached a newsstand on the corner of the already crowded main street leading up towards the cathedral, Lucy stopped to buy a copy of the local paper and opened it with trepidation.

Sure enough, there was a banner headline across the front page reading, *TENNIS STAR DISCOVERED IN TUSCANY*. Page three was filled with Tommy's scoop, along with a potted history of David's career, his injury and his unhappy marriage, as well as numerous photos of him on the tennis court and off it. The article even included no fewer than six photos of possible women who might have been responsible for his marital break-up, although the article grudgingly conceded that no proof existed to link him to any of them. Lucy found herself wondering whether her own face might soon be adorning the tabloids if they were photographed together and she started to screw up the newspaper angrily, ready to drop it into a nearby bin. As she did so, she muttered a few more choice expletives aimed at Tommy. David had been reading over her shoulder and he gently took it from her hands, removed the page with the article, and dumped the rest of the paper. After folding the article and stuffing it into the back pocket of his jeans, he took her arm and led her away.

'He's good, your friend.'

'My *ex*-friend.'

'He hasn't had much time, but he's managed to dig up almost all the dirt. I particularly like the rogues' gallery of possible sexual partners. He got that straight out of the *National Enquirer* and who knows who dreamed it up before them? I've only ever met one of those girls and that was among a group of journalists at a news conference. Still, all's fair in love and the media, as long as it sells newspapers.' Although he was trying to sound blasé, she could hear the hurt all too clearly in his voice. He paused by the front of a sports shop and stared in through the window at a full-size cardboard cut-out of himself advertising tennis racquets. He gave a heartfelt sigh and turned towards her. 'You mustn't believe everything you read in the papers. That's what my agent's been telling the sponsors for two years now.'

Lucy felt sure he was telling the truth. He certainly sounded very convincing and she found herself really hoping somebody would be able to prove that he wasn't after all cut from the same cloth as Charles or Tommy, and restore his good name. She reached across and gave his forearm a supportive squeeze.

'Sticks and stones, David. Just try to ignore it. For what it's worth, I believe you.' And she realised that she did.

He looked down and gave her a little smile. 'You do? Well, that's all that counts to me.' The smile was still on his lips as he led her off up the road again.

Ten minutes later they were standing in front of the Duomo. As with the cathedral in Siena, Lucy just stared in awe for a good few minutes. Although her mind was still churning at the thought of the ramifications of the newspaper article, the sheer outstanding beauty of the building cut through her concerns.

The soaring white marble façade, interspersed with narrow lines of deep green stone and studded all over with statues, was as imposing and fascinating as ever. The paved piazza in front of the cathedral was already crowded with tourists milling around and taking photos, although the presence of an armoured car and armed police and soldiers was a reminder of the ever-present terrorist threat that existed all over Europe these days. She intercepted a few smiles and interested glances from passers-by as they recognised David and she knew his secret was now well and truly out there. To her mortification, she also felt a number of people subject her to curious and, in a couple of cases, downright intrusive stares and her sense of not belonging in this scenario strengthened.

Inside the Duomo it was pleasantly cool in spite of the numbers of people already in there. The walls rose up immensely high and the cupola with its viewing gallery hundreds of feet above them already had energetic tourists visible up there, their heads little more than dots from down below. It was almost unbelievable to think that this magnificent edifice had been built without the help of modern engineering and machinery. They found the memorial they were looking for almost immediately, just on the left as they went inside. The sign alongside it informed them that it had been specially commissioned back in the middle of the fifteenth century and it was the work of the famous Tuscan artist, Paolo Uccello.

It was a predominantly deep ruby red and cream fresco of a serious-looking man with a strong face and long nose, holding what looked like a baton in his hand. He was seated on a magnificent white warhorse and he looked every inch the successful general he had been in real life. They stood and studied it and they both took a few surreptitious photos, even though there was a sign informing them that photography was forbidden. Very few of the hundreds of tourists milling around them appeared to have read the sign either – or if they had done, they had chosen to ignore it.

As they were standing there, Lucy heard an American woman's voice alongside them and her heart sank once more.

'Excuse me, but aren't you David Lorenzo, the tennis ace?'

Without batting an eyelid, David shook his head and smiled down at her. 'That's my cousin. I'm little Albert. I can't play tennis to save my life. Have a good day.' Tapping Lucy on the arm, he set off back out into the open air once more. As they walked down the steps into the sunlight, Lucy glanced up at him and grinned.

'Well, little Albert, what do you want to do now? Want to look for a suitable stone to crawl back under?'

He smiled back at her. 'No, no more stones, no more crawling. Mind you, that's as far as I'm concerned. If you feel uncomfortable being seen with me, just say the word and we can head for home. I wouldn't blame you. Even after years of it, I still don't feel comfortable being recognised wherever I go.'

She stood there for a few moments, genuinely torn. She knew she was enjoying his company, but she certainly didn't enjoy being the object of indiscriminate scrutiny by complete strangers. She had enough experience of the magnetic way rich men managed to attract good-looking girls to have no illusions as to what was going through the heads of many of those who saw her with him. It made her feel uncomfortable and dirty.

Finally she reached out and gave him another little squeeze on the arm. 'I'm very happy to be with you.' And she was. 'But I'd be lying if I said I felt completely comfortable. Apart from anything else, don't forget that I've just come back from years in the middle of nowhere, so finding myself surrounded by crowds of people was bound to be a bit unsettling. How about we go some-where a bit less crowded?'

'I completely understand. To be honest, after my last few years as a hermit, I feel exactly the same way.' He sounded as if he meant it. 'Let's go and find somewhere quiet so we can sit down and have a coffee. Then, unless you have plans, how about I take you for lunch in one of my favourite restaurants in the whole of Tuscany. It's in the hills just outside of town and it's very discreet.'

Chapter 19

At first sight, his favourite restaurant looked anything but discreet. It was a stunning hilltop villa, surrounded by cypress trees, approached up a long, curling, tree-lined drive off a minor road. It was situated about ten kilometres outside Florence, just over the first range of hills on the south side of the city. Even though the bustling conurbation of Florence was so close-by, here everything was much more peaceful. Everywhere they looked, there were olive trees, some still with the nets used to collect the ripe olives lying at their feet since the last harvest the previous autumn. A little three-wheeled farm vehicle came coughing and spluttering along the drive towards them, leaving an unhealthy trail of blue smoke in its wake. As the driver passed the Ferrari, Lucy saw him kiss his fingers and shout something. Whether this was a compliment directed at the car, the driver, or herself, was unclear to her, but she felt her cheeks flush all the same.

She found herself wondering what Miriam, her invaluable clinic manager and close friend back in Mabenta, would have thought if she were to see her here in this flashy car. The last time Lucy had seen her and the other locally employed staff had been several months ago as they disappeared into the bush in the hope of escaping the advancing fighters. Lucy had her sent numerous emails and text messages since leaving the DRC, but without success, and she feared the worst. Yet again, she found herself dwelling upon the gross unfairness of life and she actually sighed.

David manoeuvred the car into a space in the car park behind the hotel/restaurant and it came as no surprise to Lucy to see it filled almost exclusively with luxury cars. David, apparently unaware of her reservations, jumped out to come round and offer her a helping hand. As he reached down with both hands and caught hold of hers, he gave her a little grin. Seeing him smile cheered her up. A little.

'Been feeling a bit conspicuous?'

Lucy rearranged her clothing after being hauled back onto her feet and nodded. 'I feel like a goldfish in a bowl when I'm in this thing.' She risked a personal question. 'Did your wife like riding in it?'

'Riding in it and driving it; she loved it. More than me, probably.' He hung his head and stared at his feet as he replied. 'But she didn't use it that much.'

'I thought you said she liked it.'

'Oh, she liked the car all right. I bought it only a short while before my accident, but by that time she didn't like me. She had pretty much already left me by then and she went to live on the coast on her own for a while. After the accident she came back for a bit and then, finally, when she realised I was a hopeless mess, she went off and left me. The car stayed here and, like I say, I stopped going out so I stopped driving it.'

Lucy grabbed hold of his arm with both hands — it felt rather good — and subjected him to her sternest look, while doing her best to keep her tone light. 'Don't say that sort of thing. The only mess round here is my hair after the ride in your car.'

'Back then I really was a mess, but there was more to it than just the accident. I'll bore you with the story some time, but not today.' He looked up and she was very pleased to see a more positive expression on his face now. 'Today's a day for celebration. My jail term's over and I'm a free man.'

Lucy gave him a smile in return and wondered if she dared press him for more information about what had happened between him and his wife but decided it was best, for now, to avoid poking at what was evidently still an open wound.

They walked into the luxurious hotel, not dissimilar to David's Villa Castelnuovo, and were greeted by an obsequious lady in a designer dress, with gold-rimmed glasses dangling from a thin gold chain around her neck. She led them out through a charming lounge to a terrace at the rear of the villa, shaded from the sun by a rambling rose and luxuriant vines that looped and curled their way in and out of the crossbars of the wooden canopy that spanned the whole width of the terrace. Tables with other diners were spread out in the shade a good few feet apart from one another and David's chosen table even had a massive lemon tree in a terracotta pot between them and their nearest neighbours. He had said discreet and it certainly was that.

It was a gorgeous setting. An army of bees flitted from bloom to bloom and their buzzing provided the only constant background noise, drowning out the conversation going on at the other tables. Otherwise, apart from the occasional car on the road in the distance, it was quiet and refreshingly peaceful after the hubbub of Florence. Lucy sat back and did her best to relax, enjoying his company now that they were out of the public eye, but she couldn't help being concerned for him that his hitherto peaceful existence was about to be well and truly shattered, and was still feeling guilty at her part in it.

As if to reinforce her fears, his phone started ringing. He gave her an apologetic smile and answered it. She only heard his side of the conversation, but she had no doubt what was being said.

'Hi, Sammie, this is early for you… You've what?'

Lucy saw his face harden.

'How did they get hold of the story?… All over the news?… Already?' He gave an exasperated sigh. 'Well, so what? I couldn't expect to stay out of the limelight forever.'

She could see him biting his lower lip as he listened to whomever was on the other end of the line and her heart went out to him. The conversation went on for another minute or two and by the time he hung up, it was perfectly clear to her that his whereabouts were not only out of the bag but being trumpeted all over the media. He dropped the phone onto the table and grimaced.

'And so it begins. That was my agent. It's all kicking off again.' He sounded weary but she saw him take a couple of deep breaths and rally. 'Anyway, enough of that for now, what're we going to eat?'

They both had the same thing; air-dried bresaola beef drizzled with extra virgin olive oil and lemon, and covered with rocket leaves and shavings of Parmesan cheese. This was served with a huge mixed salad and would have been enough for Lucy if she hadn't already ordered grilled lamb chops. When these arrived, they were so very tasty that she managed to find room for them, but then very definitely refused a dessert. It was as they were sipping their coffees at the end of the meal that his phone rang again. This time it was Armando with bad, although not totally unexpected, news. The gates to the Villa Castelnuovo were now being besieged by a pack of paparazzi and journalists from as far afield as the USA. How the Americans had managed to get there so quickly was a complete mystery. As David set the phone back down again, he looked across the table at her.

'I was going to suggest you might like to come up to the villa for a swim this afternoon, but I think it might be better if I drop you off at your place before you get caught up in the feeding frenzy. I'm used to it by now, but it isn't pretty.'

'I didn't realise you had a pool. The idea of a swim definitely appeals, but I'm sure you're right. Just kick me out when we get to my house.' An idea came to her. 'Or you could leave your car at my place and make your way home across country. I'm afraid you're just too big to fit in the boot of my little Fiat or I could have pretended I was delivering something and sneaked you into the villa that way.'

He smiled. 'Nice idea, thanks, but I'm going to face the music. I've had enough of ducking and diving. I've had a two-year break and it's time I move on. When all's said and done, all I've done is to injure myself and manage to get caught up in an unhappy marriage. In the greater scheme of things, it's not exactly mass murder. They're bound to get fed up and leave me alone before too long.'

Lucy did her best to look blank. 'How come your marriage was so unhappy?'

His eyes caught hers for a fraction of a second before dropping to his now cold coffee. 'It's a long, sad story. Like I said, I won't bore you with it now. What I can tell you, though, is that your ex-friend's version of how it happened is a million miles from the truth.' He reached into his back pocket and handed her the folded newspaper article. 'Read this when you get home by all means, but, remember, don't believe a word of it.' He resurrected a smile. 'Well, the details of tournaments I won are hopefully correct, just not the personal stuff.'

Once again, it was on the tip of her tongue to press him for more information, however, she knew she would be stepping into sensitive territory. She would be fooling herself if she tried to pretend she wasn't fascinated to find out the real reason for the break-up, but today wasn't the day to ask. Today had been fun and interesting, if excruciatingly uncomfortable at times, and this had been an excellent, if ostentatious, place to have lunch. There was no point in spoiling it with a cross-examination, particularly as ordeal by media was waiting for him back home. What she did find herself wondering was if the newspaper article alleging his infidelity as the reason for the collapse of the marriage was false, then what had been the real reason? Had it even been his fault? Had it maybe been his wife's fault in spite of the allegations in the paper? Of course, she had to accept the possibility that he wasn't telling her the truth, in spite of her gut feeling. After all, she had trusted Charles at one time...

They drove back through the hills, passing by San Gimignano but not stopping. From what she could see of the jam-packed car and coach park alongside the quaint walled hilltop town with its famous towers, it would probably have been even more crowded than Florence in there. They got back to Castelnuovo around four o'clock and he dropped her by her front door, chivalrously getting out to haul her to her feet once again. She gave him a smile and reached up on tiptoe to kiss him on the cheeks, giving his biceps another little squeeze as she did so.

'Thank you for a lovely day, David. I really enjoyed myself, and the lunch was super. I just wish I could help you in some way. Listen, you've got my number now. Just call me if there's anything, anything at all, I can do to help. Good luck when you get up to the gates.'

He smiled back at her. 'You already have helped me, Lucy. You may not realise it, but I owe you a lot.'

'Like for allowing some casual man friend of mine to recognise you and reveal your whereabouts to the entire world? With friends like me, who needs enemies?'

He was still smiling. 'You'll never be an enemy, Lucy. Ciao.'

He slipped back into the driving seat and set off up the hill. As he did so, she saw him deliberately remove his baseball cap and sunglasses, ready to face the cameras. She crossed her fingers for him.

She let herself into the house and put the kettle on. As it came to the boil, she opened the back door to check that her lovely rambling rose hadn't dried up in its pot and found that Armando had already been round and had constructed a fine cat's cradle of wires around the doorway for the rose to climb. She went out to the little old brick shed at the bottom of the garden and located a spade, determined to dig a hole and plant the rose in the ground that evening once the full heat of the sun had diminished.

As she came back out with the spade in her hand, she was startled to hear a dog bark right beside her. She glanced around and saw a black nose and two paws just peeking over the stone wall between her and next door. She went across to say hello and, as she did so, she registered that her neighbour's shutters were now open. Evidently the proprietor, the Florentine who worked at the university, was now in residence.

'Ciao, dog. So what's your name, you handsome beast?'

She held out her hand for the dog to sniff and received a friendly lick in return. It was yet another black Labrador. Somehow she wasn't so surprised. Evidently the offspring of Roberto's Labs had populated most of the homes in this area.

'His name's Barolo, but he answers to Bari – if I'm holding food. Good afternoon.'

Lucy looked up from the dog. The dog's master was standing at his back door. He was a middle-aged man with glasses, and he was wearing a baggy pair of sand-coloured shorts and a short-sleeved check shirt. From the look of his pale arms and legs, he had probably spent most of the past few months indoors working, rather than out in the sunshine. His accent was unmistakably Tuscan and he looked friendly. She gave him a smile and a wave.

'Good afternoon. I'm Lucy, Lucy Young. I live here now.'

They shook hands across the wall and for a moment it reminded her of the end of a tennis match which, in turn, reminded her of David, and she spared him another thought as he tried to fight his way into his home through a media scramble.

'My name's Guido Scandicci. I'm very pleased to meet you. Did I hear you speaking English with my dog?'

'That's right. I'm English, but I work here now. I'm a doctor.'

They stood and chatted and she found him very approachable. One thing he said made her ears prick up. It was when she asked him what he did.

'I'm a professor of Medieval History at Florence University.'

'Did you say Medieval History? That's my field of interest as well.' She was quick to correct herself. 'Purely as an amateur of course. But I've just come back from checking out the fresco commemorating Giovanni Acuto, John Hawkwood, in Florence.'

'Well, well, well. One of my doctoral students is doing a thesis based around Hawkwood and his mercenary army, the White Company, so I've also been doing a considerable amount of research on him. You'll have to come round for a glass of wine some time and I'll see if I can give you any pointers.'

That sounded amazing. 'That would be wonderful. Thank you so much.'

Chapter 20

The next day marked the start of a week of night duty. Lucy had already done this the previous month and had managed pretty well, although, as always with nights, the first was the most difficult until the body began to get used to the change in timetable.

It was a quiet night and she spent a lot of it in the empty patients' lounge, flicking through the comprehensive collection of newspapers in a variety of languages, ranging from Italian to Arabic. It came as no surprise to find that all of them, without exception, mentioned David to a greater or lesser degree. Even the *Wall Street Journal* had an article headed 'Tennis Ace Emerges From Hiding'. Some alluded to his failed marriage, but most were fairly positive or at worst, neutral towards him. All acknowledged that he was one of the all-time tennis greats, and most appeared genuinely sorry for him that his career had been brought to an end by injury.

The Times added an extra dimension to the mystery of why he had chosen to go into hiding by adding an oblique reference to stories of his having had a mental breakdown as a result of his injuries. Although she had checked out his physical record, she hadn't spoken to Franz the psychiatrist about him but, if this were correct, it might well explain why things had gone sour between him and his wife. Depression can be tough on partners.

After exhausting the newspapers and doing yet another round of the patients, Lucy went to the kitchen area to see her Syrian friend, Ahmed, the night porter. As he spotted her, his face split into a smile and he greeted her in his remarkably fluent English. He was on permanent nightshift here and she often met him on his way out as she was just arriving at work.

'Hi, Ahmed, how're you doing?'

'Fine, thanks, Lucy. Can I get you a coffee? Black with just a drop of cold milk, right?'

'You know me so well.'

She sat with him and they chatted. He was one of the fortunate ones who had managed to survive the perilous crossing of the Mediterranean from Turkey to Greece and then had made his way – mostly on foot – into Italy, where he had been even luckier to find this job. Many of his fellow asylum-seekers were languishing in detention camps or worse. He was sending almost all the money he earned back to Syria to help support his elderly parents and his three sisters, and Lucy knew how hard life must be – for him and for them. He had trained as a secondary school teacher, but his school had been destroyed in an air strike and he had only just escaped with his life.

His news tonight was that he had met a girl – another refugee from Syria who was working as a cleaner in Siena – and it was clear he liked her a lot. Lucy was delighted for him. If anybody deserved a bit of happiness it was Ahmed, after all he had gone through. As they talked, he asked Lucy if she had a husband and when she shook her head, he expressed surprise.

'Why aren't you married? Any man would be proud to have you as his wife.'

She smiled at him. 'That's very sweet, Ahmed, but I've been busy.'

'Too busy for love?'

She shook her head ruefully. 'I've tried that, but it didn't work out.'

'Don't you worry, Lucy, you *will* find somebody.'

She wondered if he was right. Of her dreams for the future, all she had so far was the house and the rambling rose by her door, while the other elements in the package remained frustratingly absent.

When she surfaced just after lunchtime the next day after sleeping off her night shift, she found a letter lying on her doormat. She opened it and was delighted to find the formal invitation to Nicole's wedding in September. Nicole and her fiancé François had decided to tie the knot and she was really happy for them. The wedding would take place in Nicole's home village in Provence and the invitation was to *Lucy and Companion*. For a moment she wondered what it would be like if she turned up on the arm of a world-famous tennis star, but immediately discarded this as wild fantasy. However, on checking her phone, she found a message waiting for her from David and her heart gave another involuntary leap.

> Hi Lucy. Hope you slept well after night duty.
> If you feel like a swim, you're very welcome
> here this afternoon. Give me a call if you're
> interested. D

She called him straightaway.

'Hi, David, thanks for the invite but first, how did it go on Friday? Was it awful?'

'It was okay. There was a lot of pushing and shoving, but most of them were pleasant enough. I even recognised some of them. A few of them were a pain in the ass, but it wasn't so bad. How was night duty?'

'Pretty quiet, thanks. No emergencies, I'm pleased to say.'

'That's good. Unless you're going back off to bed again, do you feel like a swim this afternoon?'

'I'd love a swim. It's certainly hot enough.' She glanced out of the window. The sky was unbroken blue and the distant hills barely visible through the heat haze. 'Shall I come up in the car?'

'You can if you like, although it might be a bit of a struggle to get through the gates and you'd probably find lots of people taking your picture. Armando tells me there are two TV trucks parked there as well today. I have another idea. How about you walk up through the olive groves and we meet up where I met you with Boris that time? We can then get in through the side gate in the fence.'

When Lucy got up the hill to the fallen tree an hour later, she found him already there with his dog. Boris came bounding across to greet her, tail wagging furiously, and Lucy had a hard time trying not to let her own tail wag too much as she went over to kiss David on the cheeks. There was no doubt about it; she was really pleased to see him, millionaire or not. As she stepped back and released him, she was delighted to see him smiling as well.

'Lucy, hi. It's great to see you.'

'And you, David.' She sat down on the fallen tree trunk and patted the spot beside her. 'Come and tell me all about it. I must have read a dozen newspapers last night from all over the world and I reckon you've come out all right.'

He sat down beside her. 'It could be worse. At least I can stop ducking and diving and live my life – give or take a pack of paparazzi.'

They chatted for a while before he suggested heading for the pool. Boris led the way and they entered the villa grounds through a galvanised metal gate set in the fence only a few hundred yards further on from the clump of broom bushes where she had almost been caught with her pants down. She felt her cheeks flush at the memory.

Once they were inside, he locked the gate behind them and she felt sure it was a sensible precaution. The pool was on the far side of the villa and as they walked through the ruins of the castle to get there she told him about her next-door neighbour, the professor. As she did so, she had a thought.

'Now that you're no longer a hermit, how would you feel about coming round some time? I could invite him as well and we could talk history.' This would also rather neatly get him back into her house without it having to be considered as any kind of date.

'That would be great.' He sounded genuinely interested. 'Whenever you like.'

'I'll see if he's around next Saturday. I'll have finished nights by then so I could cook you both a meal.' She glanced towards him. 'I'm not the best cook in the world, but I promise not to poison you.'

'Don't go to any trouble. And let me know if I can bring anything. You'll be getting a bottle of champagne whether you want it or not.'

'Wonderful, but that's all, and do bring Boris with you. I'll get Guido, my neighbour, to bring his Lab. That way the two brothers can be together.'

'Talking of dogs, I'd better drop Boris back to the villa. He's not allowed in the pool. His hair clogs up the filter.'

The pool was almost hidden from view by a dense hedge made up of oleander bushes, all now in flower. The pinks, reds and whites made a lovely colourful barrier, as well as no doubt forming a useful windbreak on windy days. The pool was also completely screened from the road. Lucy was already wearing her new, pricey and fairly minimal bikini under her clothes. She had purchased this from a rather posh shop in the middle of Siena the previous evening on her way to work, in the hope of another invitation to swim in David's pool. Now, as she stripped off her shorts and her top, she was feeling more than a little nervous. Although she had seen, touched, and operated on his body already, seeing him in his swimming shorts in this environment, and feeling his eyes on her gave her a thrill and she wasted no time in stepping down into the pool and ducking her shoulders below the waterline. It was heavenly and she abandoned herself for what felt like ages, just floating idly around with her eyes closed. The millionaire lifestyle might be artificial and contemptible, but there could be no doubt it did have its compensations.

Finally, she roused herself from her somnolent state and climbed back out of the water. David was lying stretched out on a sunbed. She was just dabbing herself dry when she heard his voice, this time sounding suddenly serious.

'Lucy, come with me, quick!' He jumped to his feet remarkably nimbly, caught hold of her arm and hurried her across to the door of the little pool house. For a moment she wondered what his intentions might be as he dragged her along, but he soon explained. 'Drone, there's a drone coming. Can't you hear it?'

She couldn't hear a thing, but she followed him without question. As they stood close side-by-side inside the little cubicle, he peered out of the half-closed door and pointed. 'See, up there. Armando said he'd seen one buzzing about.'

She leant forward and stared along the line of his arm. First she heard the noise. It was barely audible, not a lot louder than an angry bee and she was impressed he had heard it, although, after years of media attention, no doubt his ears were attuned to this sort of thing. Sure enough, a star-shaped drone the size of a substantial bird of prey was hovering over the pool, an object strapped to its underside that was obviously a camera.

'Bastards!' There was real feeling in his voice. 'I'm going to tell Armando to get his shotgun out.'

As they waited there for the drone to lose interest, she was very conscious that their near-naked bodies were so close she could feel the hairs of his forearm against her bare skin. She found herself wondering what she would do if he moved his mouth only a few inches down towards hers and kissed her. Just as she was coming to terms with the realisation that, in spite of all her reservations, she would have no hesitation in kissing him back, he straightened up and, maybe realising they were too close together, moved a few inches in the other direction, leaving her with a sensation almost of abandonment.

'It's going.' He glanced back down at her. 'Sorry about that, Lucy. These guys just know no boundaries. Seriously, later on I'm going down to the gate to tell them I'll shoot the damn thing out of the sky next time I see it. Anyway, for now we should be okay, but maybe best to stay under the parasol.'

They went back out into the full heat of the sun and lay down side by side under the shelter of a wide parasol. Lucy's heart was pounding in her chest and she knew this had nothing to do with the drone. She couldn't fool herself any more. She definitely found David very attractive and the sensation of his naked flesh against hers had been highly stimulating. This threw up a number of problems.

First, there was the continued uncertainty about whether he was a cheat, although the more time she spent with him, the less credible this appeared. In fact, had it not been for her experience of infidelity at the hands of Charles, she would already have dismissed it as impossible. Equally annoying was the simple fact that he hadn't demonstrated the slightest sign of attraction as far as she was concerned. She had always considered herself to be a modern, self-confident woman, but she knew that in this case there was no way she was confident enough to make the first move. It was frustrating, but she knew this was the way it had to be.

Chapter 21

The week passed slowly as she worked by night and rested by day. To her disappointment, David went off to Paris and London for five days to meet with his agent and to do a series of media interviews. She was in the guest lounge of the clinic, watching his interview on Sky Sports being replayed in the small hours of Thursday morning when she was called away for an emergency. She found herself having to attend to a charming elderly man, recovering from a prostatectomy, who had somehow managed to dislodge his catheter, and by the time she had successfully reconnected him to his plastic bag and sat with him to reassure him and calm him down, the interview was over.

All week she had been thinking a lot about David, not least because on Tuesday she had finally signed on the dotted line, handed over the balance of the money, and bought the cottage. David's place in the notary's office had been taken by his lawyer so her delight at finally becoming a homeowner had been somewhat tempered by David's absence.

As a result, by the time Saturday came round, she was feeling quite apprehensive. As she had told him, her skills in the kitchen weren't that great, although Daniela's mother had given her an introduction to Tuscan cookery when Lucy had been over here as a teenager. Since then, Nicole and Geneviève had also taught her how to cook a number of French dishes during their time together in Mabenta, but she was still far more comfortable with a scalpel in her hands than an egg whisk. She asked Daniela what she suggested and decided to go with her advice to serve cold food as it was suffocatingly hot with August dawning.

She went down to see Donatello in the village shop and returned with fresh figs, slices of ham, *porchetta* and *finocchiona*, a dozen quails' eggs and a big handful of broad beans still in their cases to be eaten raw with the *salame* the traditional Tuscan way. She made these into the antipasti, and for the main course she prepared a big mixed salad with pieces of cold chicken, olives and hardboiled egg, followed by a chunk of aged Pecorino cheese and a much fresher, soft goat cheese made by Donatello's cousin. She even bought a packet of bone-shaped dog treats for her canine guests. In the fridge she had more of Roberto's rosé and a couple of bottles of crisp, fruity white wine from a little producer in the next village. As a final touch, she bought a tub of meringue ice cream and planned to serve it with a fresh fruit salad of white flesh peaches, apricots and nectarines.

She set the table upstairs in the loggia and put on the new dress she had bought specially for the occasion. It was made of light cotton, which was just as well as it was a very hot evening.

The doorbell rang at just after seven thirty and she found both men standing there with their respective dogs, having just met on the doorstep. Lucy fended off the joyous greeting afforded to her by Boris, patted Barolo on the head and then kissed both men on the cheeks. Guido, the professor, looked slightly surprised, but she didn't mind. There was no way she wasn't going to kiss David, so it was a logical extension of her welcome to include her next-door neighbour. As it turned out, Guido didn't recognise David and, if Lucy hadn't introduced them, he would probably have remained in a state of ignorance as to the celebrity status of his fellow diner.

She led them upstairs to the loggia, opened a bottle of sparkling rosé and they sat down to talk while the two canine brothers on the floor renewed their acquaintance. As the humans chatted, it soon became clear that Guido was a real authority on the English mercenary. He gave them a potted history of John Hawkwood's career, his regular changes of allegiance, his tactical acumen and his total ruthlessness. It was clear Hawkwood had been very good at his job, but he probably wouldn't have made a very sophisticated dinner guest. The bad news, however, was that Guido had heard nothing that indicated the Englishman might have had anything to do with David's castle. However, all was not lost.

'It's fascinating to hear that the castle used to be referred to as the Englishman's Castle. The thing is, Hawkwood was by no means the only Englishman over here in those days. The White Company itself was a very cosmopolitan group and there would have been numerous Englishmen among them. Even if the one in question wasn't Hawkwood, maybe it was one of his colleagues. Leave it with me and my doctoral student. We'll see what we can dig up.'

The meal turned out to be a great success and by the time she had distributed cups of coffee to the men and dog biscuits to the Labradors she felt confident her efforts had been appreciated. By now night had fallen and all they could see were occasional lights dotting the hillsides. She had lit a couple of candles and there wasn't a breath of wind to even make them flicker. She sat down and stretched her legs, encountering a warm hairy body with her feet as she did so. There was a satisfied grunt from under the table, followed by an unmistakable farting noise. She was wondering whether to comment, to specify that the source of the flatulence had been canine rather than human, when Guido saved the day.

'Barolo, really! I can't take you anywhere, can I? Sorry, Lucy, but he must have eaten something earlier that disagreed with him.'

On the other side of the table she could see David grinning and then he burst out laughing, followed by Guido. It was really good to see David so relaxed. Maybe having his location plastered all over the internet and national and international papers really had been good for him after all.

Guido finished his coffee, checked his watch, and rose to his feet. 'I'm sorry, Lucy, but Barolo and I have to go, I'm afraid. Thank you so much for a wonderful evening. Next time at my place.'

Lucy accompanied him and his dog to the door and as she climbed back up the stairs to the loggia, she could feel a sensation of anticipation building at the thought of finding herself all alone with David by candlelight. However, she was disappointed to see him on his feet, leaning against the balustrade, staring out at the handful of lights dotting the dark hillside. She went over to his side.

'All well, David?'

He turned towards her and in the candlelight she could see he was smiling. 'Fine, Lucy, just fine. This has been a lovely evening. I like Guido. He seems like a good guy. Who knows? Maybe he'll be able to shed some light on the origins of the castle.'

Lucy nodded, although she would have been far more interested to hear him tell her about any feelings he might be developing towards her. Still, conversation was conversation, so she rose to the occasion.

'Well, if anybody can find out, it has to be Guido.'

She saw him look at his watch. 'Here's hoping. Anyway, I suppose I'd better go, too. Boris needs his walk.'

Boris was stretched out comatose beneath the table and Lucy seriously doubted whether he needed an urgent walk, but she went along with it. Clearly David was feeling uncomfortable finding himself here alone with her. She picked up the cheese plate and a few other bits that needed to go in the fridge and, as she did so, he collected the rest and loaded them onto a tray. She was impressed – millionaire or not, he was certainly housetrained.

'Thanks, David. I could have done that. So, tell me, did you walk down through the olive trees?'

'Yes. There are just two die-hard paparazzi left by the gate in a camper van, but I thought I'd better take no chances. Imagine if they followed me here and got a shot of you and me together. Who knows what story they might invent?'

'What story, indeed!' Although she was increasingly coming round to the conviction by now that she would enjoy being part of that story if it ever came to fruition. 'Well, if you're walking back through the fields, I might walk with you partway if you don't mind. It's such a lovely night.'

David easily roused the dog with the magic word and they set out on their walk. The near-full moon had risen above the hills and it was bright enough to cast shadows among the olive trees. Lucy soon found it was quite easy to follow the track as it wound its way up the hillside.

It was almost completely silent up here and she started to make out little yellow dots of light among the olive trees. As Boris stopped to mark his territory, she stopped as well, watching the fireflies and reflecting what a wonderful place she had chosen for her new home.

She was very conscious of David beside her in the dark and she found herself yearning for his touch. She was even seriously considering at least catching hold of his hand, when a sudden movement barely a few yards away from them startled her. She actually did reach out and grab hold of his arm, but this was with no romantic intent. There could be no doubt about it – something big was lurking in the bushes just off the track to the right of them.

'Well, well, well, are we lucky or are we lucky? Can you see it?' David's mouth was so close to her ear as he whispered that she could feel the warmth of his breath against her. 'Look, there it is.'

Still clutching his arm, she followed the direction of his pointing finger and gradually managed to make out a light-coloured wedge shape moving slowly through the bushes, roughly parallel to them. It was the size of a dog, but it very definitely wasn't a dog. As she focused, it emerged from the bushes and there could be no mistake. What she was looking at was a porcupine. She swivelled her head up towards David.

'I didn't know they had porcupines here in Tuscany.'

'Not that many. We've been very fortunate.' Then, to her regret, he pulled away from her and bent down to catch hold of Boris by the collar. She heard his voice, still whispering. 'Come here, dog. You don't want a porcupine quill in the end of your nose.'

Hearing the movement, the porcupine stopped and then, seconds later, scuttled back into the bushes once more. David waited for a full minute before releasing his hold on the dog and straightening up. Boris, apparently blissfully unaware that he had been close to a potentially dangerous animal, set off up the track once more. David turned back to Lucy.

'That's one for your diary.'

'How amazing! When I first heard the noise I was afraid it might be a wild boar.'

'I'm glad it wasn't. They can be dangerous if you get in their way, or between a sow and her little ones.'

'Well, I'd count on you to defend me if that happened.'

She saw him grin in the moonlight. 'After your time in the wilds of Africa, I bet you'd be better than me at defending yourself – and me for that matter.'

'Don't you believe it. Not without a helicopter.' As they started off up the track again, she went on to tell him about her fraught final days in Mabenta and how worried she still was for her friend Miriam, the patients and colleagues she had left behind. As they reached the top of the olive grove where David had to turn off onto a narrow path, he stopped and looked down at her.

'You're a very caring person, aren't you?' His voice was gentle.

'I'd like think so. It comes with the job.'

'It's more than that with you, though. I really admire that in you, Lucy.'

And then, to her considerable surprise, he leant down towards her and kissed her softly on the lips.

'This is where Boris and I have to leave you. Are you going to be okay walking back on your own?'

She nodded mutely, still under the spell of that little kiss. Finally managing to regain the power of speech she replied. 'I'm just fine, thanks, David. I mean that. Just fine.'

'Goodnight, Lucy and thanks. Not just for tonight. Thanks for everything.'

And he turned away, following Boris into the shadows.

Chapter 22

When she awoke next morning, she lay in bed for a while and reflected on the events of last night. Wonderful as it had been to see a porcupine for the first time, the stand-out moment had to be that kiss. Never in her life, not even with Charles, had such a minimal, fleeting touch managed to cut straight to her heart like that. There could be no doubt in her mind that she was developing serious feelings for David but, more importantly, did this kiss now maybe indicate that he also felt the same way about her?

This was the big question going around and around in her head, but there was no point agonising about something over which she had no control, so she decided to do her best to dismiss it from her mind and move on – at least for now. She got up, took a fairly cool shower to freshen her up after what had been a particularly muggy night, and went downstairs to wash last night's dishes and tidy the house. After that, she went out into the part of the garden which was still in the shade and did a bit more digging before it got too hot. Fortunately the pile of old timber she had propped against the ramshackle back gate was still in place and the wild boar had not put in another appearance. Her recently planted flowers and bushes were still intact and she watered them before the full force of the sun fell upon them.

She came back in again around mid-morning and made herself a coffee. As she did so, her phone started ringing and, to her delight, she saw it was David.

'David, hi. How's it going?'

'Good, thanks.' His tone was warm. 'I wanted to say thank you again for last night. It was great.'

'You're very welcome and I enjoyed it as well, all of it, especially our little walk – not just seeing the porcupine.' She hoped he would read between the lines of her reply.

'I wondered if you have plans for today.'

'Nope. I've washed the dishes and it's getting too hot for any more gardening, so I'm completely free. Did you have something in mind?' Various ways of spending a sleepy Sunday with him had already occurred to her, but she chose not to voice them.

'I was wondering if you might like a trip to the seaside and a *fritto misto*?'

'That sounds amazing. I love *fritto misto*. I used to dream about all that lovely seafood when I was in the wilds of Africa. Where were you thinking of going?' She knew that from Siena to the west coast was an hour and a half, or twice that long going east, over the Apennines to the Adriatic.

'I know a good restaurant down at Punta Ala if that sounds okay.'

'I have no idea where that is but it sounds fine to me as long as you don't mind a long drive.'

She heard him laugh. 'It's not that far, I promise. Listen, it's almost eleven now. Would you be ready to go in, say, half an hour? If so, I'll call ahead and book a table for one o'clock.'

Lucy was ready and waiting well before eleven-thirty and she shook her head in quiet resignation as she saw him arrive in the Ferrari. She had been hoping he would bring his anonymous Mercedes with the tinted windows, but such was not the case and she realised she would once more be on display. This only served to highlight to her the abyss that existed – and would always exist – between the two of them and she felt a flicker of regret.

She had checked out Punta Ala on Google Earth while she waited and had found that it was a little tree-covered promontory on the west coast of Tuscany, roughly opposite the Island of Elba. It looked lovely, but she had little doubt that in August, the month when Italy traditionally closed down for the summer break, it would be heaving with holidaymakers. Still, she would be with David and, for now, that was all that mattered to her, whether he was a multi-millionaire or not.

As the car came to a halt outside her front door, she climbed into the passenger seat and lent towards him. He kissed her on both cheeks, rather than the lips, and she felt a little shot of disappointment but, she told herself, the day was still young. He was wearing shorts and his strong brown legs were very much in evidence. He looked very good and he even smelt good.

'Hi, Lucy. You look gorgeous as usual. Look out for your ears.'

'My ears?' A second later, she realised what he meant as a cold wet nose nudged the side of her head. She turned to find a very happy dog positioned directly behind her, squeezed onto the tiny back seat, his lead secured to the door pillar so he couldn't jump out. 'Hi, dog. Seen any more porcupines?' She made a fuss of him and then turned back to clip her seat belt in, gently fending off Boris's attempts to kiss her ear. Now if it had been his master…

She did her best to dismiss the thought. 'How about you, David? All well?'

'All very well, thanks. Last night was great, really great. It was good to get out and meet a new person after my self-imposed isolation.'

He set off back down through the village and they were soon on the main road heading for the coast. At first as they travelled along Boris leant his head over the side and occasionally barked at passers-by, nearly deafening Lucy as he did so. As he gradually calmed and settled down to sleep, she and David got chatting and he told her more about Punta Ala.

'We rented an apartment there right up until last year, but I was away playing so much that I rarely managed to go. After my injury, I gave up going there completely, but my wife used it a lot. The port's a bit in-your-face, but the coastline's beautiful.'

Lucy discovered what he meant by 'in-your-face' as they drove down through the pine trees into the little seaside town just before one o'clock. Every available parking space was crammed and it was evident even to somebody like herself with no great interest in cars that there weren't many little Fiats to be seen. Everywhere she looked there were big, flashy cars – including several other Ferraris – and she began to get a bad feeling about Punta Ala. Of course, she told herself, she was in the company of a multi-millionaire and this was the sort of place they frequented, and she decided to give him the benefit of the doubt – for now.

They drove down the steep hill towards the sea until they came up against barriers and a sign saying that the port area was a restricted zone. He leant out and fiddled with something and, seconds later, the barrier magically lifted. He turned right and drove along the side of a crowded marina full of small boats, threading his way carefully through a host of holidaymakers at walking pace, many of whom stopped to stare at the luxury car until he found a parking space. As he turned off the engine he swivelled around towards her.

'You hate this car, don't you?'

'I wouldn't say I hate it. It's very pretty and I'm sure it's a wonderful bit of engineering, but I do feel terribly exposed when I'm in it.'

He smiled at her. 'Want to know something? It's probably heresy, but I hate this damn car too, now. It's too big, it's too low and if you're going uphill you can't see a thing in front of you, and don't get me started on how much fuel it guzzles up. But, above all, it's far too ostentatious. It's crazy, I know. I used to love it, but it no longer does it for me. Somehow I reckon it'll be years before I take it out of the garage again, if ever.'

She was genuinely surprised, and she smiled back at him. 'So how come the change of heart?'

'Age, I suppose, at least partly. And maybe you.'

'Me?'

'Talking to you about your life, the difference you must have made to hundreds or even thousands of people, it makes me realise how superficial this sort of thing is. Maybe I've just outgrown it.'

'The sad fact is that almost all the people wandering past us would give their eye teeth to own a Ferrari. I sometimes think the world's gone crazy. We've lost our sense of perspective about the really important things in life. Like health for example.'

'Amen to that. Come to think about it, that's also a major part of the reason I'm moving on from this car.

213

When you're younger, you feel you're immortal. It's only when your health takes a hit that you realise there's more to life than the superficial stuff, like money for instance.'

Lucy nodded in agreement and was very impressed to hear what he said next.

'That's something else I've been thinking about a lot recently. I'd really like to use my money for a good cause, not just for my own creature comforts – like this damn car. Anyway, don't let it spoil your day and don't let the crowds put you off. It's not as bad as it looks here. The food's good and I promise this afternoon I'll take you to somewhere a hell of a lot quieter.'

Greatly cheered by his words, she walked with him along the quayside to a restaurant where the waiter showed them to a table under a broad white parasol only a few metres from the water's edge. It looked as though all the other tables were full and it was buzzing with conversation, but, for now, nobody appeared to recognise David, or if they did, they were civilised enough to leave him alone. Boris was persuaded to lie down at their feet as the waiter took their order. After a brief exchange of pleasantries, they ordered *fritto misto* for two and settled back in their seats. Down here by the water there was just a hint of a breeze blowing. A digital thermometer on the side of a low building just beyond the restaurant indicated it was thirty-six degrees today, but the breeze made that just about bearable.

They chatted some more and relaxed. All around them were people enjoying their holidays and – at least in a good few cases – the chance to show off their expensive designer clothes. Over her bikini, Lucy was wearing shorts bought at the market and a plain white top. Even when she added in her sandals, the total cost of what she was wearing was almost certainly a good bit less than this meal was going to be. She sneaked a peek at the designer logo on his shirt, which looked decidedly pricey. She really did like him a lot, in spite of her reservations about the mega-rich. After all, it wasn't his fault he fell into that category and, unlike many others, he had at least got there by his own legitimate efforts and, from what he had just said in the car, maybe he would really do something good with his wealth rather than just sit on it.

The *fritto misto* was excellent, no doubt due in no small part to the freshness of the little fish, prawns, squid and tiny octopus which the chef had dusted in flour and quick-fried. They shared a half-bottle of white wine and a big bottle of mineral water with the meal while they carried on chatting. Lucy would have loved to ask him for details of what he had described as the 'long, sad story' of his separation, but she decided to let him take his time about telling her. Instead, as they sat back at the end of the meal, she brought the subject round to tennis.

'I'm delighted to see you walking quite normally again. What happens next? What did Doctor Saeed say? Will you be able to play again?' She already knew the answer to this, but she didn't want it to look as though she had been too nosey.

'Play, yes – at least a bit. Compete, no.' He took a little sip of wine. 'It was pretty much what everybody's been telling me for almost three years now, but I've finally come to terms with it. Let's face it, irrespective of my injuries, I'm an old man as far as tennis is concerned. You probably know I'm thirty-seven.' Lucy did, but she gave no sign. 'After three years out, there's no way I could have gone back to the top of the rankings even with a perfect knee and, when all's said and done, I love winning. A return to top level competition now would mean a lot of losing, I'm sure.'

Lucy was delighted to hear him talking about this so rationally and calmly. If it was true that he had really had a breakdown two or three years ago, this marked a major improvement. Once again, she spared a thought for Franz who had helped her so much in combating her own demons. It sounded as though he had done the same for David.

'So what happens now? Are you going to settle down and become a wine producer? I can think of worse ways of making a living.'

He smiled and shook his head. 'No, well, yes to the wine part, but that won't be enough in itself. Apart from the past three tough years, I've spent almost all my life involved with something that occupied me body and soul. The worst thing about my injury has been the massive hole it left in my life. I'm too young to retire. I need something to focus on.'

'So what might that be? Coaching? TV commentating, maybe?'

He smiled again. 'You wouldn't believe the offers I've been getting via my agent. The latest is a range of leis- urewear for "men who want clothing that performs".' Seeing Lucy grin, he went on. 'That's nothing. Last year there was a big Italian lingerie company who wanted me to endorse their new line of sports bras. Now, I may have put on a few pounds since I gave up competitive tennis, but my boobs don't need support that badly yet.'

'Having seen you with your shirt off, I can confirm that. Apart from sponsorship deals which, I'm sure, can be very lucrative, is there something you'd really like to do with your life?'

He nodded. 'Definitely one… well two, no three really. First – don't laugh at me please – I'd like to go back to college and maybe do a doctorate in medieval history. What do you think of that as an idea? I notice you didn't immediately burst out laughing, and I thank you for that.'

'I wouldn't dream of laughing at something like that. If for some reason I had to give up my medical career, I'd jump at the chance to do the same. Where would you do it? In the States?'

As she asked the question she found herself wondering if this might take him away from her and she felt a cold stab in her stomach as she realised how much she would miss him.

'There are some great universities in the USA, but the Middle Ages happened before the US as we know it even existed. No, I'd stay in Europe, for sure.'

'What about Siena? There's a very good university here. Or maybe even Florence? After all, you now know Guido. He could help you, I'm sure.'

'Yes, indeed, or maybe your native land. Some of the best universities in the world are in the UK.'

'You said there were three things you'd like to do. What're the others?'

'The second is that I'm actively considering setting up a charity of some sort. I don't just want to be remembered for what I did on the court.'

'That sounds wonderful.' She was genuinely impressed. 'What sort of thing?'

'I really don't know – maybe providing sports scholarships for underprivileged kids or support for injured athletes or something like that. It all depends on money and that in turn depends on how things pan out with my third wish.'

'And that is…?'

'I want to get a divorce.'

'You aren't already divorced?'

'No, my wife would like nothing better and she keeps on hassling me, but I've been hanging on, hoping she might maybe change her mind and give it another go. Until the lawyers sort out the financial side of things I won't know how much I can spare for the charity.'

'What's changed your mind about the divorce?'

He looked up from his plate, straight into her eyes. 'You, Lucy.'

'Me?' The mouthful of wine she had just swallowed almost came back up again. She could hardly believe her ears.

'You. Now, listen, please don't be alarmed. I'm not proposing marriage or anything as radical as that. I'm just saying that I like you a lot and being with you has made me realise how much was missing in my marriage – like being able to talk to each other about something other than tennis and trivia for instance.'

Lucy seriously considered draining her glass of wine in one, but she settled for another sip while she tried to get her head around what he had just said. 'Well, I enjoy talking to you, too, and we do talk about a lot of different stuff.' It sounded a bit lame, but she was pleased to manage to get at least a few words out.

'Meeting somebody who shares my love of history has been a breath of fresh air, but there's so much more to it than that. Like you say, we do talk about all sorts of subjects.'

She was gradually regaining the power of speech. So he really did like her. She felt her heart soar. She reached across the table with both hands and caught hold of his.

'Well, for the record, I'm not proposing to you either, but I do like you an awful lot as well.'

She felt him squeeze her fingers. 'I'm glad we got that sorted out.' He smiled again. 'And now, if you're really sure you don't want dessert or even a coffee, what do you say we head somewhere a little quieter?'

A few minutes later they set off along the quay, but not in the direction of the car. Barely a hundred metres further on, they stopped by a sign marked *Noleggio Motoscafi*. A heavily tattooed man lazing under a faded red and white parasol advertising Campari looked up from his newspaper and beamed as he recognised David.

'Ciao, David. Long time no see.' He looked genuinely pleased to see him. 'I've kept one for you, like I promised you on the phone. Ready to go?'

David nodded and Lucy wondered what he meant. This was soon revealed as they followed the tattooed man down a sloping ramp onto a pontoon moored alongside the quay. As they reached a smart RIB, a rigid inflatable boat, the man pointed.

'This okay? It was new in June. It runs as sweet as you like.'

Boris answered for them. He was clearly accustomed to boats and he wasted no time in jumping in, before turning back towards them, legs splayed, tail wagging, his tongue hanging out, clearly delighted to be on the water. Lucy took a seat on an upholstered bench alongside David at the wheel and the engine purred into life. The tattooed man cast them off and they slowly eased away from the quayside and out between the forest of masts of moored yachts. There was very little wind and most of the yachts hadn't moved from their berths, their owners no doubt enjoying a little siesta after their Sunday lunch.

As they reached the entrance to the marina, David opened the throttle some more and the boat sped smoothly away, producing a very welcome breeze after the clammy heat of the shore. As she cooled down, Lucy found herself analysing her feelings. She still didn't know if he really had been the guilty party in the separation, but the more she got to know him, the less she believed him capable of betrayal. Yes, he was undisputedly still a very rich man from a different stratosphere, but all his talk about setting up a charity had been very heartening. And he was also very, very attractive. Her musings were interrupted by his voice.

'I thought we could go out to that little island out there.' Lucy followed his pointing finger with her eyes and spotted a rocky lump with a little tower on it, probably about a kilometre or two away. 'It's very pretty and it's unlikely to be too crowded. And, most important, there's a tiny area of gravel beach; not for us, but for Boris. He loves the water, but getting him back into a boat like this again is a real struggle unless there's a bit of dry land handy.' He shot her a smile. 'If you want to slip into your swimming things, I promise I won't look.'

Lucy stood up and smiled back at him. 'Already got them on.' She pulled off her top and unbuttoned her shorts, letting them fall to her ankles. She glanced down and was reassured to see her bikini still attached in all the right places. As she looked up again, she saw his eyes on her body and her smile broadened. 'Your turn.'

'Here, take the wheel, will you?'

Before she could object, he slipped the kill cord off his wrist and clipped it onto hers, slid off the seat and reached for his T-shirt. She made a grab for the wheel before the boat could veer off course. It was going quite fast and it was fun to drive, although it meant keeping her eyes on the water ahead, while she knew he was stripping to his shorts. A few seconds later, he slid back alongside her, but made no attempt to take over the steering. Instead, his bare arm encircled her shoulders as he pulled her gently towards him. She felt her whole body tingle as he kissed her softly on the neck and then turned her face towards him and kissed her properly.

At this point, nobody was in control of the boat, but she couldn't care less. There was nobody else close-by and the rocky island was still quite a long way ahead. She felt totally transported by his touch and his kiss. It was almost like an out-of-body experience and she found she could hardly breathe. Her head was reeling with the fact that there could be no doubt now that he liked her, a lot. His hands on her bare shoulders felt good and the kiss genuinely made her head spin. Finally, reluctantly, after a long while she pulled away enough to glance ahead of them and was relieved to see the island still several hundred metres off and the boat still heading roughly towards it. There were three or four other boats anchored around it but otherwise it looked quite deserted. She glanced back at David from close range and smiled.

'Well, Mr Lorenzo, that was rather nice.'

'Rather nice?' His voice was even a bit hoarse. 'It was incredible.' He looked genuinely moved.

She leant forward and pecked him on the lips, letting her smile broaden. 'We'll have to do it again, then.'

David gave a heartfelt sigh and then glanced forward, reaching for the throttle control to slow the boat to a standstill. Suddenly all she could hear were the screams of seagulls high above and the soft lapping of the wavelets against the rubber sides of the boat. He turned towards her, looking suddenly serious. 'Listen, Lucy, I need to tell you my side of the story.'

'What story?'

'The story of why my wife and I broke up.'

Lucy listened, spellbound, as he launched into his tale. The overriding thought going through her head as he spoke was that this – coupled with that amazing kiss – marked a watershed in their relationship.

As he had told her during their visit to Florence, it was miles away from most of the newspaper accounts.

'The final break-up was my fault – well, to a great extent – but not for the reasons people have been saying. I was away a lot – that comes with the territory in my occupation – and I assumed Rosy, my wife, would have realised that. At first she came with me to tournaments, but she soon got tired of traipsing around the world from one hotel room to another and she started to get bored. She came back to Tuscany and spent a lot of the time in the apartment we rented here in Punta Ala or in Rome with friends, or back in the States. We saw less and less of each other and we didn't even talk on the phone that much. Things might still have worked themselves out if it hadn't been for my injury. One moment I was a set and a break up against Rafa Nadal at Roland Garros and the next I was lying in agony on the court looking at my knee bent completely out of shape with my lower leg sticking out sideways.'

Lucy nodded mutely and caught hold of his hands in hers. She knew full well the pain that torn cruciate ligaments could cause. She gave his fingers a little squeeze, but he didn't seem to notice as he picked up his tale again.

'In my defence, I hope you can understand just how much of a crushing blow this was. From the very start the doctors who treated me told me it looked almost certain that my career was over. Can you imagine what it feels like to spend your whole life totally focused on one thing, to the exclusion of all else, and for that to be torn away from you in a matter of seconds? Just think – I first started playing tennis when I was five and I was winning junior tournaments by the time I was ten. All the way through school and college, tennis was the single most important thing in my life – not my parents, not my studies, not even girls; just tennis and the desire to become world champion. It was all-consuming, the only thing I knew. Being told it had come to an end came as a hammer blow to me.'

Lucy nodded mutely.

'As the significance of this gradually sank in, I'm afraid to say I totally lost it. I freaked out and spiralled down into a morose, uncommunicative state where I didn't want to see anybody or talk to anybody. And that included Rosy. I hauled her back to the US with me while I went to see specialist after specialist, trying all manner of miracle cures, but with no success, and all the time I was getting more and more depressed. By this time the villa was finished so we moved in and that was the final blow for her. She didn't speak much Italian and she found herself alone in the wilds of the country with a monosyllabic hulk. The hope was that moving to the villa would snap me out of it, but it didn't. Rosy stuck it out for a few months and then, after a series of flaming rows, she left me and came here to the apartment at Punta Ala.'

'So no naked romps with cheerleaders?' She was trying her best to cheer him.

'No naked romps with anybody – at least not for me – but I feel very responsible for the break-up. It wasn't fair of me to expect her to put up with a man who probably didn't utter more than two or three words each day. I certainly don't blame her for leaving.'

'And at which point did she start asking you for a divorce?'

'Maybe eighteen months ago. She was living down here at Punta Ala and she told me she'd met some guy with a yacht. She said she'd fallen in love with him and she wanted out. I was so low, I didn't want to lose her as well, so I kept saying no, hoping she'd come to her senses.'

'So, technically, the unfaithful partner wasn't you at all, it was your wife. So why not set the record straight?'

'Back then I couldn't care less what anybody thought. I didn't read the papers, I didn't watch the news, and I certainly didn't get involved with social media. Besides, what was I going to say? She left me because I was a wreck. Nobody could blame her.'

Lucy shook her head. 'I'm not convinced. What about the whole "in sickness and in health" thing? Didn't that matter to her?'

For the first time she saw a glimmer of a smile on his lips, albeit ironic. 'You see it that way because you're such a caring person. Don't forget I come from a very egotistical way of life where the only thing that matters is to win, to be better than the opposition. I suppose, thinking back, Rosy was out of the same mould. I'm going to do my best to change now, to become a better person – with your help – but back then, I didn't hold it against her.'

Lucy didn't know what so say, so she kissed him. When they finally pulled apart, the smile was back on his face – this time a broad, genuine smile.

'You're amazing, Lucy. Being with you just makes me want to smile all the time. Shall we go and visit the island, the *Scogli dello Sparviero*? Know what a *sparviero* is?' She shook her head. 'It's a sparrowhawk. There are nesting pairs high in the cliffs – at least there were last year.'

'Not a bad place to live.'

She clung to his arm as he brought the boat closer to the daunting cliffs. The little stone tower was clearly visible, perched on the top, and her historical interest was whetted for a moment before her head returned to the far more interesting prospect of what might be going to happen between her and the handsome man alongside her. History could wait – at least for today. Millionaire he might be, but he had said he wasn't an adulterer and she trusted him. She knew she couldn't help herself now. She had fallen for him hook, line and sinker and she knew it wasn't just for his body, but for his gentle kindness towards her and the way he had been able to voice his feelings so honestly.

He turned the wheel to the left and they rounded the side of the little island. As he did so, he throttled back until there was just a gentle bubbling noise from behind them and he cautiously nosed the RIB in towards the rough beach he had mentioned. There were three other boats already there and a few heads bobbing up and down in the water and Lucy felt almost disappointed she wasn't going to have him all to herself. Still, considering it was the busiest holiday month of the year, it was remarkably quiet.

On his instructions, she took the kill cord off her wrist and stationed herself at the bow, staring down into the crystal clear water, pointing out any possible hazards as the water grew ever shallower until she heard the engine die and, simultaneously, the underside of the nose graze the beach. She lowered herself over the side into the warm water and, as she did so, a shadow flashed over her and she was drenched by a canine tsunami as a large black body belly-flopped into the water beside her like a bomb going off. She turned towards the impact zone and saw Boris come back up to the surface, snort, and then treat her to a broad canine grin of happiness. Grabbing the end of the mooring line, she waded ashore and tied it to a hefty rock a bit further up the beach. Once she was happy the boat was safely secured, she walked back into the water and sank down into it, relishing the refreshing feel on her skin.

She and David played an enjoyable game of catch with a piece of driftwood while Boris doggy-paddled hopefully from one to the other. Every now and then they would throw it further for him and he would swim after it, snuffling happily as he did so. She soon discovered that although he invariably retrieved the stick, he evidently hadn't inherited the full retriever gene and he would refuse to hand it over, even allowing himself to be dragged bodily into the air by his master without giving it up. Needless to say, this necessitated constantly going back and forth to the beach to find ever more pieces of wood and by the time they came out of the water for a rest, she was feeling quite tired. She sat down on a boulder alongside David and reached up to kiss him again.

'This is paradise.' And she meant it. 'I can't think of any way this could be better.' Well, maybe if the other people hadn't been there, but she didn't want to sound churlish.

At their feet, Boris the dog rolled around on his back in the damp gravel, grunting to himself. He looked almost as happy as she felt.

Chapter 23

The night that followed was amazing. Lucy felt as though she was living in a dream and she knew she couldn't be any happier. She stayed with him at the villa in his lovely big bedroom. Early next morning she was there, resting on her elbows, gazing out through the lace curtains that fluttered gently in the breeze. The view was even better than from her cottage and she could clearly see Siena in the distance with the unmistakable bulk of the cathedral distinguishable among the red roofs of the old town. Beyond that, the hills continued until a vague dark strip on the horizon where the Apennines were virtually hidden by the haze. She sighed with real pleasure and couldn't help comparing this view to the orange dust and sun-scorched scrub that extended for miles all around the Mabenta clinic with hardly a single house to be seen amid the trees.

'A penny for your thoughts.' She was roused from her daydream by the feel of his lips on her neck. 'You looked miles away.'

She turned towards him and kissed him softly. 'Just thinking.'

'Let me guess: about Africa?'

'Yes, but also about just how happy I am right now. You'd better keep your distance, I think I might explode.'

He grinned down at her. 'We wouldn't want that to happen, now, would we? If it helps, I haven't been this happy for years and years, maybe never.'

As he settled back beside her, she decided the time was right to ask him a direct question.

'So does that mean you're feeling healthier mentally, as well as physically? I know about your knee, but what about inside your head?'

'You mean my depression? I'm fine now. And it's down to three things. First, less than two years ago, after Rosy had been gone for a few months, Armando and Fioretta persuaded me to get Boris.' He glanced across at her and grinned. 'To be honest, they didn't give me much choice. Armando just turned up one day with a little black ball of fur in his hands and said I needed him. And I did. Labrador puppies should be available on prescription. He did wonders for me, just as a friend and a silent, non-judgemental companion who forced me to get off my ass and outside into the fresh air. Second, Franz Berlin. That man's a miracle-worker. He has a knack of helping you get to the root of your problems all by yourself – or so it seems. He's been invaluable to me.'

As Lucy leant against his shoulder, her eyes were drawn to the curve of the cypress trees alongside the drive leading down to the gate. A sudden movement revealed what had attracted her attention. This time no fewer than three red squirrels were chasing each other from branch to branch, tree to tree and she felt herself smiling as she watched their antics. 'Franz helped me so much too. My experiences in the Congo – particularly those last really scary weeks – were weighing me down more than I was prepared to admit at first. I was still having awful nightmares even after weeks had gone by, but he sorted me out. Yes, Franz is a good guy.' She reached over and kissed David softly on the lips. 'And so are you. And the third thing? You said there were three.'

He smiled down at her. 'Need you ask? The third, and most important was you, Lucy.'

'But you and I have only just got together.'

'I knew it from the first moment I saw you.' He ran a finger gently across her cheek and she rubbed her face against his hand. 'Honest, I mean it. Even as I was lying there bleeding from that stupid bullet wound, it registered with me that you were something very special.'

'But you were so grumpy the first few times I saw you.'

'You think that was grumpy? You should have seen me a few months earlier. Believe me, what you saw was sweetness and light compared to the bad-tempered wreck of a man I was before I met you.'

'You really must have been in a bad place. And you must have been on your own for ages. So how did you spend your time here after your wife left?'

'Walking the dog and reading history books, and doing a hell of a lot of nothing.'

'Well, it worked out in the end and if I've helped in any way, then I'm pleased, and I'm sure Boris would like me to say the same on his behalf.'

'You and Boris are great, but you're even better than him. Apart from anything else, your breath smells a whole lot sweeter and you don't pee on the plants.'

'Erm, I might need to talk to you about that…'

The only bit of bad news that morning was that he told her he had to fly back to the States the next day for almost a week and she realised she would miss him tremendously. Still, they would have tonight, so she went off to work with a smile on her face. It remained on her face even when Charles joined her at her table at lunchtime.

'Hi, Lucy. You're looking tanned. Been out in the sun?'

'I had a trip to the seaside yesterday. What about you? Cheered up since we last spoke?'

He hung his head. 'Not really. I still feel the same way and she hasn't changed. I didn't realise it could be so hard.'

Lucy choked back the urge to tell him it served him right after his behaviour towards her and no doubt countless other women, but she bit her tongue. Instead, she kept the smile firmly on her face. 'Give it time. You'll get over it. It worked for me.' And she returned to her ginseng.

Mid-afternoon, just as she was coming out of theatre after a fairly routine appendectomy, she was met by Bruno with a request.

'Hi, Lucy. I don't suppose you could do a few nights for me this week, could you?'

She thought quickly. Tonight was a definite no, but then David would be away until the following Sunday or Monday. And if she did nights while he was away, she would be able to spend more nights with him when he got back. It was a no-brainer. 'Yes, of course. Not tonight, but any other nights this week. The whole week if you like. What's the emergency?'

'Not really an emergency. Virginia wants me to take her away for a few days. There's some stuff we need to sort out.'

Lucy wondered if this might be the occasion that he finally asked Virginia to marry him and she was happy for them – even more so now that she had David. 'Well, why don't I do Tuesday to Saturday? Come to think of it, I might need a day or two off next month as a friend's getting married in Avignon, so if I scratch your back…'

'It's a deal. Thanks a lot, Lucy.'

That evening, she insisted that David come to her house and she prepared dinner for him. Although food was secondary to what she had in mind, she stopped off at a fish shop in Siena and bought some fresh crabmeat and served it, according to one of Daniela's mum's recipes, mixed with grated apple and avocado, accompanied by a tomato salad made with wonderful aromatic big tomatoes from Donatello's shop. While she was there she also bought strawberries and ice cream. If the way to a man's heart was through his stomach, she felt sure that on a swelteringly hot night like tonight this cold spread would do the trick.

It was fortuitous that she chose to serve cold food, as the first thing she did when David appeared at her door was to give Boris a big bowl of dog biscuits, specially bought the other day when Boris and Barolo had come to dinner, while she dragged his far-from-unwilling master upstairs to her bedroom. They didn't sit down to eat until after nine, but he didn't complain, and neither did she. By this time Boris had made himself at home and they found him sprawled across the sofa, snoozing happily. As they came down the stairs, one eye opened and his tail started thumping lazily against the cushions.

'Boris, dogs are meant to be on the floor, not the furniture. Shame on you.' David wagged an admonitory finger at him but that only made the tail wag harder. Lucy was in such a good mood, she just went over and patted the Labrador's head.

'You stay there, Boris. It's an old sofa anyway.'

But, needless to say, as she retrieved the food from the fridge and set it on the table, Boris conveniently forgot that he had eaten barely two hours earlier and jumped off the sofa to position himself under the table with an expectant look on his face.

As they ate, they chatted some more and she asked David something she had been thinking about for a week now.

'David... just say no if you don't want to, but... a good friend of mine called Nicole, one of the nurses I worked with in Mabenta, is getting married next month. She's French and the wedding's going to be in Avignon. The invitation is for me plus one. I don't suppose you'd like to come with me, do you?'

He didn't hesitate. 'Absolutely. I'd love that. I love France and, the way I feel about you, I'd be happy just to be wherever you're going to be. Count me in.'

'You're sure? I mean, people are going to recognise you.' She had a sudden thought. 'Come to think of it, what if somebody takes a photo of the two of us together? They might post it on the Internet. Shouldn't we maybe wait until you've got your divorce settled?'

'You sound like my attorney.'

'You've spoken to your attorney about me?' She didn't know whether to be pleased or intimidated.

'Indirectly. Meeting you has been the kick up the ass I needed to make me get on with my life. I spent an hour on the phone with him this afternoon. That's the main reason I'm going back to the States. I want to get the divorce papers settled as soon as possible and, like I told you, the sooner the divorce settlement gets done, the sooner I'll be able to think seriously about setting up some sort of charity. As long as you don't mind, if people see you and me together before that, so what? As both you and my lawyer say, the break-up was technically Rosy's fault every bit as much as it was mine – in his eyes a good deal more.

Being seen with you isn't going to hurt – and it means we'll be together.'

'Well, if you're sure. I'm just happy to be where you are, too. Does this mean you'll be seeing your wife this week?'

'I don't know. I'll find out in the next few days.'

Lucy found herself wondering what the reaction of his wife was likely to be when she found her husband once more looking and sounding normal. Might this rekindle the love she presumably must once have felt for him? The thought that this might mean losing him so soon was unsettling, even though Lucy kept reminding herself that getting together with him, amazing as it was, would ultimately have to end anyway. She knew only too well that her conscience would never let her settle down in the lap of unashamed luxury when so many people were suffering in squalor. Once again, her thoughts were drawn to the people she had left behind in Africa and she found herself struggling, caught between these two so very different worlds.

Carpe diem, she told herself. Enjoy the moment, because sooner or later these wonderful days are bound to come to an end.

Chapter 24

The following day she had a long lie-in to help get her ready for night duty starting that evening. David had gone off at the crack of dawn for his early flight and she had been left with time to reflect on the whirlwind that had carried her away in the past forty-eight hours. Suddenly her whole life had changed for the better. She now had a wonderful man in her life – albeit maybe just temporarily – and a permanent smile on her face. Compared to those final days in Mabenta, this really was a dream come true. Her escape to Tuscany had turned into something far, far better than she could ever have imagined.

That afternoon she met up with Daniela for tea before going to the clinic to start her night shift. When she passed on her amazing news, Daniela beamed.

'I've been feeling awful about the fact that it was my newspaper, and my colleague, who revealed your tennis player's whereabouts. I'm just delighted it's worked out so well for him and for you. Tommy's been avoiding me since the article came out and he knows I'm going to give him a real telling-off. Even if we're journalists, we need some sense of morality.'

Lucy patted her hand. 'Don't waste your breath, Danni. Even David says it needed to happen so he could get on with his life.'

'Are you seeing him tonight?'

'No, he's on his way to Boston for a few days. He went off this morning. I'm going to be working nights until Saturday and then he'll be back and I'll see him again. And once he's back, I'd really like to have you and Pietro round for dinner one night so you can meet him. Anyway, how are you? How's the bump?'

'I'm doing well. To be honest, I just want to get on with it now and have the baby.'

'Still no idea if it's a boy or a girl?' Pietro and Daniela had decided they didn't want to know.

'No. Just so long as it's healthy. That's all that counts. By the way, you know that next week's the Palio, don't you?'

'How could I forget? The local news has been full of it for days. This one's the Palio dell'Assunta, seeing as it's August, isn't it? In this heat I'm happy to give it a miss. Now that I'm going to be a permanent resident here, there'll be other opportunities to see it again. Are you going?'

'I don't think so. I'm feeling less and less sociable, and the idea of standing up for several hours in a crowded room really doesn't appeal at all. The paper organises a party every year and I could get invites for you and David if you'd like to go along. It's in an apartment overlooking the square and the view's great.'

'Thanks, but no thanks. I remember Tommy telling me about that. I'd rather not meet him again because I might feel tempted to tip him out of the window.'

That evening at work, she met up with her friend Ahmed again, but there was no smile on his face tonight. She was quick to ask why. It soon transpired that his new girlfriend, Rahel, had a big problem.

'She's sick and she needs medical help, but it's not easy to get.'

'Can't she just go along to the hospital in Siena?'

Ahmed shook his head morosely. 'The problem is she's an undocumented migrant. She has no right of residence in Italy and the authorities have been clamping down. I would hope they'd treat her at the hospital, but she might then find herself in trouble with the authorities as a result.'

Lucy made a quick decision. 'I'll take a look at her, Ahmed. What about after we finish our shift tomorrow morning? We could go together in my car.'

Ahmed's girlfriend was living in a squat in the less salubrious part of the outskirts of town, not the sort of area the multitude of visitors to Siena ever saw. While Lucy parked between a burnt-out van and an old car with no wheels, resting on bricks, Ahmed climbed out and went across to a couple of men squatting in the early morning sunshine and spoke to them for a minute before returning.

'It's all right, Lucy. They'll keep an eye on your car. Would you like to come with me?'

Lucy nodded. No doubt, without these unofficial guards, she would have returned to find her Fiat also minus its wheels.

He led her up three flights of concrete stairs and into an open plan area that had probably started life as an office or factory space. Now, from the plaster falling off the ceiling and walls, and graffiti all over what was left, it was clearly earmarked for demolition. It was warm and sticky in there and it smelt of drains – or, rather, the lack of them. There were probably five or six little clusters of people up there, huddled together with their meagre possessions. Rahel was in the far corner along with a couple of older people and she was curled up in a ball, wrapped in a thick blanket in spite of the heat.

Ahmed knelt down beside her and whispered softly in her ear. Lucy saw her stir and look up, her bloodshot eyes full of gratitude.

'Thank you, doctor.' Her voice was very weak, but she even managed to summon a little smile.

Lucy gave her a thorough examination and very quickly diagnosed appendicitis. Rahel needed to have the offending organ removed as soon as possible to avoid the risk of peritonitis, which would be a far more serious matter. She reached for her phone but then remembered that Bruno and Virginia were away. Gritting her teeth, she called the clinic and asked to be put through to the director, Professor Gualtieri Della Torre, Virginia's father.

'Good morning, Professor Gualtieri. It's Lucy Young.'

'Good morning, Doctor Young. How can I help?'

Rapidly, she outlined the situation, explaining that in her opinion an urgent operation was needed. 'I could take her to the main hospital where I'm sure they'd treat her, but Ahmed's terrified that the authorities might subsequently have her arrested and maybe even deported. I honestly don't know if that would be the case, but they're both dead scared. Might there be a free hour of theatre time today and a bed for two or three nights at the clinic? I'd be happy to do the operation and I'll also pay for her stay there. I'm sure I could persuade an anaesthetist and a nurse to help out.' He didn't respond immediately, so she hurried on. 'The thing is, she's the girlfriend of one of our staff members. I don't suppose…'

There was the briefest of pauses before he replied. 'After what you did for Mr Lorenzo, we owe you, and

Ahmed's always been a dedicated member of staff. Fine. Bring her here.' She exhaled in relief.

'Thank you so much, *Professore*.'

'That's okay and, Doctor Young, there's no need for you to pay.' There was a gentle note to his voice. 'Tell Ahmed we're glad to help.'

'Thank you so very much.' Lucy reflected that he really was a good man.

Together with Ahmed, she helped Rahel down the stairs and they laid her in a foetal position on the back seat of the little car which, fortunately, still had its wheels. Back at the clinic she found that Professor Gualtieri had already put things in motion and they were able to wheel Rahel straight down to the operating theatre. The operation was very straightforward and a complete success and at the end Lucy went out to give the waiting Ahmed the good news. He was grateful, but she made it clear where thanks were due.

'All I did was a routine operation. It was Professor Gualtieri who authorised everything and who's paying for it.' She gave him a hug as she saw tears of joy running down his cheeks. 'You and I have a good boss, Ahmed. We're lucky to work here.' She realised she meant it.

It was midday by the time she got home and she went straight to bed, setting the alarm for seven o'clock so she would be able to take a shower and eat something before hurrying back to work. In spite of feeling tired after so long on her feet, she also felt elated. After months here in Siena looking after the privileged few, it had felt good to do something for the less fortunate. Importantly, it underlined what a fine man Professor Gualtieri was. Whatever reservations she might have been having about private medicine, she knew she was proud to work for a man like him.

She was woken just after six o'clock that evening by her phone. As she reached lazily for it, she was delighted to see it was a call from David in the States. Her tiredness disappeared in a flash and she sat upright.

'David, hi. It's so good to hear from you.' And it was. 'How was your journey and how's everything?'

'It's great to hear your voice too, Lucy.' He went on to tell her that he had had his first meeting with his 'legal people' and he hoped everything was going to be concluded by the end of the week. Apparently most of the groundwork had already been done by his wife's lawyers in the hope of a speedy conclusion. As the end of the week was little more than two days' away, Lucy crossed her fingers that he was right.

'And are you going to be meeting up with your wife?'

'Friday afternoon, I believe. We both need to sign some papers.'

Lucy found herself yet again wondering what reaction his wife might have when she saw him. Might she find she still loved him and want to get back together with him? If so, Lucy wondered where that would leave her. Still, she told herself, there was nothing she could do about it, so she just had to hope for the best, although it was an uncomfortable feeling.

They chatted for almost half an hour before, reluctantly, she told him she had to get ready for work. Before ringing off, he came up with an invitation.

'My sponsors – who, I'm pleased to say, are sticking with me – have invited me to a Palio party next Wednesday. I wonder if you'd like to come. We can watch the race from above the crowds.'

'That sounds great, but it's not the party organised by the local newspaper, is it? I've already turned down an invitation to that as I really don't want to bump into Tommy… you know, the guy who ratted you out.'

He assured her it was a totally different party and she said yes, willingly. In fact, she didn't really mind where she was going to be as long as wherever that was she would be by David's side.

Back at the clinic later that evening, she found Rahel sitting up in bed and looking much better. Lucy sat and chatted to her for some time, listening with rapt attention to her first-hand account of the arduous journey she had had to undertake to get away from the war zone with her elderly parents. They came from the ten percent of Syrians who were Christians and things had been getting increasingly tough for them in their home town of Aleppo by the time they left. Lucy was also fascinated to learn that Rahel had been a trainee nurse.

Rahel told Lucy her plan was to try to enrol in a course here in Italy so she could finish her nursing studies and make enough to look after her parents. The problem was that almost all the precious money she and her family had, had been used to pay the extortionate fee the people-smugglers had charged to cram them onto a frighten-ingly overloaded inflatable for the crossing to Europe. In consequence, she had had to take any job she could find until she could save enough money to let her carry on with her plan. Lucy knew it was going to be an uphill battle and urged her to waste no time in applying for asylum. She also offered to act as a referee if necessary. In the meantime Ahmed had managed to find modest accommodation for her and her parents which was much better than the squat.

Lucy thought about the Syrian woman a lot during the final days of the week and when it was time for Rahel to be discharged on Friday morning, she pressed several hundred euros into her hands. Brushing away her protests, she told her to consider it a loan that she could repay once she was a qualified nurse with a full-time job.

Chapter 25

David was due to return on Sunday lunchtime and Lucy spent the morning in the garden, anxiously waiting for the call telling her he was home. She had food and wine in the fridge in the hope that she would see him. She hadn't heard from him since the day he was scheduled to have his meeting with his wife and she was desperate to know how it had gone.

She soon found that she had company in the shape of Barolo the Labrador from next door, who stood up on his hind legs, snuffling at her over the wall, tail wagging. As she was petting him, his master appeared.

'Ciao, Lucy. All well?'

'Ciao, Guido. Yes, all good. And you?'

They chatted over the wall for a bit and then he gave her a fascinating piece of news.

'We think we may have a candidate for the "Englishman" who used to own the Castelnuovo.'

'You have?'

'In Hawkwood's mercenary army, the White Company, the next most important man was the treasurer. It turns out he was another Englishman: William Thornton. Very little is known of Thornton or of the fortunes of the White Company after the death of Hawkwood, but it's clear they continued to operate for some years, no doubt amassing a considerable amount of wealth in the process. As treasurer, Mr Thornton would have had access to this. For all we know, he might have taken Hawkwood's place as leader.'

'So you think the castle might have belonged to him?'

'That's the theory we're investigating. As this is Siena territory, there may be mention of it in the Siena archives and my student is diligently sifting through the records in the hope of finding confirmation.'

Lucy thanked Guido and asked him to pass her thanks to his postgraduate student and then had to rush indoors as she heard her phone start ringing. It was David.

'Hi, Lucy, I'm in the car and on my way home. I should be back in an hour or so.'

Lucy resisted the temptation to query how it had gone on Friday afternoon and instead asked if he would like to come for lunch. He accepted readily and she felt a sensation of relief. Hopefully, if he was about to announce a rapprochement with his estranged wife, he would hardly have agreed to have lunch with her. Nevertheless, she awaited his return with apprehension.

Any doubts she may still have harboured were swept away when he arrived, jumped out of his car and immediately picked her up and hugged her tightly to him.

'God, Lucy, it's so good to see you again. I've really missed you.' He kissed her until she was ready to subside into a heap in his arms. Finally, gasping for breath, she beamed at him.

'I've missed you, too. Lots and lots.'

Managing to restrain her natural instincts to take him upstairs and ravish him, she sat him down at the table and produced the cold spread she had prepared. As they ate, he told her all about his week in the US and, finally, got to the bit she had been waiting for.

'I saw Rosy on Friday afternoon.'

'And how did it go?' Lucy did her best to keep her tone neutral.

'It was okay. I think she was so relieved I was finally giving her the divorce – and a whole heap of money – that she managed to be extra sweet. We didn't argue – the legal people had already done that. We both just signed on the dotted line in front of our respective lawyers and that was that. All that's left now are a few odds and ends to tie up.'

'So you just met up with her in the lawyer's office?'

He nodded. 'To my considerable relief, she said she had to dash off, and it was all over in less than half an hour. But she did tell me one thing; she's seeing another guy.'

'No longer the man with the yacht?'

'No, apparently that didn't last. No, this is somebody else: an American.'

'So if she's seeing somebody else, she can hardly complain if you're doing the same.'

He grinned. 'Exactly. Takes the pressure off a bit, doesn't it?'

It certainly did. Lucy was so relieved, she decided to leave the ice cream in the fridge and immediately hauled him upstairs to bed.

Considerably later that afternoon he went off to the villa to see Armando and Fioretta and, of course, his beloved Boris. As he had just spent hours in an aircraft and was feeling jet-lagged, they agreed that he should get some sleep and so she wouldn't see him again until the next day, but she didn't really mind. The important thing was that he appeared as pleased to see her as she had been to see him.

As it turned out, it was just as well he wasn't there that evening as she had an unexpected visitor. She had just emerged from the shower and was tidying away the last remnants of lunch when she heard a car outside, followed by a knock on the door. It was Bruno.

She gave him a big smile and invited him in. As he walked in past her, she couldn't miss the expression on his face. Bruno definitely wasn't a happy man. She put the kettle on and waited for him to tell her what was troubling him. It didn't take long.

'Listen, Lucy, I hope you don't mind, but I need your advice.'

'Of course. What's the problem? A surgical matter?'

He shook his head. 'I wish it were. No, it's Virginia.'

'What about Virginia?'

She saw him hesitate before unburdening himself. 'She's been having an affair with another man.'

Lucy was genuinely amazed. Virginia had always struck her as being devoted to Bruno and certainly the first few times they had met socially, there had even been a certain amount of tension in the air as Virginia had made clear to Lucy that she was staking her claim to him. What could have gone wrong?

'Are you sure, Bruno? What makes you think that?'

He sighed, looking quite deflated. 'She told me.'

'She told you she's been unfaithful?'

'That's why she wanted us to get away together. We've just had four great days on the Island of Elba and everything was going so well, I mean, really well. I'd even finally decided I was going to ask her to marry me. It's about time, after five years together. But then last night, before I had a chance to pop the question, she opened up to me about her affair.'

Lucy was puzzled. 'But why would she insist on a romantic getaway with you, only to tell you she's found somebody else? It makes no sense.'

Bruno looked up and Lucy could see that his eyes were bloodshot. 'She wants me to forgive her.' To give him time, Lucy went across to the worktop and turned off the kettle. This was a subject that deserved something a hell of a lot stronger than tea. She dug in the cupboard and located the still unopened bottle of grappa Guido had brought with him the previous Saturday night. Pouring Bruno a shot of the fiery liquor, she slid the glass across the table into his unresisting hand.

'Tell me what she said.'

He took a mouthful of grappa, grimaced, and picked up the story once again. 'It was an aberration, a moment of madness. She went to a conference in Rome a couple of months back and that's where it happened. She was tired, they'd all had a bit too much to drink, and she'd got this crazy idea into her head that I was going to dump her.' He caught Lucy's eye. 'And for you, of all people. Apparently she thought there was some kind of chemistry between us and she was very upset. Anyway, whatever the reason, she ended up in bed with one of the other delegates.'

Lucy was appalled. 'She was jealous of *me*? But there's nothing between the two of us… apart from friendship of course.'

'That's what I told her and she said she knows that now but, at the time, she was convinced there was something going on. I've a feeling some of our friends must have told her how madly in love with you I used to be way back when we were teenagers.'

Lucy could now see why Virginia had been a bit standoffish back in the early days. 'So it only happened the once?'

He nodded. 'So she says. When she woke up in the morning, the first thing she did was to put a stop to it. She told the man she regretted what had happened and she didn't want anything more to do with him. And she says the reason for this was me. She realised she loved me, not him, and she wanted to be with me…' His voice tailed off and he took another little sip of grappa while cogs were beginning to turn inside Lucy's head. Surely not…

'Who is this other delegate?'

'I didn't ask. It doesn't matter, does it? What counts is that she did it.'

'When did she tell him it was all over?' A little bell had just started ringing inside her head. It couldn't really be, could it?

'That morning, but then again more recently as he was still pestering her. They finally had it out a couple of weeks ago and she laid it on the line to him. She says she's been feeling terribly guilty ever since it happened and she knew she had to come clean and tell me all about it.'

Lucy breathed deeply. A couple of weeks earlier had been around the time Charles had come to her for advice, telling her he had fallen for a woman who had spurned him. She also now remembered Charles telling her some time ago that he had been at a conference. He had described the woman with whom he was now besotted as being 'not exactly married' and the situation as 'complicated'. Joining the dots was looking all too easy and inevitable. She reached for another glass and splashed a little grappa into it for herself. She rarely touched the stuff, but these were exceptional circumstances.

As the grappa scorched its way down her throat, she debated what to do. If she told Bruno of her suspicions, it might scupper any chances of a reconciliation between Bruno and Virginia. As long as Bruno believed it had been some random, unknown man, hopefully it would be easier for him to come to terms with it and forgive her, if that was really what she wanted.

'And you're sure she wants you to forgive her?'

'That's what she said, or rather, pleaded. A moment of madness, never to be repeated, she called it, and she sounded sincere.' He looked up from his glass. 'I'm so confused, Lucy. That's why I came to you. You know both of us and you're the most sensible person I know. Tell me what I should do. What would you do?'

That, of course, was the question. Lucy knew what she would do because she had already done it, and with the same man – assuming she was right in her suspicions. After what Charles had done to her, she had had no hesitation in telling him that was the end of things between them. Should she tell Bruno to do the same? Was Virginia being honest when she said she chose Bruno over Charles? To give herself time to think, she went over to the fridge and started pulling out the remains of the lunch she had prepared for David. By the time she had set the table and put a big helping of mixed salad and some slices of porchetta onto Bruno's plate, she had reached a decision. She filled her glass with ice-cold mineral water, took a big mouthful, and made a start.

'It's a decision only you can make, Bruno, but if you really want my advice, here goes. You just told me the two of you got on really well when you were on the Island of Elba and you were about to ask Virginia to marry you. That's a huge step, so surely you can be in no doubt that you love her, or at least you did then. Do you want to throw all that away because of her one moment of madness?'

The more she thought about it, the more convinced she became that Virginia deserved the benefit of the doubt. She reached across the table to give his hand a little squeeze.

'We all do stupid things, Bruno, but the main thing is that she owned up, apologised, and meant it. Let's face it, she could have said nothing to you, married you, and taken her secret with her to the grave. All right, we all know it would have been better if she hadn't done it, but having the courage and the integrity to own up indicates to me that she's serious about her remorse and about wanting to stick with you. Like I say, it's your decision, but if it were up to me, I'd give her another chance.'

'You would?' He looked up from his plate. 'Really?'

'Really.' She squeezed his hand once more before releasing it. 'Now eat up. You look as though you could do with a square meal. When's the last time you ate?'

'Um, not sure. Yesterday, I suppose.'

'Then eat.' She gave him a smile. 'Go on. Doctor's orders.'

Chapter 26

The next few days were wonderful as far as Lucy was concerned. She spent almost all her free time with David and he even started giving her some tennis lessons in the evenings. Although she was very rusty, she managed to get the ball back over the net to him most of the time and he gallantly told her she had talent. Best of all, she saw he managed to move around the court without too much obvious difficulty, although her shots didn't exactly put him under any stress. They ate together, swam together, walked the dog together and spent their nights together. The last paparazzi finally packed up and left, and peace descended upon the villa once again.

One evening, David insisted upon inviting Guido and his Labrador for dinner at the villa and this time Guido brought something much better than a bottle of grappa. Upon arrival, David and Lucy led him round to the side of the villa to show him the vestiges of the castle, and as he stood there, surveying the ruins, he turned towards them and revealed what he had brought: information, fascinating information.

'I have some interesting news. We now know all about the Castelnuovo.'

Lucy gawped at him. 'You do? You know who built it, who owned it? What's the story?'

He leant against a bit of ancient stonework and smiled as he broke the news to them. 'It was started, but never finished.'

David looked as astounded as Lucy felt. 'What? The castle? I don't get it. I mean, the foundations are still here.'

Guido was still smiling. 'Ah, yes, the foundations – but not a lot more. We were right in our guess about William Thornton, the treasurer. My researcher found a reference in the Siena archives to a bill of sale for a plot of land on the hill here. It was bought by a W. Thornton in 1399, five years after the death of John Hawkwood. So it really was an Englishman who intended to build the castle here.'

'Intended to…?'

'As far as we can ascertain, building started almost immediately after the sale, but it all stopped barely a few months later. A contemporary chronicler reports the death of William Thornton in the summer of 1400 and it emerges that the building work finished with his demise. The White Company either disbanded or moved away from this area shortly after that and gradually disappeared from the annals of history.'

'But why call it a castle if it never was one?' Lucy was hanging on his every word and felt sure David was similarly enthralled.

'That's the interesting part and it was Giulia, my postgraduate research student, who hit upon the answer. She thinks it was called Castelnuovo because that's where William Thornton came from. You're English, think about it.'

'Castelnuovo… New Castle… Are you telling me William Thornton came from Newcastle and he gave that name to his new home in Tuscany?'

Guido nodded. 'She tried Newcastle-upon-Tyne but found nothing, but then she tried the town of Newcastle-under-Lyme in Staffordshire, England, and found a record of his birth in 1350. It all fits.'

'So the castle never was a castle...' Lucy was fascinated. She looked across at David who had a similar expression on his face. 'But you told me many of the houses round here are made of stone from the castle, how could that be?'

David nodded. 'That's what I heard, and certainly there are similar bits of stone all over the village.'

Guido had an answer. 'I imagine after building work stopped, the locals helped themselves to any materials left lying around and pulled down some bits of what walls had already been erected. So, David, you are indeed living next to the foundations of a castle built by an Englishman, but it died along with William Thornton.'

The rest of the evening was spent talking history and when, at one point, David happened to mention that he was thinking about going for a doctorate in medieval history, Guido was very supportive.

'Please come and talk to me about it. We would love to have you.'

Lucy glanced across and couldn't miss the delight on David's face. She grinned at him and squeezed his fingers.

'How about that, David? You could study in Florence and stay living here.' Which would also keep him conveniently close to her and her place of work. It sounded perfect.

The next evening she invited David, along with Daniela and Pietro, to her house for dinner so they could all meet up, and she got the distinct impression that her friends approved of her choice of man. David told them what Guido had said about the castle and they looked fascinated. Piero in particular had even played among the ruins as a youngster and knew them well. As for Lucy, she couldn't have been happier – apart from a nagging worry, deep down, as to where this all might be leading. Could she have a future with somebody as wealthy as him without sacrificing her principles? Sooner or later something was going to have to give but, for now, she did her best to relegate that to the back of her mind and just concentrate on enjoying the moment.

She saw nothing of Bruno or Virginia at work on Monday, but that afternoon she ran into Charles, who had some surprising – and welcome – news.

'Hi, Lucy, I want you to be one of the first to know – I'm leaving.'

'What, permanently?' Lucy looked up in surprise.

'Yes, I've been offered a position with MSF in Chad. I thought, if you can do Africa, so can I.'

'Good for you, but why leave now?' Although she felt pretty sure she knew what he was going to say. She wasn't wrong.

He dropped his eyes. 'I need a change, and it's sort of to do with that thing I told you about.'

'That thing or that woman?'

'That woman. I need to put some distance between me and her.'

As far as Lucy was concerned, this proved it. And his decision to leave was the best thing that could happen. For once in his life, Charles was doing the right thing and she was pleased to see this sign of positive personal development in him. She didn't press him for any further information and went off feeling relieved. She heard later that day that Bruno and Virginia had returned to the

Island of Elba to continue their holiday for another few days and she crossed her fingers, hoping they would be able to resolve matters between them.

On Wednesday evening she and David went down to Siena for the Palio. This four-day event had been running since Monday with practice sessions, processions and ceremonies, including the all-important drawing of lots to see which *contrada* got which horse. Thursday was the main event when jockeys from ten of the seventeen *contrade* would race bareback around the main square. Siena was packed out with locals as well as tourists. Even though she and David took her little car, they still had to park a long way from the centre and as they walked into the old town, the crowds became thicker and thicker. It was a tight squeeze to get down the main street towards the piazza and Lucy was very glad that the access to their drinks reception wasn't from inside the square as she knew from experience that this would have been packed out since lunchtime or even before. The hefty doorman immediately recognised David and they were ushered up three flights of stairs and into a fine old apartment overlooking Piazza del Campo.

It was a suffocatingly warm night and although the windows were wide open, it was still sweltering in there. Lucy was glad she had put on her lightest dress and open sandals, but she was still hot. Definitely no place for a heavily pregnant woman – Daniela was well out of it. The voices of the crowd in the square reached up to them and added to the noise as they entered the apartment. Bands of drummers down below were making the glasses on the bar rattle. David was greeted enthusiastically by a horde of elegantly dressed people, among them a number of famous faces, including a very well-known Hollywood actress whose plunging neckline threatened to distract attention from the race.

Lucy would happily have hung back, but David insisted she accompany him as he did the rounds, shaking hands, hugging and kissing the people he met. He introduced Lucy to everybody, but she hardly caught any of the names because of the din. Flashlights popped and she found herself photographed alongside him. There was little doubt their relationship would now become public. There was also little doubt in her mind that this glitzy environment felt wrong. How could they be here, sipping expensive French champagne, while millions of people around the world didn't know where their next meal was coming from? She glanced across at David and saw him smiling. Of course, he was used to this lifestyle, but that didn't help her. She liked him a lot, but coming face-to-face with his world was challenging.

Finally, clutching their glasses of champagne, they stationed themselves by one of the windows to watch proceedings. There were thousands of people crammed into the centre of the square and a racetrack of hard-packed clay had been laid down around the edges. The traditional pageant had already been in full swing for over an hour with men and women in brightly coloured medieval costumes riding horses and on foot, bullocks pulling carts, people marching, twirling and tossing flags into the air. It was a stunning spectacle and Lucy and David watched it in fascination.

As they did so, waiters came round with canapés, and Lucy suddenly got a surprise. A silver platter of delicious-looking nibbles appeared at her elbow and she saw that it was being carried by none other than Rahel. As they recognised each other, Rahel's face broke into a smile that broadened all the more when Lucy gave her a hug, taking care not to tip the platter over in the process.

'Rahel, how are you? You look great.' In spite of the operation barely a week earlier, she really did look good; a whole lot better than the last time Lucy had seen her. 'I didn't know you were a waitress.'

'Hello, Lucy. Tonight I'm a waitress, tomorrow morning at seven o'clock I'll be a cleaner again. Like I told you, I need all the work I can find.'

Lucy introduced her to David and she looked at him in awe.

'I've never met a real celebrity before. I know your name and I've seen your picture in the papers. I'm so very pleased to have met you.' She glanced around. 'Please excuse me, but I have to keep moving or my boss won't be happy.'

After Rahel had left, Lucy told him all about the emergency appendectomy the previous week and he listened to the story with considerable interest. 'Just like I said, Lucy, you're a very caring person. It's ironic that I'm supposed to be the celebrity when all I can do is to hit a ball over a net. For my money, you're the real star.'

Lucy shook her head. 'No, Rahel's the real star. She has a dream and she's already suffered so much just to get here and, God knows, it isn't going to be easy from now on. She's not only got to look out for herself, but for her parents as well. I have nothing but respect for her and, I suppose, a lot of guilt. Why her, why not me?'

'You mustn't think that way. At least you're doing something that helps mankind. What about me? Just lazing about, without lifting a finger to help the less privileged.'

'That's not…'

Their conversation was interrupted by the boom of a cannon that scared the pigeons for miles around and made most of the people in the room jump. They later learnt that the Hollywood starlet had been so startled by the noise, she had emptied her glass of champagne down her front – luckily there wasn't much dress there to stain. The cannon announced the arrival of the horses and riders, and all necks craned for the first sight of them as they paraded around the square. Before long, the track was cleared and the jockeys lined up behind a hefty rope. An expectant hush fell across the tens of thousands of spectators. After a brief delay while the horses were all mustered into position, the rope was dropped and the race was on.

The noise levels rose to a crescendo as the competitors circled the square three times at the gallop, skidding around the bends. At one of the early corners, the rider for the *contrada* Selva, dressed in orange and green, was thrown off his horse into the barrier but, amazingly, the horse kept on going, making its way up the order until it even overtook the leader right at the very end and won by a whisker, in spite of being without its rider.

'How about that? They say it's the horse, not the rider, that counts.' David had to put his mouth close to her ear in order to make himself heard. He then took the opportunity to kiss her neck and she was smiling as she replied to him.

'I'm not sure it would work that way in many other horse races. I'm just glad no horses or riders were injured too badly.'

As the fans mobbed the victorious horse, and the unhorsed Selva rider found himself a hero – admittedly a seriously bruised hero – David's phone started ringing.

He pulled it out of his pocket, glanced at the caller ID and she saw his face become more serious.

'Sorry, Lucy, I need to take this.'

He gave her an apologetic shrug and headed back towards the door and then through it, presumably to get as far away from all the noise as possible. Lucy stayed by the window, still clutching her untouched glass of champagne, feeling like a fish out of water in the midst of all this opulence. Glimpses of Rahel, hard at work, didn't make her feel any better. She wondered if Nicole and Geneviève back home in France were having similar crises of conscience. She had spoken to Nicole recently to confirm that she would be coming with her plus one and had been very pleased to hear her sounding untroubled – apart from wedding planning. She was still thinking of her two nurse friends a few minutes later when she felt a hand on her shoulder.

'Hi, are you here alone?'

She turned to find herself looking up into a familiar face. It took her a few seconds to remember his name. It was this year's biggest Hollywood heartthrob, no less, and she felt sure millions of women around the world would have been prepared to sell their souls to the devil – or worse – just to be able to get this close to him. But movie star or not, she was very happy with the man she already had.

'Hello. No, I'm here with a friend.'

'A boyfriend?' There was something predatory in his eye, not dissimilar to the looks she had caught from Tommy for time to time. She shivered, but did her best to remain civil.

'Yes, my boyfriend. He's just gone out to take a call.'

'Pity. You're so beautiful.' The look he gave her was no doubt designed to charm the proverbial – and actual – pants off the women in his sights and she felt sure it probably worked more often than not. Just not with her tonight. Resisting the temptation to tell him what she really thought, she just murmured a less than genuine, 'You're very kind.'

To her surprise, he reached into the top pocket of his linen jacket, produced a card, and pressed it into her hand. 'If you get tired of him, do give me a call. I'm filming in Rome for a month. Could be fun… Ciao.' With that he turned and walked off into the crowd, leaving her with an unpleasant taste in her mouth.

David didn't come back for quite some time. In fact, the winning *contrada* had already shouldered the silk banner of the Virgin Mary and set off in triumph with it towards the cathedral before she saw him again. She gave him a smile.

'That was poor timing. You missed the last part of the show.'

'No problem. At least I got to see the race. That was my lawyer on the phone. The divorce papers are all going through and Rosy's legal people have finally finished arguing about money.' He gave her a shrug. 'It's all so distasteful.'

Lucy nodded. She had been harbouring similar thoughts about her actor 'friend', as well as the crowd surrounding her here, all decked out in their expensive finery. She caught hold of David's forearm and gave him an encouraging squeeze.

'But at least it's all settled now.'

'Here's hoping. Hey, shall we get out of here? After two years as a hermit, I'm finding the crowds a bit heavy going.'

Lucy was equally pleased to get away.

Together, they did the rounds of the room once more, shaking hands and saying goodbye. The Hollywood starlet with the revealing neckline, now wiped down and dried off, gave David a far from casual kiss and Lucy felt her hackles rise. The actor who had propositioned her was nowhere to be seen and she shuddered again as she wondered if he had already found himself some other woman for a tryst. As they left the apartment, she dropped the visiting card into a waste bin. She was relieved when they were back out in the street following the crowds, as they made their way towards the main gates of the old town and then from there to the Fiat.

As she slid into the driving seat, David reached over and caught hold of her hand before she could turn the key in the ignition.

'Lucy, I know we said we'd go out for dinner, but I'll be quite honest, I think I'd be happier just going home.'

She gave him a big smile. 'You're not the only one. I've had it with crowds for a while. I felt like a fish out of water back there among all those celebrities.'

He caught hold of her hand and squeezed her fingers. 'I'm sorry. It's an artificial world and very different from the one you know. Maybe it might be better if we avoid that kind of thing for a while.'

'Thanks, David, that'll suit me down to the ground. Now, if you're happy with ham and melon, pecorino cheese, and the remains of the ice cream, let's go back to my place.'

'Manna from heaven.'

Chapter 27

Lucy went into work on Thursday morning feeling pensive. After David had gone back to the villa and his dog just after dawn, she had lain in bed, reflecting on her experiences the previous evening. On their return to her house, they had enjoyed a delicious homely meal together and a wonderful night, but she couldn't stop thinking about what he had described as the artificial world in which he lived. Was there any way she would ever be able to fit into such company?

Yes, she liked David a lot, maybe even loved him, and she enjoyed being with him immensely. The fact was, however, that her whole life up to now had been a million miles away from such luxury and privilege, and with a serious job to do. Care for others was her raison d'être and she knew she was committed to it. Did she really see herself settling into that sort of lifestyle, where all that mattered was winning – whether at sport, in love or financially? No sooner did this thought occur than she remembered that he had told her he was thinking about setting up a charity. That wasn't the action of a heartless and selfish man. Just because he had taken her to the Palio party didn't mean he was out of the same mould and she would do well to be a bit less judgemental.

Something that brightened her day came from Bruno. He reappeared at work, looking tanned and relaxed, and took her to one side. To her delight, he told her he and Virginia had spoken at length and he had forgiven her. What was more, he had carried out his original plan and had asked her to marry him. She had said yes and Lucy was very happy for both of them. The idea that she might inadvertently have been responsible for splitting them up had been bothering her and it was a relief to hear that relations between them had been restored, hopefully better than ever. She felt even happier an hour later when Virginia took her by the arm, walked her out into the gardens and hugged her. There were tears in her eyes as she thanked Lucy.

'Bruno told me he went to you for advice and you told him he should give me a second chance. I'm so very grateful, Lucy and when I think that I was worried you'd try to take him from me… You're such a lovely, lovely person and I hope you'll forgive me for thinking badly of you.' She kissed Lucy on the cheeks and hugged her warmly once more. 'Thank you so very much.'

That evening Lucy and David, accompanied by Boris, walked down to the Cavallo Bianco for dinner and, to her relief, there was no sign of Tommy. Although Boris appeared to recognise his sister, there was no great show of affection and in true Labrador tradition he appeared much more interested in the enticing aromas all round. David was immediately recognised by the owners and most of the other diners, but nobody bothered them, apart from a couple of people who asked him, very politely, if they could be photographed with him. Lucy had little doubt that word would soon get back to Tommy that the two of them had been sighted together and, no doubt, he would ensure the news appeared in his paper. Still, she told herself, this kind of exposure was part and parcel of dating a celebrity, like it or not.

After a very good meal, they walked back up through the olive trees to the villa. The temperature was high and the humidity in the air even higher. There were clouds in the sky obscuring the moon, but they soon got accustomed to the dark and had no trouble finding their way. Boris occasionally disappeared from sight completely, only for his eyes to then appear amid the bushes, glowing an ethereal green colour. David was holding her hand and as they reached the spot where they had seen the porcupine, he stopped and pulled her gently towards him.

'You're a bit quiet tonight, Lucy. Is everything okay?'

'I'm fine.'

She heard him snort. 'I used to be married, remember? I know what that word means. Even I know that fine doesn't mean fine. What's the matter? Come on, we know each other well enough by now. What's eating you?'

She hesitated but then gave in. 'I suppose if the truth be told, I'm scared I'll never be able to come to terms with the whole celebrity lifestyle thing. You know – being recognised and photographed, rubbing shoulders with people with all the money in the world but the morals of a tomcat. I've become very fond of you in a very short space of time and I love being with you, but sometimes it's hard.'

His arms stretched around her shoulders and he hugged her to him. 'I've become very fond of you in a very short space of time as well, Lucy. Listen, what we have is too good to lose. I've never felt like this before about anybody, and that includes Rosy back in the day. I'll do what it takes to make you happy. Just say the word and I'll happily go back to being a hermit if that's what you want.' He lifted her chin with a finger and kissed her softly on the lips. 'Really, don't worry. Whatever it takes, okay?'

She kissed him back and did her best to convince herself that, with time, she would be able to settle into his life, but she knew it wasn't going to be easy.

Over the next few weeks, she experienced some of the happiest days of her whole life as her love for him grew – yes, she had even started using that word, but only inside her head for now. The stress and fear of the Congo disappeared completely along with the nightmares, as she did her best to carry out her stated aim of living for the moment. She found herself settling down even more at the clinic, although she still remained uncertain about the ultimate direction of her future. But, for now, she really did manage to enjoy life on a day-by-day basis.

At the beginning of September her parents came over to stay with her for a week. Although she had already told them she was seeing David, they were pretty star-struck – particularly her mother, still a keen tennis player – when they met him. For his part, David was charming, communicative and generous as always. He insisted on taking them for lunch at the villa outside Florence where he and Lucy had eaten on the day he was first outed by Tommy, and her parents were most impressed with the place and the food. He drove them there in the Mercedes – the Ferrari, apart from being too small for four people, had not been out of the garage since the day they went to Punta Ala – and Lucy could sense her father's fascination with the luxury vehicle.

That night, after David had returned to the villa, Lucy was surprised to hear her father tackle the subject of relationships; something he had scrupulously left to her mother all her life so far.

'Lucy, sweetheart, are you sure you're going to be able to cope with being with somebody like David?' Seeing the expression on her face, he was quick to clarify what he meant. 'Don't get me wrong. He's a good man, and your mother and I like him a lot, but he comes from a very different world, you know. Is that going to be a problem for you?'

'It's something we think you should consider, Lucy.' Her mother laid a comforting hand on top of hers.

'Oh, I've been considering it all right, I can assure you. Not a day goes by without me wondering whether we can make it work and how.' She gave a frustrated shake of the head and a sigh escaped her lips. 'It's complicated. I really do like him an awful lot and I'm pretty sure he feels the same way about me. If he were to get really serious, I honestly don't know what I'd do. I know I want to be with him, but I also know I'd want to keep on working. And if I took another job somewhere else, what then? What if I decided to go back to MSF?'

'You'd work it out, Lucy.' He mother gave her hand a squeeze. 'You're a bright girl and he's a good man and you'd come up with a solution, I'm sure. Don't forget, you can't expect to have everything the way you want it. Life – and relationships – demand compromise.'

'I'm sure you're right. Yes, as far as the practicalities are concerned I expect we could sort something out, but, deep down, it's a question of principle. I know what I think about the injustice of most of the world's wealth being in the hands of the very few and that isn't going to change. Sooner or later my principles are going to come up against my feelings and it's going to be tough.' She shrugged, trying to release some of the tension creeping into her shoulders, and did her best to sound positive.

'Anyway, I've only just started going out with him and everything's going so well at present, so I'm going to let the future look after itself for now.'

On their last night before flying home to the UK, David invited Lucy and her parents up to the villa for dinner. She and he had been keeping chastely apart while her parents were here and she had been missing him a lot. To her surprise when they got there she found that he had prepared the meal by himself, rather than asking Fioretta for help. There was ham, melon, *finocchiona* and fresh figs as a starter and then he had made a wonderful mixed salad, all apparently grown in the vegetable garden on the estate. They ate outside on the terrace in front of the villa from where they had a spectacular view out over the hills as far as the distant mountains. He had decided to do a barbecue and, assisted – or at least tailed – by Boris, he grilled a fine selection of meats, along with skewers of prawns and octopus interlaced with baby tomatoes. To drink there was champagne, followed by Armando's red wine, and it was a lovely evening. As the sun sank below the hill behind them, they sat back and enjoyed the peace and quiet, while Boris noisily crunched his way through the remains of a massive T-bone steak at their feet.

'And when's your friend getting married?' Lucy had told her mum all about Nicole's upcoming wedding.

'This time next week in Avignon. David's going to come with me, so I'll have my plus one for a change. Normally at weddings I end up all on my own.'

She saw her mum smile contentedly. 'It's about time you got yourself a plus one, Lucy. You're very lucky to have found David.'

'I'm the lucky one.' David reached over and caught hold of Lucy's hand. 'She's the best thing that's happened to me for years and years.'

Fortunately it was dark enough for Lucy's blushes not to show, but she chose to downplay the significance of his remarks. 'Ssh, don't let Boris hear you say that. I wouldn't want him to get jealous.'

Later on, as he walked with them back down to her cottage, David took her by the arm and slowed his pace, letting her parents go on a little way ahead. She pressed herself against him, curious to see if he had something to say. As she waited, she watched the fireflies dancing underneath the trees and breathed in the scent of lavender in the air. His voice was little more than a whisper, but the message was unmissable and her heart leapt.

'I meant what I said about you being the best thing that's happened to me. The fact is, Lucy, in case you hadn't realised, I'm afraid I've fallen in love with you.'

Hearing him use the L-word for the first time gave Lucy an overwhelming desire to leap on him and roll him into the bushes but, in deference to her parents, she restrained herself and just raised herself on her toes to kiss him softly on the cheek. As she did so, she almost tripped over Boris who was trotting along at their feet.

'Love me, love my dog. And I do, David, both of you.'

Chapter 28

The following Friday after she had finished work, David picked her up and they set off for Avignon in the Mercedes, stopping for the night in a luxury hotel on the Tuscan coast, just north of Viareggio. This was a very stylish modern hotel and their room had a broad terrace looking out over the tops of a forest of umbrella pines towards the deep blue of the Mediterranean with its unbroken sweep of golden sandy beach. Behind them, the view was even more spectacular up into the nearby mountains which, at first sight, looked as though they were covered in snow. In fact the hotel was very near Carrara, home to Italy's famous white marble quarries, and the setting sun shed a gentle pink glow across the dusty white slopes. It was a very romantic spot.

Their room was huge, with a massive – and inviting – king size bed. The bathroom was as big as her bedroom at home and unsurprisingly in there the floor, walls, basin and shower were all clad in marble. Everything was spotlessly clean, ultra-modern and doubtless vastly expensive. Dinner that evening on the immaculate rooftop terrace was excellent and she couldn't fault any of it. The service was impeccable, the wine exquisite, the view stunning. Her companion was cheerful, attentive and very appealing. It should have been a wonderful evening except that her annoying Jiminy Cricket of a conscience kept snapping at her heels throughout, as thoughts of Ahmed and Rahel, and her good friend Miriam – now missing for months – threatened to dampen the mood.

After a long, languorous, loving night, they both went for a swim in the sea in the morning and the cool water finally managed to clear her head. As she swam idly about, relishing the refreshing feel of the water on her skin, she gave herself a serious talking-to. She was going to a good friend's wedding with the man she loved. So he was rich; she knew that he was a good man at heart. Money didn't always have to be a bad thing if it was in the right hands. She was alive, she was healthy, and she had every reason in the world to be happy. And that was what she was going to be. As she had told her parents, the future could look after itself for now.

She swam over to where David was floating on his back, caught hold of him and hugged him so tightly, they both disappeared under water. Trying to kiss him underwater was a step too far and they both emerged coughing and spluttering, but she was still hanging onto him.

'What was that in aid of?' He was grinning at her.

'That was me telling you I really do love you, David Lorenzo, and I never want you to forget that.'

'And if I promise never to forget it, you promise not to try to drown me again?'

'It's a deal.' She kissed him again and she knew she had meant every word of what she had said.

The wedding took place in a lovely old Romanesque church in Nicole's charming Provençal village, just outside Avignon. As they walked in and took their seats, she saw a number of faces turn towards them and recognition dawn on many as they caught sight of David's tall form. But, for once, Lucy barely noticed as she suddenly stopped and stared. There, sitting in the second row, was a very familiar face. Breaking the respectful silence of the little church, Lucy set off down the aisle at a run and almost threw herself into the arms of her friend.

'Miriam, it's you. You're alive.'

'Lucy, Lucy, Lucy, it's so good to see you, my gorgeous girl. Nicole told me you were coming today so I thought I'd give you a little surprise.'

Lucy looked around and smiled apologetically at the other guests as she grabbed David's hand and pulled him down alongside her to sit with Miriam.

While the organ continued to play quietly in the background, Lucy quizzed her about what had happened. The story was almost as awful as she had feared. Miriam and her little group of patients and colleagues had ended up hiding out in a tiny encampment in the inhospitable bush, without electricity or any connection to the outside world. They had stayed there, in fear for their lives, for almost three months while rival warring factions had rampaged throughout the area. Only a few weeks ago the fighting had finally moved on and things had calmed down enough for the group to make their way once more out into open country and, ultimately, back to civilisation.

Miriam had travelled on to Kinshasa and flown from there to France barely two days ago. Lucy clung to her arm and listened intently, her delight at finding her friend alive and well threatening to make her burst into song. Fortunately for the others in the church, before this could happen the organ struck up the wedding march and the ceremony began.

The reception was in a big marquee pitched alongside the ruins of a Roman villa only a hundred yards from the church. The sun was shining, the surroundings were charming, and everything went well. As they got there, Lucy immediately spotted Geneviève and took David across to meet her. They embraced and exchanged news. Geneviève told them she had found a good job in an immigration reception centre close to where she lived in northern France. The man on her arm was introduced as Didier, her 'petit-ami', which sounded promising. Didier turned out to be a tennis coach and he appeared over-whelmed to meet David and soon the two men were chatting amicably in a mixture of English and French, which David spoke unexpectedly well.

The bride and groom appeared and Lucy embraced them both warmly. After hearing so much about François from Nicole while in Mabenta, Lucy felt she already knew Nicole's new husband well. She introduced David and saw Nicole do a double take before glancing back at her with a broad grin and a wink.

'I'm so pleased to see you looking so happy, Lucy. And – don't take this the wrong way – but you've put on a few kilos and you look a whole lot better for it.' She turned to David. 'We were quite worried about Lucy, you know. She was working herself into the ground at the clinic.'

He smiled back at her. 'I can imagine. That's the sort of person she is. That's why I love her so much.'

Nicole's eyes flicked to Lucy's, presumably as she registered his choice of vocabulary, before she winked at David. 'Everybody loves Lucy.'

'Not as much as I do.' He caught hold of Lucy's arm and pulled her close. 'She's one of a kind.'

'Stop it, you two. David, this is the bride's day. Please can we change the subject away from me?'

They chatted for a while about friends and colleagues back in Africa, and Lucy was delighted to hear that most of the patients who had disappeared into the bush along with Miriam had managed to make a good recovery in spite of the circumstances. There had even been a successful birth of a healthy baby girl. All things considered, it could have worked out far, far worse and the sense of dread Lucy had been harbouring gradually subsided. She was interested to hear that Miriam was planning on staying here in France. She had dual nationality, French and Congolese, and had studied in Toulouse before returning to her native land some fifteen years earlier. But now she, too, was calling it a day.

'I'm going to work with Geneviève at the refugee centre in Lille. It'll be good to be back in France, although I'm not looking forward to the cold winters again. Mind you, at least here there shouldn't be any more crazy men with guns.'

Nicole stayed with them for some minutes, although the subject soon returned to Lucy. One thing Nicole said to her really resonated. 'What's it like working in an upmarket private hospital? Somehow I never expected to find you in a place like that.'

Lucy nodded slowly, choosing her words carefully. 'I know what you mean. I was worried, too, at first, but I'm settling in. I spoke to Doctor Brown, you know, the MSF director in London, before accepting the job and she told me not to worry – they're all patients who need my help. So they have money, so what? All right, from time to time there are a few very questionable patients there, although the vast majority are just like you and me.' She shot a little smile in David's direction. 'And some of them are really very nice.'

She saw him smile back and she could see he was listening carefully. 'So, you aren't thinking of leaving?' Miriam sounded interested. 'You're not thinking of going back to the Congo, are you?'

'I'm not thinking anything at the moment. As a place to work, the Siena Clinic's very different from Mabenta, but I enjoy the work, I like my boss, and it's meant I've been able to find myself a little cottage, and I love Tuscany.' She reached up and kissed David on the cheek. 'And my neighbour up the hill's a pretty good guy. As for the Congo, no, Miriam, I think I'll go for somewhere a bit less violent next time.'

'Next time? So you *are* thinking of going back to MSF?' Nicole didn't miss much.

'I really don't know, Nic. I'm just enjoying things as they are for now.' She glanced up at David. 'And they really couldn't be much better.'

That night Lucy and David stayed at a beautiful old hotel right in the centre of Avignon, their room looking out over the rooftops to the towers and battlements of the medieval Palais des Papes. Once again, their room was luxurious and immaculate and once again Lucy had to suppress that same familiar sensation of not belonging. Still, she told herself as she snuggled up against him in the soft, comfortable bed, it didn't get much better than this.

Did it?

Chapter 29

The crunch came when they got home on Sunday evening. After a light meal, they ended up in the old dovecot on the top floor of his villa with a happy dog stretched out at their feet. Lucy had drunk quite enough this weekend so they settled for cold mineral water rather than champagne for a change. It was almost completely dark by this time, although the moonlight allowed them to see out over the trees towards the distant hills studded with little clusters of light from the remote farmhouses. Above them the sky was a velvety deep purple and it was very romantic and calming.

The calm didn't last long.

She and David were sitting side by side on the sofa, admiring the view and enjoying each other's company. It soon emerged that he was still thinking back to the events of the past two days.

'It was a lovely wedding, wasn't it?' He gently stroked her cheek with his finger.

'Mhm, yes.' She nestled against him contentedly.

'Nicole and François looked very settled and happy together, didn't they?'

'I think marriage is going to agree with them.'

'You know, I'm finally going to be divorced in a month or two. It's funny – one marriage begins and another ends.'

'Mhm…' She was really very comfortable and a bit sleepy.

'Lucy, I was wondering…' He sounded unusually hesitant.

'What?'

'I was wondering if you maybe felt like marrying me.'

Lucy's tiredness left her in an instant and she felt her whole body tense. 'You're asking me to marry you, David?'

'I know I should really be down on one knee, but my excuse is that it still hurts a bit.' He gently turned her face towards him in the moonlight. 'It doesn't have to be straightaway. Whenever suits you, if you'll have me. What do you think?'

What *did* she think? On the one hand, she knew she loved this man dearly and the thought of spending the rest of her life with him was appealing and immensely tempting. The trouble was that the annoying elephant called money had just lumbered into the room once more. She stretched up and kissed him softly on the lips to give herself more time before replying. His touch felt so very right. These past few days with him had been wonderful, although she couldn't hide the fact that she had found herself feeling awfully out of place in the expensive hotels, seriously questioning the fairness of a world where some human beings could live in such extreme luxury while others barely scraped to make ends meet.

'I'm going to need time to think.' She sensed tension in him now, so she hastened to do her best to defuse the situation. 'I love you to bits, David. You have to know that. These past weeks have been the happiest of my life. I've never felt about anybody else the way I feel about you and that's the truth. It's just such a big decision to make.

Could you just give me a little time? Please don't interpret my hesitation as me not loving you, because I really, really do. I just need to get my head straight.'

'Of course, take all the time you want. I'm not going anywhere. I'll wait for as long as it takes and if there's a problem, I'll do whatever it takes, I promise.'

'I know you would, David. But it's not up to you to do anything. I'm the one with the problems.'

'What problems?'

She hesitated, uncertain how to explain it to him. 'It's just that we come from very different worlds. You live in a castle – well sort of – and you mix with Hollywood stars and millionaire sportspeople. It's a completely alien environment to me, that's all. I just need to think it through.'

'But I'm still me, Lucy. And for you I promise I can be whoever you want, do whatever you want. Just say the word. Whatever it takes, Lucy. Remember that, please.'

'Of course I will and, remember, I love you so very much.'

She kissed him again and then rested her head against his chest, her eyes staring out of the window and across the dark Tuscan countryside, wondering just what she should say, just what she should decide.

She was still wondering next morning as she went off to work. The night with David had been bittersweet as she struggled to come to terms with the question before her. There was, of course, a simple solution: ask him to give away most of his money and move to some under-privileged part of the world with her. No sooner did this idea cross her mind than she rejected it out of hand. This was money he had legitimately earned and he was free to do with it as he wished and he should be able to choose where he wanted to live – and he already lived in a wonderful place. As she had told him, she was the one with the problems as far as wealth and social injustice were concerned. It wasn't his place to make sacrifices to resolve her dilemma. This was down to her and her alone.

That afternoon as she sat in the staff canteen with a cup of tea, she sent him a text message to buy herself more time.

> I'm feeling a bit shattered. I think I'll just crash out tonight. Okay with you if we meet up tomorrow evening instead? x

His reply came back almost immediately.

> Sorry to hear you aren't feeling 100%. Tomorrow's fine – get some rest. If you want to talk, I'm here. x

On her way home, she stopped off at Daniela's house. She found a very pregnant lady well into her final trimester fanning herself with a magazine as the unusually high September temperatures stubbornly refused to acknowledge that autumn was just around the corner. As she took one look at Lucy she must have realised that things weren't all right with her.

'What's the matter, Lucy? What's happened?'

Lucy took a deep breath. 'It's David; he's asked me to marry him.'

'That's amazing… isn't it? Why have you got that look on your face? If a tall, handsome, kind millionaire had just asked me to marry him, I'd be jumping for joy. What's the problem? I thought you told me you'd fallen for him big time.'

'I have, Danni. I love him to bits but the problem's not him, it's everything he stands for.'

Daniela looked blank. 'I'm afraid you're going to have to spell out just exactly what that means.'

So Lucy did her best to lay out her concerns that David's millions, and the lifestyle that came with them, just weren't for her. She told Daniela she knew it was her problem, not his, and she could only think of one way of resolving it – by saying no to him.

'I know I could take a deep breath, marry him, and stick it out for a year, maybe a bit longer, but sooner or later it would all become too much and I'd have to get out. I couldn't bear the thought of dragging him through another divorce. That would just be too cruel.'

'Crueller than saying no to the man you love and who loves you?' Daniela reached over and caught hold of both of Lucy's hands in hers. 'Listen; you need to sit down and tell him all this, talk it through with him. Being wealthy doesn't have to be a bad thing. If he truly loves you, he'll come up with a solution. It's all very well you saying it's your problem, not his, but it takes two to make a relationship, or a marriage, work.'

They talked for over an hour, but Lucy remained unconvinced. She knew herself too well and she really did fear that if she did say yes to him – and so much of her was crying out to do just that – it wouldn't be long before it would all turn sour. She drove home and decided to put the kettle on. Even the scent of the rambling rose wafting in through the open back door failed to put a smile on her face tonight. It was all just so terribly complicated.

As the shadows lengthened, she let herself out of the back door and went for a walk up through the olive groves, in an attempt to clear her head. She ended up by the familiar tree trunk where she had met Boris and then David but, this evening, there was no big friendly dog and no tall loving man.

She sat down and rested her head in her hands. She had been fighting back the tears all day, but now, all alone in the middle of the Tuscan countryside, she broke down and cried like a little girl.

Chapter 30

She slept very poorly that night in spite of a photo that arrived on her phone mid-evening. This was a close-up of Boris with the most loving expression on his face and a one-line caption underneath just reading, *Missing you*. Unfortunately, all this achieved was to make her start crying all over again.

Next morning she went off to work in a state close to blank depression, her mind still churning. The more she thought about it, the clearer it became. Much as she loved him, her conscience just wouldn't let her tie herself to a multi-millionaire. As the day progressed, the heart-wrenching lack of any solution to her dilemma took root and by the time she had finished her last operation of the day, she was close to tears once more.

As she changed out of her scrubs and splashed cold water in her face, she heard Virginia's voice. She sounded a bit strange, but there was so much going on inside Lucy's head, she didn't really pick up on it.

'Lucy, if you've finished, could you spare a few minutes to speak to my father? He says it's important.'

Lucy nodded distractedly. 'Of course. I'll go straight up to him now.'

Together they climbed the stairs back up to the ground floor and walked through the corridors to the director's office. Virginia tapped on the door and turned the handle. That was when it all started to get really weird.

As the door opened, Lucy saw not only Professor Gualtieri standing there but, beside him, none other than David, a nervous smile on his face. More unexpected than that, however, was to see her former boss, Dr Brown of Médecins Sans Frontières standing alongside them.

Professor Gualtieri beckoned them in and waved in the direction of Dr Brown.

'Ah, Doctor Young, thank you for coming. You know my old friend Hannah Brown, don't you? She's come over here for a very special reason, not just to see me.'

'Hello, Lucy. I'm very pleased to see you again.' Dr Brown was smiling at her. 'And you're looking so well.'

Shell-shocked would have been a more appropriate description from Lucy's point of view. As she shook the august doctor's hand, she managed to blurt out a greeting, but that was about all. Professor Gualtieri continued as if unaware that his surgeon looked as though she had just stepped on a black mamba.

'Do sit down, please, Doctor Young. I gather you've just come out of a long afternoon in theatre. You must be tired.'

Lucy found herself sitting on a leather sofa alongside David, while the professor and Dr Brown settled down in armchairs opposite them. Virginia took up station by the window, a little smile on her face. The professor waved in David's direction.

'We'll let Mr Lorenzo do the talking. It was his idea, after all.'

'His idea?' As a contribution to the conversation it wasn't exactly inspired, but Lucy was glad to get at least a couple of words out. She listened intently as David started, hesitantly, to explain.

'Lucy, I had this idea… Well, to be honest, it sort of came from you.'

Lucy had no idea what might be coming next. She just nodded mutely and waited.

'Over the years of my tennis career, I've made a lot of money. Now that the divorce settlement has been finalised, I know I've still got a whole heap more than I'll ever need, and the money still coming in from sponsorship deals, merchandising and investments will be more than enough to keep me for life. Like I told you, with your help I want to become a better person. I still want to do my doctorate in history, but I also want to do something with my money. Remember we talked about a charity of some kind, something that'll make a real difference to those who need it a hell of a lot more than I do?'

Lucy found herself reaching out to take hold of his hand. Words once more failed her, so she just nodded and gave his fingers a little squeeze.

'The idea came to me when I was listening to you and your friends in Avignon, talking about the work of Médecins Sans Frontières. As an organisation they do amazing work and it occurred to me that I could, and should, contribute towards making sure that continues.'

Lucy looked up in surprise. When he had spoken before, it had been about maybe doing something to help underprivileged kids or injured sportspeople. Now he was talking about MSF? She was still having trouble articulating anything so she simply listened as he went on.

'I also thought about your story of the Syrian lady back here in Siena who needed an urgent operation and that's when the idea began to crystallise. These people don't just need help back in their countries of origin, they still need it badly even after they make it across the Mediterranean. That's why I called Professor Gualtieri to run my idea by him and he told me he knew Doctor Brown.'

Professor Gualtieri took up the tale. 'I called Hannah and the three of us had a long talk, as a result of which she very kindly took the time and trouble to fly over here today to see us and to discuss things in more detail.'

Dr Brown looked across at Lucy, the smile still on her face. 'I'm sorry it's all coming as a big surprise to you, Lucy, but I hope it's a good surprise. David told me he wanted to help MSF and he outlined his innovative plan to set something up here in Siena. He told me he now recognises what you and I have always known – that we live in an unfair world. In helping us, he wants to do something to try to redress the balance, and he's been extremely generous.'

As Lucy just sat there in a state of shock, Dr Brown went on to outline what had been agreed. David was gifting an astronomical sum of millions of dollars to help Médecins Sans Frontières – aided by Professor Gualtieri – to set up a medical treatment centre for the needy here in Siena and, beside this, he was also going to use his considerable network of friends, fellow athletes and business contacts to try to obtain further sponsorship for what he saw as a wonderful charitable cause. In this way, more of these centres could be set up where needed to help the flood of humanity on the move in these turbulent times.

Dr Brown then added the icing on the cake – as far as Lucy was concerned.

'And we can't think of anybody better suited or better qualified to head up this new centre than you, Lucy. You have the background, the experience and the expertise to ensure that we make a success of it. Michelangelo, Professor Gualtieri, has offered to throw his weight behind the project, particularly in ensuring that we obtain all the necessary permits and support from the authorities – which won't be an easy task. But, as you know, he's a person of real consequence here in Italy and with his help, we see no reason why this project shouldn't succeed and prosper.'

As this all began to sink in, Lucy gradually began to feel a wave of warmth and happiness spreading throughout her whole body and when Dr Brown reached the end of her explanation, Lucy could feel tears running down her face. Quite unable to help herself, she got to her feet and went across to kiss the professor warmly on the cheeks, no doubt surprising him, but from the expression on his face, not displeasing him. She went across to hug Dr Brown who kissed her in return and then went back to David and did the same. She still couldn't manage to put her thoughts into words and sat there, smiling and crying for several minutes before the power of speech returned, even if what she managed to say wasn't exactly inspiring.

'Thank you so much for coming all the way over here to Siena, Doctor Brown.'

'My pleasure entirely, Lucy. David was particularly keen for you to hear and approve of the donation and his plans to help set up this new MSF centre and I was very keen to meet and thank him for his generosity.' She caught Lucy's eye for a second or two. 'You do approve, don't you?' All Lucy could do was nod mutely. 'Excellent. I was delighted to make the trip – not least as it gave me the chance to renew my acquaintance with Michelangelo and his charming daughter. I was also very pleased to have the chance of seeing you again, Lucy, to say thank you once more for all your efforts in Mabenta.'

It was well past six o'clock by the time Lucy emerged – still in a daze – from the director's office with David at her side. They wandered out into the garden as the sun was beginning to drop behind the hills, gradually turning the sky an enchanting rose pink. He took her hand and led her across to an old bench where they sat down side-by-side, surrounded by sweet-scented bushes. He kept hold of her hand and gave it a gentle squeeze. He didn't say anything. He didn't need to. They sat there like that, in silence, for quite some time before she finally managed to put her thoughts into words.

'David, are you doing this for my sake?' She had to clear her throat before managing to speak properly. 'It's not fair of me to ask you to make such a massive sacrifice.'

'I'm not doing it for your sake, Lucy.' His voice was gentle, but heavy with emotion. 'I'm not even doing it solely for the sake of the poor people who need medical help. I'm doing it for my sake, for me. I need this. Like I told you, I don't want my life to have been just about playing tennis and winning a few tournaments. I want to be able to sit back in years to come and know that I tried to help other, less fortunate, people.' He turned towards her and she caught the reflection of the setting sun in his eyes, turning them the rich purple colour of lavender. 'Life's been unbelievably good to me – in spite of the past few years – and you're so right when you say it isn't fair that anybody should have so much. With your help, I now know that the best thing I can do is to give something back. I want to be a better man. You make me a better man.'

'You're a wonderful man, David.' Lucy could feel the tears streaming down her cheeks again, but she knew these were tears of joy. 'And I love you so very, very much.' And she kissed him.

As they finally separated, he looked down at her with a little smile.

'Feel like taking Boris for his evening walk?'

—

Lucy drove home on autopilot, as if in a dream, jumped into the shower and then changed into a T-shirt and shorts. As she came back downstairs again, she could already hear a familiar whining scratching sound and she went over to open the door. David, now also wearing shorts and trainers, was standing there with his faithful hound at his feet.

'Ready to go?'

She dropped to her knees and hugged the big black dog, feeling him bury his face happily into her armpit, his tail wagging so hard with joy his whole body was wagging with it.

She knew how he felt.

Together, they made their way up through the olive trees, the last rays of the sun just peeking over the top of the hill casting long shadows. She and David walked hand-in-hand, happy to exchange little more than a word or two as they passed the spot that, to them, would forever be the place where they had seen the porcupine. At the top of the olive grove, they followed Boris onto the narrow path that wound its way through the rough scrub of the steeper part of the hillside. The temperature was still high, in spite of being the middle of September, and the sky was crystal clear. She knew from Armando that the *vendemmia* would start any day now and she hoped the weather would stay fine and dry until the precious grapes had been collected and ferried off to be made into next year's wine.

At the top of the rise, they walked across to the fallen tree where she had first discovered the identity of her reclusive neighbour and she found herself reflecting upon how much progress he had made since then. He had come out of his shell, had rediscovered what it felt like to smile once more, and had morphed from a bitter, grumpy victim into a confident, happy man.

And her?

She couldn't remember another moment in her life when she had been as happy as she was now. She had everything she had ever wanted, and the future, which only a couple of hours ago had looked so bleak, was once more bright and inviting. She sat on the familiar tree trunk and pulled David gently down with her until he was sitting at her side. A warm hairy body pushed in between them and she smiled as she saw Boris panting like a steam train, his head resting happily on his master's knees. She reached down with her free hand and ruffled his ears. The look he cast up at her melted her heart.

'Love you, love your dog.' She returned her attention to David who removed his hand from hers and stretched his arm around her shoulder, cradling her against his chest.

'Are you sure you mean that?' She felt him kiss the top of her head. 'I come with a lot of baggage, you know.'

'And I don't?' She twisted her face up towards him. 'I've struggled all my working life trying to square the circle, to come to terms with the fact that I've been lucky enough to have been born in a country where people – generally speaking – don't go round in fear for their lives. I was able to get a good education and enough to eat every day and yet I know that millions upon millions of people elsewhere in the world never had that and never will. I know now that it's been eating me up inside. Suddenly I feel a tremendous weight lifted off my shoulders and it's thanks to you.' She stretched up and kissed him softly on the lips. 'You won't believe how much you've helped me.'

'I've helped *you*? It's the other way round; I owe you so much.'

She nestled against him and gripped his arm with both her hands. She felt happy, she felt safe, and she felt a growing sense of pleasurable anticipation at the new life that now opened out in front of her. She looked out across the valley to the farms on the far side, the regular rows of vines among the olive groves and open fields making the scene look like a patchwork quilt. Although it was getting dark, she could see the funny little miniature tractors used in the vineyards creeping across the hillsides as the farmers prepared for the harvest to come. She hoped the wine would be good and now she knew without a doubt that she would still be here in Tuscany to sample and enjoy it. She squeezed David's arm and looked back up at him again.

'David, I'm sorry it's taken me so long, but if the offer's still open, there's absolutely no doubt in my mind that I'd love to marry you. I can't think of anything better than spending the rest of my life with you, if you'll have me.'

As she spoke, she felt a big hairy paw land on her knee, followed by another as Boris, no doubt affected by the emotion in the air, stood up on his hind legs and stretched his long black nose towards her, trying in vain to reach up and kiss her. She smiled down at him and ruffled his ears as his master leant towards her and did what the dog had failed to do. Just before he kissed her, he murmured softly.

'You can't imagine just how happy that makes me.'

But she could, and it felt amazing.